TO MURDER AND CREATE

TO MURDER AND CREATE

A NOVEL INSPIRED BY T. S. ELIOT'S
'THE LOVE SONG OF J. ALFRED PRUFROCK'

ARDYTHE ASHLEY

First Warbler Classics Edition 2023

To Murder and Create: A Novel Inspired by
T. S. Eliot's "The Love Song of J. Alfred Prufrock" © 2023 Ardythe Ashley

www.warblerpress.com

ISBN 978-1-959891-98-7 (paperback)
ISBN 978-1-959891-99-4 (e-book)

Publisher's Note
Spelling and punctuation in "The Love Song of J. Alfred Prufrock" by T. S. Eliot adheres to the original June 1915 publication of the poem in *Poetry: A Magazine of Verse,* with the exception of the substitution of "no doubt" with "withal," in accrdance with the 1917 publication of the poem.

This book is dedicated to the memory of Jim Hejduk,
who was there from dawn to sunset…leaving me with
seventy-four years of enchanting memories.
Shantih shantih shantih.

CONTENTS

"LET US GO THEN," called Mrs. Maybelle Gill, her voice loud enough to carry upwards to the farthest reaches of the staircase, "or we shall be late for evening Mass. I do not wish to arrive late for evening Mass. It is impolite to God."

She stood at the bottom of the stairs by the hall table that had been polished only the day before, but which was already showing a thin skin of dust, giving her mild offense. She refrained from touching the surface as she did not want to soil her gloves. She would attend to the dust upon their return from church.

She gave herself the briefest of looks in the hallway mirror. Firm as ever. Grey hair lightening towards white. Eyes not so bright as once they had been, faded now from chocolate brown to the color of tepid tea, but there were still some good looks lingering around those eyes. Alas, the rest of her face had sagged. Well enough for seventy, she judged, steering herself firmly away from the sin of pride.

"I shall be down in a moment," answered Lucille Davenport, from two floors above her, "My hatpin has somehow become bent all squiggly. I must find another. There will be time."

Maybelle sighed. Lucille, younger by over three decades was consistently late one way and another, always losing things, dropping things, tripping over things, and usually just as it was time for them to depart. Maybelle adjusted her own hat, a worn beige toque of which she was overly fond, it having been her mother's. She smoothed down the front of her woolen coat, a different darker hue that was strangely at odds with the hat, beige being beige. Of this sartorial mismatch she was unaware.

"I'm going," she announced to the clatter of Lucille's shoes on the upper landing and she opened the door to an early October evening, crisp enough to justify the wearing of coats.

"Are we the only ones going?" asked Lucille, rather breathless from her descent, as they stepped together onto the porch of No. 13.

"The unholy lot of them are in the parlor or in their rooms," answered Maybelle. "Times require I accept the lapsed and the heathens into my house."

"And Himself?"

"He has a mild cold."

Himself, that was how the boarders referred to the man who lived quietly below stairs, in the semi-basement chambers next to the kitchen. He had been living there for almost twenty years. If he was a relative of the landlady, she was not saying though there was much speculation along those lines, there being no Mr. Gill on the premises. Maybelle Gill sometimes referred to Himself by his Christian name, Josiah, which seemed overly familiar and was slightly discomforting to Lucille, but usually he was addressed to his face as Mr. Elder.

Lucille was second only to Himself in the length of her stay, having rented the two top floor rooms almost twelve years before, when first coming to Boston to teach secondary school. Nowadays boarders came and went with more frequency, sometimes remaining only for a few weeks, although one month was the absolute minimum stay required by Maybelle Gill, and with payment collected in advance.

The two women moved as shadows then, walking swiftly along Boston's cobbled streets without further conversation, preparing their hopeful hearts to be discovered by the grace of God at evening Mass.

A yellow tomcat sat on the basement stairs next the porch, halfway down to Josiah Elder's rooms and watched the ladies' skirts brush along the pavement as they passed, decided to ignore them, and licked its paw.

2.

"YOU AND I," exclaimed Winston Ward with a laugh, you and I know how to live, now don't we, Mr. Sterling?" He passed his silver flask to Reginald who was pleased to receive it.

"Why it's almost empty, Winston," objected Reginald, determining this from its light weight while admiring the engraved initials on its sleek, hard shell. "You shall have it back after I have drained it dry," and he downed the remaining liquid which was warmed by the recent proximity to its owner's hip, and which burned hotly as it washed into his throat and passed down into his chest, inducing an unwelcome cough. "Yes, we do know how best to spend an evening," he agreed, when he was able to speak again. "Let the ladies say their prayers in church, and let the gentlemen talk of more important matters."

"Which important matters, do you say then?"

"Why of younger ladies who are not inclined to prayer."

"And how might these ladies to whom you refer be *inclined*?" Both men laughed.

These two boarders were sunk comfortably, each to each, into the two oldest and best chairs in the parlor, awaiting their supper, which would be served as soon as Maybelle Gill and her companion returned from Holy Mass. The gentle odors of roasting chicken and potatoes crept up through the seams of the floorboards and the threads of the worn carpet from the kitchen below. They had been talking of horses and business and women as young men do when hungry and waiting, each enjoying the forbidden pleasures of cigarettes and whiskey while the landlady was elsewhere, most likely on her knees.

Winston and Reginald had been working as a team for just over a year, moving from city to city and settling in together at each new location. They sold kitchen appliances for a midwestern company and were quite successful.

They found their shared room at No. 13, rented the month before, to be comfortable, and they were working their way through the city touting sinks and iceboxes to both restaurants and wealthy homes.

"Where shall we go after dinner?" asked Reginald, the younger man. He was tall, thin, blond, a perfect male specimen except for a slight limp, the result of a childhood encounter with an angry dog. But it was Winston, the more weighty and worldly of the two, who most easily attracted women. There was something feral in his nature, something that said here lies a good time with no strings attached.

"Not much doing in Boston on a Sunday night, you know," replied Winston. He was a sturdy man with a ruddy complexion, and with his slightly flattened nose he looked more like a boxer waiting for a punch than a suave salesman.

There was a small part of Winston Ward that disliked Reginald Sterling for being better looking than himself, and small part of Reginald that was judgmental of Winston for his rough talk and callous treatment of women. Reginald, whose mother had died giving birth to him, had always longed for a woman he could love, not one to use and discard. He kept his disapproval to himself in the interests of comradeship, so the two of them bumped along alright.

"This city is laced up pretty tight," continued Winston. Better to be in Chicago or Brooklyn on a Sunday, but we could go and see if that place down by the harbor is open for business. What's it called? Rosa's or something?"

"We will find some spot by the harbor for sure. Sailors have needs…"

"…And where there is need there is profit to be made." And they laughed knowingly.

"You had best air out this room, gentlemen, as Mrs. Gill will be returning any minute now."

This warning, softly spoken, issued forth from Himself. He had just come up from his rooms to await his dinner with the other boarders. Josiah Elder stood in the doorway between the parlor and the dining room as if uncertain as to which room he preferred, leaning slightly to the left and, like a tired prophet, indicating the smokey air with weak waves of his raised right hand. He was dressed carefully as always, though one cuff of his starched white shirt was frayed where it emerged from its hiding place up the sleeve of his unfashionable frock coat. His silk tie was properly knotted and pinned, but his shoes polished to a reflective shine were worn down at the heels. Though unimpressive in stature and hesitant of voice, he nevertheless spoke the truth and Winston and Reginald were quick to respond. They hurried to open windows, ridding the room of the odor of cigarettes.

On occasion, when alone, the two men had remarked upon the curious Mr. Elder, referring to him as did the other lodgers, as Himself, although he never was known to speak of himself. Mrs. Gill, who was quite the gossip about matters outside the house, never deigned to discuss him. He came and went between the lower depths and the upper floor at breakfast and supper rather like an old ghost. (A midday meal was not served at No. 13 Milford Street.) The occasional boarders, those who came and went, could offer nothing about him, of course; not who he was, or where he came from, or what he did, or had done, for a living, and the longer term residents, following the example of Mrs. Gill's discretion, murmured only of his being in retirement. He engaged hesitantly in polite conversation if spoken to, but seldom if not, preferring to eat his meals silently and with a precision that had at times caused others to stare. His English had the ring of a good education, his voice gentle, his manner unfailingly polite. He was, most unexpectedly, likable.

As the other boarders, Captain Earnest Arlington, Miss Mary Prior, and Mr. Lionel Quill could now be heard descending the staircase, Mr. Elder, turned and stepped out onto the sidewalk for some air.

"There goes Himself," said Miss Prior, as she entered the parlor," off to avoid the madding crowds." Miss Mary Prior was the youngest and newest of Mrs. Gill's long-term boarders, a woman in her late-twenties, fetching in an elusive way, with lustrous dark hair and finely made features that arranged themselves as if they veiled a secret. Mary was slipping past her prime in full awareness of the fact. She inspected the men who came and went from the establishment carefully but with diminishing hope of finding someone compatible as the months passed. She suspected she was in the wrong place and at the wrong time to meet a man of mutual interest, but as she was on her own with only a typist's salary for support, No. 13 was it. This is where time and fortune had carved out a niche for her. At least she had the pleasure of male company at meals, something lacking in her previous abode, filled only with timid women and from which she had fled before her rent was again due. And here, no one knew of her past.

She looked about the room which still held the pleasing scent of cigarette. She didn't like Winston Ward. His rough manner put her off, and she thought him vain. She had not entirely ruled out Reginald Sterling. He was young and attractive, more of a gentleman in his behavior than his business partner, but still only a salesman, she mused. A salesman with a limp.

She could not quite fathom Captain Arlington, and she had decided that he was too old for her, although there was the heft of money about him so she would keep a watchful eye in his direction. He was a well-built, handsome man for his age, she thought. He was younger than the venerable Mr. Elder by a decade or more. He carried himself with authority and had a pleasant way of listening to her when she spoke, as if what she said was interesting.

Mr. Lionel Quill was English and was the most handsome of the lot. Money there, too, thought Mary judging by the cut of his suits and the make of his shoes. He said he was married, but where was the wife? "Back home across the waters until my business here is concluded," he had cheerfully informed them, but what that business was, or if it was ever to be concluded had been left to imagination. Sometimes a man's unavailability could arouse interest in a woman, thought Mary Prior, but not in the person of Mr. Quill who was, as her father, a dour old man who had seen it all would say, rather too light on his feet.

Had she erred coming to a city when there had been decent country boys back home willing to marry her? she wondered. Country boys that did not charm and smelled of barns. No. She had, at the very least, given herself a chance for a different kind of life. And here in Boston, among crowds of the young and anonymous, she felt she might be able to leave behind the appalling thing that had happened to her.

The group heard the front door open and the muffled sounds of greeting between the ladies and Mr. Elder in the entryway followed by the sound of the closing door, and to her assembled guests, as Mrs. Maybelle Gill was fond of calling them, the smell of roast chicken seemed to thicken in the air, urging them into the dining room just as the ancient grandfather clock chimed seven.

Mr. Elder was the last to leave the parlor, pausing to shut a window, straighten an antimacassar, and notice an out of place magazine that he picked up and put down quickly with a frown. He seemed reluctant to join the others at table, moving slowly and appearing preoccupied as he gained his chair.

No one seemed to notice Mr. Elder's distraction except Winston Ward. It is bad enough we have to sit through grace every meal, thought the salesman, without having to wait for Himself to dodder in late. He vowed that someday he would be rich enough to stay only in good hotels, eat in excellent restaurants, and drink fine wine with his dinners. The thought was a comfort as he sat with his head dutifully bowed and tried not to listen to Mrs. Gill as she rattled on about God's bountiful gifts.

3.

"WHEN THE EVENING IS SPREAD OUT AGAINST THE SKY LIKE A PATIENT ETHERIZED UPON A TABLE," read Lucille Davenport aloud, pacing restlessly in her room, alone. Sunday prayers and dinner were now things of the past. She held the latest issue of a poetry magazine in one hand and an illicit glass of wine in the other. It was white wine in case it should spill, though she preferred red.

What a nasty image, she thought, an etherized patient. How was she to inspire poetry in the minds of her young students when lines like this were the sort of thing that passed as verse nowadays? Why it didn't even rhyme with anything, although other lines in *The Love Song of J. Alfred Prufrock* did, in many of its haphazard, ill-considered stanzas. And why did the poet preface his poem with a quotation from Dante? One that she had parsed out, phrase by phrase with an Italian-English dictionary, not that she understood its relevance:

If I thought that my reply was given to anyone who might return to the world, this flame would stand forever still; but since never from this deep place has anyone returned alive, if what I hear is true, without fear of infamy I answer thee.

Dante must be endured, she knew, as part of every good education, but used as an epigraph it should be translated into a comprehensible English version to give one a running start, and here, she thought, it was only printed in the original Italian to make the author appear erudite.

Lucille had made up her mind. There was only one more poem to select for the semester ahead and she would not include this poem in the syllabus no matter what the critics were saying about it. She was a week late in submitting her selections to the school's administration. She had waited for the new issue of the poetry magazine to arrive, sent from a friend in London, hoping for something wonderful to be found within its flimsy pages. But this poem was—oh, what was it? It was pretentious. And it was depressing.

Lucille was always distressed, though not with herself, when she failed to understand something. She felt dislike for the things she could not easily grasp, and was unaware that this propensity was not to her advantage as a teacher, or for that matter as a woman hoping to be found interesting. Perhaps she would have tried harder had she not discovered, sadly, that most men did not look for intellectual achievement in a woman when it came to selecting a wife. She put down the magazine and searched out a volume from her bookshelf, first considering Shakespeare as the sonnets never failed. No, it would be Shelley. *Ozymandias* certainly prevailed over *Prufrock*, but she needed something lighter. Suddenly annoyed with the task, she quickly settled on *To a Skylark*. It was a short, uplifting poem, good for restless adolescents. The girls anyway.

Preparation for the semester now accomplished, she replaced the volume and walked to the window where she stood, glass in hand, pensively gazing at everything and nothing, over the rooftops of the houses opposite. It was quiet tonight, and already dark. The sky dimmed earlier and earlier as autumn came on, but displayed no stars tonight because of the fog. Her reflection on the glass looked back at her, vaguely pretty, pale and indistinct, offering no company. There was little movement on the streets below, the city's residents stifled by the inhalation of Sunday homilies, and grown sullen at the thought of a return to work in the morning.

Lucille Davenport did not enjoy Sunday nights, which she usually spent alone, as she was doing tonight. The enclosed quiet of her small sitting room evoked an unpleasant restlessness. She was certain there was some change she must make to bring more satisfaction into her life, but she was at a loss as to how to go about it, or even to know what sort of change it should be, controlled as she was by habit, by custom, and by her desire for security.

She remembered a younger Lucille, an adolescent still in the watchful clutches of the nuns, but one who knew how to sneak out upon the roof of the orphanage to smoke a found cigarette butt, or make her way past the rooms of sleeping women to the kitchen pantry for extra bread and honey. She had sometimes scribbled naughty poems on the inner walls on the outhouse, doggerel she had written herself. Why had that rebellious girl vanished? She knew, of course. She herself had decided to reform, to behave herself, to control her impulses not only to avoid penance but, upon leaving the orphanage to make some kind of respectable life for herself. Etherized...the word came unbidden and unwelcome to her mind. Damn the damn poem, she thought, shocking herself with her inner profanity, wondering if the poem's inherent darkness had sullied her mind. Or perhaps it was the wine.

She had come to Boston, to No. 13, in a trusting spirit twelve years before expecting to meet an interesting partner, a decent man; marry him, have two boisterous boys, and leave the classrooms behind forever, but this had not happened. She taught on. She taught on. She found little to enjoy.

Sometimes she watched the newest resident, Mary Prior, now going through the same motions, expectations, hopes, and disappointments as she had done herself, and she felt pity. What could be sadder than the life of a typist? A young woman trapped in a dreary office, her lovely hands clattering hour after hour on unforgiving keys producing words she did not care about for businessmen who did not care for her. Mary sometimes played the parlor piano in the evenings and Lucille suspected the melodies that rose from her fingertips were an antidote to her days of tuneless pounding.

Lucille believed that she had chosen a more humane profession for herself, but even though the occasional student showed interest in her, or what she taught, she could not deny a growing sense of irrelevance. Should she feel pity for herself? What would be the use in that? No one gets everything they want, she consoled herself, and some people get far less than she had managed to scrape together.

She picked up the discarded poetry magazine and read again the new poem that she had decided not to teach. She could not understand what the poet was saying. She could not understand what he meant at all.

4.

"Let us go," urged Reginald to Winston, always the more impatient of the two. But Winston was all for a second helping of dessert now that the other boarders had departed the dining room. The cook had so far overlooked the remains of the bread pudding as she cleared the table. It sat in the center of the table where it's soft innards oozed out sweetly onto the lime green dish. Reginald felt slightly queasy at the sight, whereas Winston was gazing at the messy pudding happily.

"We have the whole night before us," objected Winston. "The whole night."

"But we have an early morning appointment tomorrow, so an early start makes sense."

"I should have liked cakes and ices, but this pudding will have to do," replied Winston, ignoring Reginald's plea and scooping a mound of the lumpy whiteness onto his plate. "Take a moment to digest your chicken. I thought it very well cooked tonight though there is never enough of it. Never enough."

"There will be something or other for you to gobble up at the bar, no doubt. Let us go."

"There will be time, Reginald. There will be time."

"Oh must you repeat everything you say?" Reginald asked rather sharply, for he was irritated now, watching Winston put spoonful after spoonful of the wretched pudding into his mouth.

"Let us not have a tedious argument," responded Winston, wiping his sticky lips, and rolling his soiled napkin into the appointed ring. "We'll go."

The urgency of Reginald's need for a drink was annoying to Winston. Was the man an alcoholic? There had been signs lately of such an affliction. If this was the case then he must help his friend find some liquid relief now that the pudding was well dispatched.

Winston could not have guessed that one reason for Reginald's drinking was for the purpose of making their evenings out together more tolerable. Sometimes the younger man would rather have stayed in, perhaps play some cards or listen to the piano music of Mary Prior, but Winston was for bars and brothels every evening, and his partner felt it was the manly thing for him to go along. The alcohol took the edge off.

In her sitting room Maybelle Gill heard the men leaving the house, the door slamming unthoughtfully behind them. She was a pious woman, but she did not think "bless their souls" or "may God be with them," as she knew she ought. She muttered instead, "good riddance." She pulled her shawl close around her shoulders and returned to her knitting, remembering an earlier time when the likes of salesmen and other men whom she found coarse were turned away from her door. No. 13 in the early days was welcome only to professors, teachers, clergymen, an occasional governess, and other refined sorts of persons. Once, to Mrs.

Gill's delight, a priest had stayed while his rectory was being repainted. Genteel it had been. Well, no more, she sighed, times change, needs must, and she dropped a stitch.

I must be more charitable in my thoughts, she chided herself as she worked her way through the purple and yellow wool. The salesmen seemed, on the whole, to be decent enough. They kept their room tidy. They didn't swear or spit in the parlor. She knew they smoked and drank, of course, but not around her. Their clothes smelled of it though. She noticed the disagreeable odors when she thoroughly cleaned their room each Monday. Cleanliness was a virtue she believed, and most guests appreciated a proper cleaning. She knew her age would soon require her to hire a maid of all work, but by continuing to do the task herself she could keep a close eye on the intimate habits of those in residence. The salesmen, out each evening, were certainly not attending church services. She tried to keep from imagining where they went, and what they did, and whom they did it with...but she knew. Well, she sighed, the Winston Wards and Reginald Sterlings of the world would come and then move on having contributed nothing of value to No. 13 except their rent money, but having done no real harm.

Having reformulated the two men she prayed for their souls, she crossed herself, and went on with the tasks of elevating her spirit and dropping her stitches.

5.

THROUGH CERTAIN HALF-DESERTED STREETS Mr. Josiah Elder made his way with deliberation as was his custom, always progressing along the same route as he had done for many years. He was a man who had no eagerness for novelty. Novelty, he had observed, arrived quite often of its own accord, unbidden. One had only to be perceptive. There, on that window sill for instance, was a new blood red geranium where only the night before a sadly empty pot had sat abandoned, tinged green with age and neglect. And there a copper penny glittered by the drain. He stooped to pick it up.

Although the streets were dismal in the fog he was fond of them. He knew them well. Occasionally a housewife, spilling out of her corset, would loiter in a doorway watching him pass by without interest. Men in shirtsleeves, some he had come to recognize, leaned out of windows to smoke their pipes, but never said hello. He was sure he could walk the entire way unseen. In truth, he was sure he could walk the entire way blindfolded. This familiarity gave him a sense of ownership. His route. His streets. There was no uncertainty in it.

Tonight the fog was thick, giving his perambulation the possibility of adventure, even of danger, though any ruffian would see at a glance that he had nothing to offer. Being a prudent man he always left his watch and its golden chain, which had once belonged to his father, on the dresser at home, as well as the silver ring purchased long ago from a pawn shop for a pittance, but which cheered him when he allowed it to slide onto his finger. A gang of miscreants could emerge from the miasma, search him upside and down and would find only an old man in old clothes with a shiny penny in his trousers' pocket. Nothing so exciting as this had ever occurred during his walks, of course, but he had read in *The Boston Courier* of a rise in crime in this rather poor area of town where the houses seemed to lean together in an evil way, as if conspiring to do him some mischief…so, maybe. The idea allowed him to feel quite daring.

He did not need a cane as yet, but the length of time it took for him to complete his walk stretched longer with each passing year. The ice of winter slowed him down and he never quite recovered his former pace in the Spring. About these incremental losses he was unconcerned. He was a man who had spent his life absorbed in the minds of others, so conveniently packaged as they were, in books. It had left him philosophical about life, unsure about almost everything, but not about his ultimate place in the scheme of things. He was unimportant. In the long run he would end, be no more, just as he once had never been. Death was life's final word on itself and he was resigned to it. In the short run he would end up where he had begun, at No. 13. When it came to the meaning of life he didn't think there was one, and to him that was no great matter.

He knew that when he arrived home he would make his way down the seven stone steps and enter the kitchen by way of the servants' door, make himself a cup of tea and eat the biscuits left for him on the table by the young and clever cook, Beatrice Platt. A pleasant girl. By the time he returned she would have completed her evening tasks and left the kitchen as sterile as a doctor's operating theater, knives sharpened and shining in the rack, copper pots hanging overhead in descending order, and breakfast trays laid out for the morning on the counter. He thought there might be something to that girl. Beatrice the cook. Beatrice on the other side of his door, cooking and baking, but always thinking, he could tell. He recognized intelligence when he saw it.

In earlier days, when a family had lived in the house, the rooms he occupied, just off the kitchen, had been a butler's quarters. He found them to his satisfaction. Both the small sitting room and smaller bed chamber were spacious enough for his spare needs. They were comfortably furnished, although the line of rectangular windows, placed at the level of the pavement, allowed in only a little natural light. Fortunately, Mrs. Gill's electrifications compensated, so he could read well enough. Sometimes he switched off the lights and sat quietly in the gloom watching the comings and goings of people along the sidewalk just above his head, the feet that clicked, the skirts that trailed, the canes that thumped, the paws that trotted, and wondered where they were all going, what they might be doing and thinking. There were too many lives to imagine them all.

Mr. Elder had left the scarlet geranium far behind, and gone round the corner by the pharmacy where the young men stood in a fan of light, neither scholars nor thugs, who seemed to have nowhere else to go. He paid them no mind as he stepped carefully over the uneven cobbles, for his thoughts tonight were unusually disturbed. Lucille Davenport, the school teacher who lived on the uppermost floor, had left a poetry magazine on the parlor table. Josiah had glimpsed it only briefly as he passed by on his way into the dining room for the evening meal, but he thought he recognized the photograph on the cover as someone he knew, now older, more mature than when Josiah had last seen him. He had hoped to take the magazine down to his rooms for a closer inspection after dinner, but Miss Davenport had retrieved it and carried it up the stairs, leaving Josiah in uncertainty. Had the boy, for he seemed only a boy, become successful? Famous enough to have his face thrust flat upon a magazine cover? Perhaps he had been mistaken. Surely his eyes had deceived him. Dare he ask Miss Davenport if he might have a look at it? Would an inquiry give rise to idle speculation?

He decided it was best to keep the matter to himself, all things considered. It would be more discreet to acquire his own copy of the magazine. He wondered perhaps if the nearest bookshop might have one. That is what he would do. He would go tomorrow to the shop at the corner of Washington and School Streets, as he used to do so often in the days when he was teaching. There he would make an inquiry.

Then again it might be best to let the whole matter lie. Most probably he had been mistaken and was sending himself upon a fool's errand. Would it be worth it? The walk to the bookshop from No. 13 was a long one. On the other hand if the fog lifted in the morning as Captain Arlington had predicted, it would be pleasant to take a morning stroll. October was a kind month, filled with autumnal hues and lovely slanted light that crept away while people were at their evening meals, returning brightly in the mornings. Yes. He would traverse the long way to Washington and School Streets in the sunshine of morning. If the fog should lift.

His decision now settled, he walked along the twisting streets back to the boarding house in a calmer mood. The evening's exercise, his considerations and reconsiderations, had calmed his emotions.

As he approached the house he looked around for the yellow cat that sometimes sat upon the kitchen steps, a cat he always called Tom Cat, although he did not, of course, know it's rightful name. The animal was nowhere to be seen.

6.

THE MUTTERING RETREATS, the evening's farewells as the parlor emptied out, roused Captain Arlington from his after dinner nap. He had captured a good chair and while the others had played whist or read, his indulgence in the cook's heavy sauces and heavier bread pudding had the effect of sinking him into a troubled sleep. He dreamt of the sea as he often did.

They were gone now, all the others, excepting Mary Prior who sat dreamily by the piano, but not playing anymore. He watched her secretly through half-closed eyes. The residents had gone out walking, or out drinking, or off to their rooms for more reading or sleep. He knew them all. He had a habit of watching and listening closely to people, trying to imagine their lives, and a boarding house was an excellent place to observe humanity's whims and ways, of which he could never quite believe himself to be a part.

The sea kept one adrift, separate from the concerns of landed people; but now he was ashore, run aground, because the rogue wave had hit, the snarling winds had conspired, and his poor ship, after fighting the tempest bravely had broken up and begun to sink. "Every man for himself," he had cried out. The most mournful words he had ever uttered.

The men, his men, the drowning men, swam before his eyes. He had gone down stoically, as he should have done, never leaving the ship as it plunged deeper and deeper into the watery underworld. There had been no bravery in the moment, or fear, only a determination that his last act in the world be an honorable one. But fate had other plans for Captain Earnest Arlington and he had bobbed up like a wine cork emerging into the howling air near an over-turned lifeboat, and clinging to it, cringing at his clinging, he had saved himself. Tossed about in those terrible seas, he had not wished to live. Death pulled and pushed at him from below, and he willed himself to let go, but to sink again into the darkness, to swallow more of the black oily water was horrifying. Life clutched at him from above as, with whitened knuckles, he held onto the shattered edge of the boat. In those desperate moments he learned that a man's will to live could be stronger than his shame or his guilt.

Saved, he did not feel that God had granted him another chance at life. On the contrary, he felt marooned. He knew he could never go home to his coastal village full of seafaring men and mourning widows. The disgrace was too great. So he hid himself here in the crowds of Boston, in this ordinary boarding house, with these anonymous people, only to find he was still too close to the sea. The smell of fish and salt was carried on night winds from the harbor, and when he wandered too far from No. 13 he overheard the laughter of sailors lost in their liquors and their lusts inside the watering holes along the docks.

So he had planned to depart Boston for somewhere deep in the midst of America; to Indianapolis or Omaha where no one thought of the sea and many did not know there was one. He had determined to go at the end of the month, but his plan was now, again, confounded by fate.

He had formed an unexpected and unwanted attraction to the youngest boarder. He had most inconveniently fallen in love with Miss Mary
Prior.

It was a dizzying experience. He found himself fascinated by the
shape of her wrists, and earlobes, and lips, the glimpses of her ankles and
the curling lashes of her eyes, her delicate fingers that he knew tapped
tapped tapped all day long on unrelenting keys without complaint, but
rendered lovely melodies in the evenings. When he envisioned her in
his mind's eye she seemed to be encircled with a sparkling glow. All
this was absolute nonsense, he knew. He had been mesmerized before
in his youth and thankfully outgrown it, and once or twice he had been
stricken with lovesickness in distant ports, from which he had sailed
away with a mixture of relief and regret. But Mary was right here at
breakfast, at dinner, and after dinner, humming as she played, or
laughing during card games, then yawning before withdrawing to her
bedroom, all magical to him.

He knew that Mary Prior wished for love, but he did not think she
would wish for him, so he wished enough for the two of them, smiled
like a bewitched schoolboy whenever she entered a room, and listened
attentively when she spoke to him in the languages of youth about her
life, of a life lived upon dry land. She was too discreet of speak of love.

Foolish man, he thought. Foolish girl. He felt himself being pushed
and pulled by currents of affection, this way and that, towards and
against, like the waves unsure whether to drown him or buoy him up.
Tonight, exhausted, he had given himself the relief of sleep while she
sat first at the piano, but now, as he roused, moved to a chair nearby,
holding a book close to her slightly near-sighted, sea-green eyes.

Surely, he thought, he must speak to her of his feelings. Surely, he
thought, he must not.

7.

OF RESTLESS NIGHTS, of insomnia, and of midnight longings, Mr.
Lionel Quill had gained a most intimate knowledge. Tonight, after
dinner and cards, he prowled the length and breadth of his room, a
confining space not designed for restlessness, but for sleeping, an

experience he longed for but seldom achieved with much satisfaction. His chamber was well located at the back of the house with a separate entrance and a good lock. He always chose or declined rooms on the issue of privacy, but never, of course stating so aloud while viewing the available rooms with one landlady or another. Displaying concern for such matters might arouse curiosity in the mind of a wary female. Where had all these landladies come from? Women without men, middle-aged or older, patrolling their properties, and clutching their proprieties like lovers.

Tonight, like many nights, he was a man without a lover and so he paced up and down on the small square of carpet in what served as his home for the month, or maybe longer, unless suspicions began to arise in the mind of Mrs. Maybelle Gill or an outright discovery was made about him. Then the dismissal would come in no uncertain terms by a kindly woman turned red with outrage. In other places, when he had been lucky, a refund of his remaining rent had been slapped onto his palm in distaste, but usually not. Still, his situation was better here in America than in England. In England he would be prosecuted as a criminal. Here there was a better chance of being thought of merely as a disgrace.

He was fairly certain Mary Prior was onto him, but she was young enough not to be horrified, just mildly repelled. The younger generation was more forgiving than the old. He hoped this trend would continue in the future as it arrived, and arrived again.

He had already attired himself for bed, but this bed would not be having him tonight. The house was quiet. Lucille Davenport had finally stopped her own pacing overhead. The salesmen next door were out catting around as usual. Mrs. Gill on the ground floor was hopefully deep in sleep, and Mr. Josiah Elder was ensconced down in the lower depths. Who knew what Himself did with his evenings, mornings, afternoons, nights. The man was an enigma.

Slowly Lionel dressed again, this time in his best suit, and stepping stealthily so as not to wake the others, he crept from his room and down the back stairs, hunched like a thief with a bag full of incrimination on his back. He made his way towards the alleys near the harbor, hoping he would not inadvertently cross paths with Winston or Reginald. It was a night of heavy yellow fog, perfect for shrouding impermissible desires.

8.

In one-night cheap hotels and sawdust restaurants with oyster-shells the yellow cat was a well-known visitor. The owners of these establishments were tired working people, toiling while others slept. Lifting their eyes from washing or cooking they were always glad to see him as he made his midnight rounds. They would give him a caress or bits of fish or incomprehensible conversation. He liked best, the fish.

Tonight on his wanderings he had recognized a man who lived upstairs in the house where he stayed. The man was entering a hotel with another man close upon his heels. He understood this behavior. He often changed his own sleeping spots as a matter of safety.

The cat arrived at his favored destination, a restaurant that was always good for a meal at its back door. The cook, a short, man with a long black tail down his back, called him Herekittykitty, and gave him rice with bits of chicken. Tonight the cat ate his meal enthusiastically, let his back be scratched, and then wandered away in search of sex.

9.

Streets that follow like a tedious argument of insidious intent… Lucille read, silently. Unable to sleep, she had decided to read the poem, which she did not understand or like, once again. For some reason she was not entirely at peace with her decision to dismiss it, although she was sure it was unsuitable for young minds. Nevertheless, she had to acknowledge that something in its odd rhythms and strange imagery had taken hold of her, and its content was disturbing her mind.

She struggled out from beneath the bedclothes and stood up, letting the magazine slide from the counterpane onto the floor where she let it lie. The solemn face of the handsome young poet stared up blankly at her night-gowned figure from its paper cover into some unknown middle distance. He did not look at her.

Did she dare? With a curious mixture of righteousness and guilt she placed her bare foot directly on the image.

"Take that," she said aloud. "You have written a bad poem, and you are a bad man."

He had fooled other men, doubtless men of his own station who knew him and liked him, into thinking it was good; the self-satisfied kind of men who would take no notice of *her*. A woman alone. A spinster. He had charmed them all. Charmed them into thinking the poem was modern, and therefore, fine.

"But I am not beguiled," she declared.

She was only confused, for there was something in the wretched thing that bedeviled her. Something personal. Something terrible.

10.

"To lead you to an overwhelming question...that, and that alone, is the purpose of poetry."

This statement had been Professor Josiah Elder's signature phrase, with which he had begun every semester, and that he oft repeated whilst teaching the course in Creative Writing of Poetry and Literature to Harvard students for so many, many years.

Class after class of fresh smart boys who thought they were men and thought that they knew it all, were told by Josiah Elder to look into their hearts and minds before they dared to write a single word themselves. He had used exactly that phrase:

"Poetry," he would declare, "must lead you to an overwhelming question."

But there it was, wrenched out of context, and sent back to him in smudged typeface by his special boy, now grown to manhood with his face on the cover of a magazine looking so...looking so...feline.

He had been Josiah's golden student, a boy who had arrived at Harvard hesitant, unsteady, but with undeniable genius. He was the one who was destined to follow in his own footsteps as head of a department, philosophy was the mother's preference, but literature and creative writing was a better fit, in Josiah's opinion.

The young man's talent had been breathtaking when he first materialized in the classroom. It was *this* boy whom he had favored over all the rest; whom he had dared to love; all in a proper way, of course. It was *that* boy who had become a Judas, who had purloined his wisdom, stolen his words, and who had satirized and savaged him in the poem, turning him into a mournful caricature of himself. He had been eviscerated.

This, now, became his own overwhelming question: why had Thomas Eliot wanted to hurt him so badly?

Mr. Elder sank into his armchair and gazed up at the passersby outside his window, unseeing. It was his habit to face bad news squarely, not to turn away from suffering, his own or others, so he held the magazine's image at arm's length, where he could see it clearly without his glasses, and spoke to it, softly at first.

"For all the time and the love and care that I gave you so freely, recognizing your brilliance, your talent, you have ransacked my mind, you have belittled my ways, and you have put them to your own indecipherable, despicable purposes."

His voice began to rise as he felt the stirrings of the anger beneath his pain.

"Why? Was it because I revealed my affection for you? Is that why you have made such a vicious assault upon my person? You misunderstood! You thought I was making unwelcome, unnatural advances towards you. That was not what I meant at all; that is not it, at all!"

Josiah Elder, wounded and confused and angry, realized he needed something that he seldom needed…a strong drink. He did not keep alcohol in his rooms, for that would be against the house rules. He knew the older of the two salesmen staying on the second floor had a flask, but he would not stoop to ask assistance from the likes of Winston Ward! How standards had fallen at No. 13.

He considered inquiring of the sailor-man, Captain Arlington, who seemed respectable enough. All sailors drank, didn't they? How else to endure their fearsome lives, floating upon the skin of fathomless death. Did he dare to presume? Or to ask? He had never done anything to disobey Maybelle Gill's regulations, or any regulations for that matter, except perhaps not crossing at the designated place on Suffolk Street, but he had an urge to break rules now. To break rules and teacups and window panes. He must do something radical to calm his nerves.

He recognized that he was not himself.

He knew that if Lucille Davenport had failed to leave her copy of the poetry magazine lying unattended, if he had not seen that familiar face as he passed by it; had he not, against better judgment, bought his own copy and then read the ghastly poem, he would be having his usual, quiet evening of chamomile tea and Shakespeare, for it was his habit to read much of the night.

The vision of Lucille reading the poem, reading it aloud to others horrified him. Lucille taught young people, almost children. Would she dare to teach the poem? Surely not. She was a sensible woman. She would not fill their minds with such depressing drivel when they needed to be uplifted and encouraged.

And what if he were *recognized*!? The idea shot through him like an arrow of steel carrying fear on its gleaming tip. No. No. No. He reassured himself. It won't be so. Tom has had the decency to render me anonymous to all but myself. He has disguised me with a ridiculous name. He stared at the title: *The Love Song of J. Alfred Prufrock*. Surely no one but myself will connect the honorable Professor Josiah Elder with the pitiful J. Alfred Prufrock. This is an entirely private attack. Taking a deep breath he let the fear drain out of the hole in his lungs where the arrow of thought had pierced him, leaving only an aching emptiness.

His frayed nerves would have to be soothed with a swallow of cooking wine. He tiptoed from his empty room into the darkened kitchen and drank straight from the bottle in the pantry. He coughed, then shuddered as the acidic liquid went down into his chest. He saw that his hands were shaking as he replaced the bottle. The alcohol had done him no good.

"It was I who had first believed in him," he whispered into the night. "And it was I who believed that I had something to teach him. I believed in him, and I believed in me, and I have been played the fool."

II.

"OH, DO NOT ASK, WHAT IS IT?" cautioned Maybelle Gill to Captain Arlington with a laugh, holding up the bulky woolen square of ill-chosen colors to show her progress. "It will be a scarf to begin with, but it may knit itself into a blanket over the winter when the nights are long." He smiled and nodded in tactful approval. "And might you be staying with us for the duration?" she asked. "I do hope so."

Maybelle was pleased with the acquisition of Captain Earnest

Arlington as he was both an attractive man and a clever one, and would be amusing to talk with in the dark, cold evenings that were in the offing. He stood in the open doorway of her living room. It was the room in which she spent most of her evenings when not in church. It fronted the house and stood across the entryway a little apart from the guests in the parlor but near enough so that she could gage the temper of their murmurs and note their comings and goings.

She appreciated the look of the Captain who was tall, upright, graying at the temples with a fine healthy complexion, no doubt from his years in salty air. He smiled easily and listened well. She sensed that he might have come from good family before going to sea, and rising to Captain is not an easy accomplishment whatever his background. She wondered what had put him into dry-dock here in No. 13. Perhaps his age? He got on well with the other tenants and did not make trouble for her, so he would be an excellent addition should he choose to extend his residency into the winter months.

"I am thinking that I might remain here, but my room is rather small for a long stay," he replied. "Might there be another available in the near future? Perhaps one with a fireplace?"

"Let me see what I can do, Captain," she responded. "The salesmen, Mr. Ward and Mr. Sterling, might leave Boston for warmer climes along with the first gust of a strong New England wind, and I don't know yet about Mr. Quill. His room at the back of the house is quiet with a separate entrance. It has no fireplace, but stays very cozy in winter as the chimney from the kitchen runs up along the south side of the house."

"Well, I do like a good fire," he said glancing longingly at the embers glowing in the fireplace near to where she sat. "It was something I missed at sea all those many years. I could pay a little extra for the coal if a room with a fireplace were to become available." He saw that the offer pleased her, and he was emboldened to ask: "Are the ladies staying on, if you don't mind my inquiring?"

Maybelle raised an eyebrow. So that was it. He'd taken a fancy to Lucille Davenport or Mary Prior, she thought. She had seen it all before, seen it all. Maybelle hoped it was Lucille whom he had set his eye upon, for she appeared to be dwindling of late, worn down by too many disappointments and too many hours spent with other people's clamorous children.

"Both my lady lodgers have booked for the winter ahead," she replied," raising a wagging finger, "though I am wrong to tell you."

"I apologize for giving you any discomfort, Mrs. Gill."

"A woman in my position must learn to be discreet, Captain Arlington, but she must also know when to make exceptions." She smiled at him conspiratorially. He returned her smile, made a slight bow, and left the living room, closing the door politely behind him.

Yes, she liked the Captain, this man who had blown in off the waves. He was too young for herself, far too old for Mary Prior, but like Goldilocks' porridge, he was just right for Lucille Davenport. She wished to be encouraging in the matter of Lucille's hopes for marriage.

Maybelle Gill never felt disappointment in regards to her own prospects in life. This was because she allowed herself none. Long ago when Mr. Leon Gill, her newlywed husband, who was a fine young man from a wealthy family, had been killed on their honeymoon by a falling tree she found that she had no further inclination towards romance. She had loved Leon and been loved in return. She felt that their courtship and subsequent union, albeit short, was quite enough for one life, and so she had closed the book on such attachments, or more accurately, she accepted God's will in the matter of ending her honeymoon in so abrupt a manner. Her graceful acquiescence had allowed another life to emerge.

The brief marriage had secured her financially, so with her considerable inheritance she had purchased this house for a substantial sum and set about decorating it with her own tastes which ran to the ornate in her private rooms, homely in the public rooms, and austere in the rooms she let out. She installed solid oak furnishings that would endure for decades even with the wear and tear of careless boarders. There were good thick curtains in all the rooms that could be pulled back in summers, but when drawn close they kept out the damp and cold of Boston winters, saving on coal. The carpets were durable wool, and the indulgence of modern electrical lamps, were of shining brass with etched glass shades.

The house was rooted in a solidly middle-class neighborhood, though bordering a less auspicious area. It was, however, within walking distance of some attractive shops, and a library was nearby for the more scholarly of the boarders. It did not put on airs or get above itself in style, but fit in snuggly with the neighboring houses, two of which also offered rooms for rent, though not so nice as hers, she presumed. From the front door with its stained glass insets one stepped from the narrow porch down two wide stone steps to a well-maintained sidewalk along a quiet street. In the back a small garden had once held the outhouse, but Mrs. Gill had installed running water and a modern water-closet on each floor including the basement, her biggest and boldest expense, so now the little garden with its rich soil offered a small patch of shade in summers, and the pleasant scent of lilacs in Spring.

Over the years the reputation of No. 13 for quietness and cleanliness had allowed her to fill the house with companionable people, and it had proved worthwhile financially, offering her a steady income to supplement her savings, and as a bulwark against loneliness. God had helped her through her mourning and with her transformation into a respectable widow, the Mrs. Maybelle Gill, of No. 13. She was a woman who, within these walls carefully chose the players, issued the directions, adjusted the scenery, influenced the plots, and enjoyed the passing show of genteel humanity as it paraded in and out of her front door.

Her happiest find had been Himself, Professor Josiah Elder, now retired, who had lived quietly underneath her living room floorboards in the basement rooms for two decades. He was a kind man and they had come to care for one another in a somewhat formalized way, rather like an old married couple she imagined, but without the disappointments of romance, the messiness of marriage or, God forbid, the embarrassments of sex.

Mrs. Gill offered up a prayer of gratitude to her generous and forbidding God, unaware of the troubles beginning to brew both upstairs and down. She continued knitting the woolen strands of her ill-defined creation.

12.

"Let us go and make our visit," whispered Mary Prior with a conspiratorial smile. She was allowed two days off from her job at the patent office each year, besides July Fourth and Christmas, and she had chosen this bright, unusually warm, October Monday as one of them. Mary was downstairs in the kitchen where she should not be, having cajoled the cook, Beatrice Platt, into preparing sandwiches for their mutual outing.

"Mrs. Gill will fire me for certain if she hears an inkling of this," replied Beatrice.

"We are not planning a murder," chided Mary, "and how would she ever know? Winston and Reginald won't talk."

Beatrice nodded in the direction of Mr. Elder's closed door.

"He is a nice gentleman," said Mary. "He won't tell, even if he knows."

"Himself knows everything that goes on in this house, just as Mrs. Gill does. They talk, those two."

"Well, I shall stand between you and any rebuke whether from Maybelle Gill or Himself. I shall take all the blame on myself. A bit of cheese and a roll or two will never be missed and I've an apple for each of us." An act of petty larceny excited Mary, but not Beatrice. Mary was the more modern and more daring of the two.

Her nervousness not withstanding Beatrice was eager for the afternoon's planned adventure. Mary had asked Mr. Sterling and Mr. Ward, to take them to the new wing of The Museum of Fine Arts which had recently opened on Huntington Avenue. It was too far to walk, even on a nice day. The men had willingly obliged, probably to seem important and to show off the Model T automobile that their company let them drive, supposedly only for business purposes. In her opinion it showed their lack of character, but she wanted very much to see the paintings which she had read about in the *Boston Evening Transcript*.

Beatrice might be obliged to earn her living as a cook, but she had a good brain which longed for knowledge and for the cultured life that accompanied a well-educated mind. Mary Prior, she judged, was more interested in Winston Ward or Reginald Sterling than in art, and was probably flattered that the two men were breaking company rules to transport the women on their lark.

Had Mary known of Beatrice's thoughts, she would have agreed. She was quite excited, mostly about the ride itself, her first in an automobile. After the museum visit they would enjoy a picnic in the surrounding park-like grounds if the weather held. Then they would board an omnibus for their return journey, for the men had emphasized that they must get on with their work after the morning's drive. The two women would be back in plenty of time for Beatrice to serve up the juicy roast beef that was now coming slowly to perfection in the oven.

Mary was aware that, although there was no particular rule against it, Mrs. Gill disapproved of her friendship with Beatrice who she considered to be staff, below stairs, and quite unfairly, lesser than her boarders. Mary held more enlightened notions, and she did not give a hoot about Maybelle Gill's middle-class prejudices. They were both working girls, one in an office, one in a kitchen. Both were accomplished at their work but were left unsatisfied by what they did. They differed in their prospects for salvation, however. Mary pinned her hopes on her good looks and a marriage. Beatrice, unaware of her attractiveness, was counting on an education.

Well, if we survive the automobile ride, we will see the new paintings, thought Beatrice. It was a consoling prospect. Mary will be free to flirt if she chooses, and I will enjoy the art, though I will fret about being discovered, which could cost me my job. Would it have been worth it to venture out if she found herself unemployed with tuition to pay next week? By nature, Beatrice Platt tended to overthink things. Her seriousness went into her cooking, and into her lessons at the night school she attended, resulting in excellent meals and high scholastic marks, but it took its toll on her ability to fully enjoy her life.

She wondered what it would be like to be as carefree as Mary who seemed light-hearted about everything except finding a husband which she considered a very serious endeavor. Beatrice didn't think much about husbands. There will be time for one to turn up, she supposed. In the meantime there was history and literature and art and the menu for next week about which to be concerned.

13.

In the room the women come and go talking of Michelangelo, and of other artists of which he had no knowledge, for about art he knew next to nothing. What did a man who had spent his life upon the oceans know of paintings? Of sculpture? Of what was fine, and what was bad in art, in poetry, and in all the things that interested pretty young women? The Captain knew he shouldn't be here at all. Infatuation had led him astray. The Boston Museum of Fine Art was large, solid, stuffy and, for a man such as himself, intimidating.

Captain Arlington had overheard Mary Prior making her plans for this visit with Winston and Reginald as he had awakened from one of his after dinner dozes in the parlor. Envy of the two younger men, and jealousy of which he was not proud, had propelled him to the museum on impulse, and now he hated himself for his lack of self-control; for coming to this place, this repository of beauty where in every work of art he found only his own incomprehension.

At sea Captain Arlington had seen beauty, recognized it, even reveled in it; the beauty of magnificent sunrises over watery horizons, at dolphins emerging and remerging like mermaids within the twilight waves of black and white, at the stars at night sparkling like sea spray splashed across the heavens so clear and bright one could believe they were the eyes of angels; but about colors daubed on canvas trapped in gilded squares he knew nothing; of stony men with their bottoms embarrassingly bare, even less.

Suddenly, seized with a need for air, real air, outdoor air, he decided to escape the cloistering rooms before he embarrassed himself by crossing paths with the two young women he had so furtively followed. He felt himself to be a love-struck old man, out of his element, almost out of his mind.

Awash in these unpleasant thoughts and admitting to himself this had all been a mistake, Captain Arlington made for the museum doors and, as the fates would have it, ran directly into Mary Prior and her companion, the cook from downstairs whose name escaped him, but in whose sharp eyes he read awareness that this could be no coincidence. The two salesmen, thank God, were nowhere to be seen.

"Why, Captain Arlington," exclaimed Mary, "what a delightful surprise. You know my friend Beatrice Platt who works for Mrs. Gill, preparing our delicious meals. I knew you were a man of refinement. Not like those two rascals who brought us out here and then scurried away as though dogs would burst out of a hunting scene and bite them. But the ride in their automobile was great fun. Are you leaving? Perhaps you will join us on our picnic and then accompany us back to No. 13 on the trolley."

How self-possessed are the young, thought Captain Arlington while he himself, caught in his duplicitous act, felt thoroughly unbalanced, as if he stood upon undulating waves that were trying to send him staggering. He fought to steady himself, appear normal, speak properly.

Aha! thought Beatrice. The Captain is smitten with Mary, plain as day. He actually followed us, the old scoundrel, and has been caught out. She wanted to laugh but stifled her amusement. He was, after all, a guest of Mrs. Gill.

"I shall be best pleased," the embarrassed man managed to say with a correct smile, relieved that his words were coming out in the right order. "Best pleased to accompany you two lovely ladies on the return journey." What he actually wanted to do, was, like a ruthless pirate, seize Mary Prior, throw her over his shoulder, carry her off protesting (only slightly) onto a waiting ship, hoist anchor, and sail away with her forever.

The three walked sedately from the museum together, all passions suppressed, into the late afternoon air, already thickening with wisps of evening mist that carried with it the scent of the sea. Too far away.

14.

THE YELLOW FOG THAT RUBS ITS BACK UPON THE WINDOW PANES was a comforting sight to Lionel Quill, for like the fogs of London back home, they hid his ways, hid his means, hid him from the eyes of the men and women who might understand, and if they understood would disapprove. Now, in the waning light of evening he made his way back up to his room, both satisfied and shaken by the night and day just passed with the gorgeous young man whose real name he would never know. He admitted that he was tired; not from the indulgent idyll, but tired of hiding and pretending. Pretending to be normal. Tired of being Lionel Quill, a fictional husband to a distant, imaginary wife.

He was a good looking man. This he knew. Attractive women turned their attention to him often with their wants and wishes. He played along with an agreeable smile, laughed with them, held a hand or two, all the time not wishing. Not wanting.

Then he would politely slip away into the evening's welcoming shadows, as the world prepared for sleep, unwrapping itself from a day of propriety; as the decent women with their unfulfilled wishes peeled off their dampened clothes, and brushed their teeth, and clipped their toenails, and cleaned their ears, Lionel would walk into the night, wanting what it was that he wanted.

If fortune smiled, out of the darkness would step another like himself. They would find their way to privacy, and then would come the moment when, safely behind locked doors, he could step into an embrace, rest his head gently upon the stranger's shoulder, and let his mind, stuffed with the world's judgments and disapprovals melt away into the relief of what was light and right. For him.

Why then, as he returned, so satisfied in so many ways did he think of suicide? Why in such moments did death seem better than life. It would be easy enough, the belt off his bathrobe wrapped round the doorknob, a quick push, but it would take more nerve than he could summon. Better to step in front of a trolley. Yes. That was a better idea. He could do it one day when he least expected it, surprise himself before his resolve could weaken. He could let a sudden impulse take him, and in a few quick steps be out of this pretense of a life into something that was genuine. The shock of impact, the deafening squeal of brakes, a flash of red, and then blackness before the pain could find him. He would lie on the pavement, still and broken, while all around him people gathered. And wept. And cared. He could see it all in his mind's eye like a painting.

15.

THE YELLOW SMOKE of innumerable chimneys arose from the tired city and mingled itself with the fog coming in from the sea; a fog that returned each evening trailing the setting sun, thickening the autumnal air to a quivering marmalade. Winston Ward and Reginald Sterling stood outside on the steps No. 13 and added the smoke from their cigarettes to the gathering miasma.

The men had enjoyed a grand day. Daring to take the two young ladies for their outing in the company automobile had been an adventure. When they left the women at the museum and turned their minds to work, they had been met with success. Two ovens! They had sold an oven to each of two restaurants, which would return a fine commission.

"I think our Mary has set her cap for you," said Winston to Reginald, watching him closely to measure his reaction.

"*Our* Mary, is it?" replied Reginald giving Winston no clue as to his feelings, which happened to be icy in regards to Mary Prior, whom he found ordinary. A nice enough girl. A typist. He yawned.

"Well, I think she could be *your* Mary, if you have a mind for it."

But Reginald didn't smile. His feelings were disturbed this evening by having made the formal acquaintance of Beatrice Platt. Beatrice the cook, whom he hadn't looked at twice as she was serving up his meals over the past few weeks, seeing only the trays of food, not the woman who offered them. How could he not have noticed her before? The lovely rounded breasts, the slim hips, the arms downed with light brown hair, the delicate ankles. And the hands! Surely her hands were made to offer caresses as well as creamed potatoes. Reginald was unaware that it was her intelligence which had attracted him as she made pleasant conversation about poetry and art. He did not think of himself as particularly intelligent, or interested in the life of the mind. He did not think of himself much at all. Mr. Elder would say he was still finding himself, but of this opinion he was unaware for he seldom conversed with Josiah Elder.

Winston, however, often made comments about his partner, not always complimentary. Today he had seen the spark before Reginald had registered it himself. "So it is Our Lady of the Kitchen that's got hold of you," he taunted.

"You don't miss much, do you?"

"Your mind didn't seem on business today."

"We did well enough!" he protested. "But don't you ever get bored with the work, Winston?"

"Bored? No, never. I like the challenge of starting each day at zero, with a good paycheck waiting at the end of it if we meet the challenge."

"Most jobs will give you that."

"True enough, but it's best to stay on the horse you know."

"I don't think we are very well liked by the other boarders. Salesmen are not highly thought of." This had not troubled him in the past, but how others viewed him had taken on sudden importance with his attraction to Beatrice.

"Why on earth would you care? One of the great advantages of sales is getting to know people you can leave behind without a care. They are entertaining in the moment, but their opinions don't count for much.

And I like being able to travel on when we have had enough of them, free to try our luck selling in another city."

"Ovens. Iceboxes. Sinks."

"What would you rather?"

"Ladies undergarments would make a nice change."

"If you want to start up a conversation with Beatrice Platt down in the kitchen, you'll do better with ovens than corsets, I reckon. Ladies don't discuss what's underneath until they are married."

Reginald sighed. "Well, I suppose we must go and find some women who are not ladies then," he said, feeling less interested than on past evenings, but knowing this suggestion was expected of him.

"I've been thinking about Lucille," said Winston.

"Lucille? The lavender scented ghost of a woman who always bores us silly going on about some gent named Prufrock that we don't even know? She's thirty if she's a day. She doesn't seem your type at all, Winston."

"True enough."

"I'd say, she's a real lady. What thoughts could you be having about her?"

"I was thinking I might be able to put some rose in her cheeks."

"Well, aren't you the sly dog. But she'd never have you. All she thinks about is church and poetry. She's all laced up with only proper behavior inside."

"Thought I might unlace her."

"You wouldn't. No. You couldn't."

"Bet's on?"

"You're serious."

"I'd be doing her a favor."

"Okay, Winston. If you succeed I'll take you to a steak dinner. But if she refuses, as she most certainly will, you will buy the steaks."

"And whiskey to go with the steaks."

"How will you prove your success?"

"I shall bring you an undergarment with the scent of lavender."

"You are a villain!" declared Reginald. He patted Winston on the back, but at heart he was not at ease with the part he was forcing himself to play in the interests of their comradeship.

The two men stepped on the butt ends of their cigarettes and began walking towards the docks without the need of another word between them.

Winston was smiling, certain he would win his bet, but Reginald was downcast. Playing so fast and loose with another person's feelings, as Winston was proposing to do, troubled his conscience. And as for himself, he didn't have the slightest notion of how to talk to Beatrice Platt.

16.

"THAT RUBS ITS MUZZLE ON THE WINDOW PANES, LICKED ITS TONGUE INTO THE CORNERS OF THE EVENING, LINGERED UPON THE POOLS THAT STAND IN DRAINS, LET FALL UPON ITS BACK THE SOOT THAT FALLS FROM CHIMNEYS, SLIPPED BY THE TERRACE, MADE A SUDDEN LEAP, AND SEEING IT WAS A SOFT OCTOBER NIGHT, CURLED ONCE ABOUT THE HOUSE, AND FELL ASLEEP."

After reading this section aloud in her most scholarly voice, Lucille stopped for a moment to breathe and, without looking up from the magazine asked Maybelle Gill: "Now why is this poet writing about smoke? Why is he pretending that the smoke is a cat?"

Only the sound of a stentorian snore issued forth from her friend for she, like the smoke had fallen asleep. Lucille had wanted to discuss the troublesome poem, so she had come downstairs to Maybelle's sitting room to share it with her. Well, she had gotten a second opinion, if not a discussion. Whereas the poem made Lucille want to throw things and scream, it had put Maybelle out cold.

Mrs. Gill could be forgiven, Lucille thought charitably. She was a landlady, not a teacher or writer or artist or the sort of person to care about poetry. She was a woman who worked hard all day long keeping the place immaculate, believing cleanliness was next to Godliness and Godliness was all that mattered. She supervised the cook, dealt with tenants' complaints, paid the bills. Most importantly, she was always kind to Lucille. I never had a mother, mused Lucille, but if I did, I couldn't do better than Maybelle. She deserves a quiet evening of knitting and chat, not the demands of intellectual discourse that are above her abilities.

Perhaps that snore was just what she had needed to hear. Lucille was painfully agitated by the whims of the modern world, spinning away in new directions, leaving her behind and bereft in some bygone era, an era in which poetry was sane and beautiful and lifted you up out of the mundane only to deposit you on a cloud or in a meadow or in the sweet sadness of a broken heart. Not in someone's unpleasant neurosis.

The frightening thing, Lucille was beginning to admit to herself, was that the dreadful poem must have some truth inside it, or it wouldn't have taken hold of her so fiercely. It was, she had determined, a poem about a feckless man, middle-aged, probably. A lonely man, a well-mannered, self-conscious, shy man who could not make up his mind about anything, who second-guessed his every move, his every trickle of emotion. A poem of hesitations. She, herself, was a very determined woman who had built a decent life out of nothing. So how could Prufrock's fumbles and foibles be speaking to her so insistently? What was he trying to tell her?

A log fell in the fireplace grate sending a flurry of sparks upwards through the chimney into the night air. It was time to ascend the stairs to her lonely room.

17.

AND INDEED THERE WILL BE TIME, thought Josiah Elder, time to make a plan. A plan of action. It might be months, years even, before Tom Eliot returned again to America, now with a war hotly underway in Europe, and with the risk of submarine attacks on passenger ships in the Atlantic. He had risked a crossing in August on the St. Louis, so Josiah had been told, but it was now too late, for he had already sailed back to England. Yes, it might be years before the boy, the apostate poet, this Judas of an acolyte, dared to cross the sea and return to Boston once again. I have missed my immediate chance, he thought, but perhaps it is for the best. My plan must be well made.

Tom *must* come back, of course, he assured himself. The Eliot family summered on the Cape where on one splendid occasion, not so very long ago, Josiah had been a welcomed guest. He had greatly enjoyed the visit, marred only by witnessing the attentions Tom had shown to a girl there, Emily Something. She had seemed a rather self-possessed girl, and Josiah had not liked her at all. He noticed that she had concealed her feelings for Tom, whatever they might have been, and this had secretly pleased him. Of course it might have been better if she had showered him with attention, then perhaps Tom would not have rushed back to Europe and made his o'er hasty marriage in London.

Tom had once been destined to become a professor at Harvard. "To follow in *my* footsteps!" Josiah said to the air. That mother of his, surely a force to be reckoned with, had decreed his destiny. She had known of his talent. Her own poetry was puny by comparison. Nevertheless, she had insisted on his becoming a respectable teacher, in spite of her awareness of his genius. Perhaps because of it. And Josiah had wished for this too, with all his heart; for then Tom would be close as his marvelous gifts were unfurled, his talent revealed; and he would become a companion for Josiah in his last years. They would talk of Shakespeare together, and Marlowe, and Milton long into the nights as they drank good wine and enjoyed fine cakes. So he had imagined. So he had hoped.

Well, Tom might escape for a while, studying in Europe, seeking other challenges, trying on different identities, but he will come again, and next time I will be alert to his arrival, he consoled himself. I still have people at the college, friends of many years, lines of communication that were still operating and through which I shall hear of his coming, and then there will be a reckoning.

The bitterness he felt about Tom's poem sustained Josiah. His anger warmed him in the crisp October air, where the cold winter winds would soon swirl the fogs of winter. He walked the night, sometimes in a fever, without feeling the chill. He walked his usual route and then walked it again. He sought exhaustion. He was determined to walk away his anger and the pain that lay beneath it, and when he finally stumbled down the steps of No. 13 his wounded soul was waiting for him in the gloom, holding wide a shroud of melancholy to enfold him. He went to his bed and there he lay, peering upwards into the miasma outside his windows, and did not sleep—

18.

FOR THE YELLOW SMOKE THAT SLIDES ALONG THE STREETS, RUBBING ITS BACK AGAINST THE WINDOW PANES obscured all of Josiah's hopes, all the nights he had dreamed of reunion. Now only soot and ash fell upon his heart, so full of memory and desire. Mr. Josiah Elder alone in the darkness of his basement rooms, turned his face into the pillow and wept.

19.

THERE WILL BE TIME, thought Captain Arlington, buoyant at the prospect of the long winter ahead, closed snugly into No. 13 with Mary Prior. The other boarders will be here too, of course. He sighed. But they are just the extras, the bit players, needed for propriety, needed for distraction, while in reality there will exist only the two of us, anchored in our safe harbor, protected from the ravages of the New England storms.

Mrs. Gill had failed to secure a room with a fireplace for him. Unexpectedly, the two younger men had decided to stay in Boston for the winter months leaving no vacancy. It was not too large a sacrifice for him to remain in his small chamber, for the solid exterior walls of the house would enclose them both. And Mary's room had a fireplace. So she had said. He imagined them entwined before the hearth, more heated than any fire, her youthful beauty bending to his mature will, melting into one another. He rubbed his hands together in anticipation like a villain in a farce.

And lately she did appear to fancy him. He caught her glances at his weathered face, his salty hair, his muscles still strong from a man's hard life on the seas.

Their union must be so. It was fated, he knew; though, as yet, she suspected nothing of this. For the present he would continue to play the attendant lord, to listen dutifully to her daily chatter about the small pleasures and problems of a young woman, of the tedious typing work where words were pounded into being from her fingertips. No one else seemed to care about her daily experiences. It was, it must be admitted, a banal life. His own mind often wandered when she breathlessly reported of office intrigues, of her employer's stinginess. How could one really care about such matters? But he could *seem* to do so, and thus his appearance of unfailing attentiveness and her deep loneliness would intertwine. He would have her. Yes! He would have her, and then he would be able face life boldly again, his head held high, with his arm entwined with hers, walking home through the bustling city, leading Mary to their bed.

20.

There will be time, Beatrice muttered under her breath, trying to reassure herself. Mrs. Gill had ordered a Thanksgiving feast, which she would have to produce just as her mid-term paper for English literature was due. She knew she was a good cook, talented, gifted perhaps, but the ability to roast a savory duck or mash the perfect potato was for her nothing compared to the pleasures to be found in her night school classes where she could plunge into the greatness and the beauty of the past, the books, the art, the poems.

She worried over the timing, but willed herself to manage. Turkey, stuffing, trimmings, vegetables, gravies, sauces, pies; nothing that took any great skill. And while these things baked and simmered she would consider *The Love Song of J. Alfred Prufrock*, the poem that had so disturbed poor Lucille Davenport. This poem would make a fine subject for Beatrice's paper, and she was glad Lucille had made such a fuss about it, bringing it to her attention. There was not much in the house that escaped her notice as she silently served the meals, fetched tea and cakes for Mrs. Gill, and overheard the parlor talk as she tidied the dining room.

It was doubtless a daring choice for her to write about this particular poem. It was new and was considered modern, startlingly original, and she didn't know if her professor would approve. But she felt she could critique it well, compare it to other poems they had studied in class. She thought she might even come to understand it.

She knew people who seemed, in their fashion, to be similar to Prufrock; people who could not get out of their own way and second-guessed everything they did. If she was honest, she herself was some-times a bit like Prufrock. Why she was fretting even now! She disliked this trait in herself. Fortunately she had discovered that the demands of work combined with the concentration of study often pushed her cares off to the side. It is old people who have the time to worry, she thought.

How did so young a poet know enough about an older man to write about his distress with such perfection?

Suddenly an idea occurred to her. Perhaps Mr. Elder, just the other side of the door, would discuss it with her. She had watched Lucille's fruitless attempts to draw him out about the poem over dinners, but Beatrice reckoned she had a better relationship with Mr. Elder than Lucille. She always left him treats on the kitchen table when she went home for the night, so he would have something to eat with his evening tea. A cake, some toast, a peach. He always smiled at her, and she at him, when he passed through the kitchen on his way to and from his rooms.

And Josiah Elder had taught literature and poetry and creative writing at Harvard! That was a lofty thing indeed.

Could she ask him? Did she dare to presume?

21.

To PREPARE A FACE TO MEET THE FACES THAT YOU MEET was a necessity for Lionel Quill. He knew how to do it well. He readied himself to go down to dinner with care. He was well acquainted with all the residents now; the two cocky salesmen, so enamored with matters of trade that they held no interest for him; the hesitant spinster up the final staircase; the young, self-satisfied typist without the distinction to merit it; the Captain without a ship; Mr. Elder, Himself, so much a part of the furniture of No. 13 that one might sit on him by accident; and at the head of the table, the matriarchal landlady who watched them all like a patient barn owl as they crawled through their ever so predictable lives, his own being the exception.

He actually liked Americans on the whole, finding them a bit coarse, too outspoken, and vastly under-educated compared to Europeans, but friendly, open, and usually honest. He would have preferred to be living in France where he had, not so long ago, happily studied painting. There were times in Paris when he thought he might actually have a notable talent, but fate in the form of love in the form of a beautiful young man had called him back to London. When the romance had failed, plunging him into despair, he had decided he needed a change of scene. It was not wise to be in either France or England now because the god of war had crawled up over the horizon line eager to destroy his generation. If he was going to die, he preferred it to be by his own hand, not in some meaningless battle engineered by pompous royalty and self-serving politicians. He had journeyed to America to wait out the hostilities and hopefully to mend his shattered heart.

Lionel was the black sheep in his aristocratic family, but as a male he could depend on the ironclad English inheritance laws to assure him of an income, though not so princely as his elder brothers. He did not have to work, so here, among the incurious Americans he simply said he was an efficiency consultant, a vague made-up term which seemed to offer an acceptable explanation for his unpredictable comings and goings.

The depth of his depression the previous week frightened him as he looked back upon it. He had considered suicide, and not for the first time. He suffered from these descents into despair less often now than when he was in England, but they were still profound and perilous. He knew that continuing to pursue anonymous sexual experiences was dangerous because the loveless encounters reminded him of how much he still longed for the man he truly adored and who wouldn't have him, but the adventures were also a kind of drug, offering the illusion of solace, and of course, there was the real physical pleasure.

He had recovered his spirits slowly after the last plunge and now his drug of choice was once again calling to him. As he stood before his bedroom mirror he liked what he saw. Yes. He was still very attractive. Much depended on this. He could continue to imagine himself as a Greek God when next he shed his clothing in front of yet another stranger in yet another cheap hotel; no longer the young Apollo perhaps, but the mature and powerful Zeus. Should he grow a beard?

At meals, in the succession of boarding houses he inhabited, he kept his divinity hidden. He wore the disguise of a mere mortal…normal, rather uninteresting, a bit obtuse. He made himself be as ordinary as the rest, but privately he knew he would continue to believe himself to be special, unique, extraordinary and magnificent, for if he failed to polish his own armor he knew from experience that his will could suddenly collapse, as it had so recently done in this very room.

In those terrible moments when all his energies failed he felt all too mortal, revolting, worthless, hopeless, and he wished to be dead. Not tonight! Tonight, after a satisfactory dinner, he would enter into darkness. Lionel Quill, talented artist, wealthy English gentry...and a God of Love.

22.

THERE WILL BE TIME TO MURDER AND CREATE the carefully wrought alibi that I will need, thought Mr. Elder. At first his sadness had spiraled him downwards into a black hole of exhaustion where he believed he would die, but then, like a patient recovering from a terrible illness, he had felt his strength slowly returning. Anger hardened into resolve, leaving him with one overwhelming question: *How to do it?* For Tom (no longer his special boy); yes, Tom (not the cat who lived in the kitchen); but Thomas Stearns Eliot, the poet, would have to die.

23.

AND TIME FOR ALL THE WORKS of God, thought Maybelle Gill, quietly observing her boarders come and go from where she was sitting by her living room window. It was such a peaceful time at No. 13. The guests all seemed quite content and able to get along well with one another. Always a blessing. Dinners were companionable with light conversations and excellent fare. Two more blessings.

Would it be God who would have his way with each of them as time chimed on, she wondered, or some evil force? She had read of a doctor in Vienna or Paris whose name she could not rightly recollect, Feud, perhaps, or Fried, who said that everyone had thoughts going on below the surface of their minds, the unconscious, he called it. Quite right, agreed Maybelle, and if you watch people, if you pay close attention, you can discern there is more to a person than meets the eye. Well, she could anyway. It was a necessary talent in her profession.

If a landlady wasn't careful all the wrong sort ended up in the rooms that surrounded you. She was very careful. Very discerning. And over the years the rare bits of hanky-panky she had not predicted or obstructed were few and far between. One petty thief. One girl in the family way with no family. One unsavory homosexual. She had dispatched them all, returned them to the streets from whence they had come, and where, she was certain, God awaited them with his own judgments though He might be more forgiving than Maybelle of their immoral ways. Better on His hands, than hers.

Here, in her home, she asked only for peace and occasional amusement, and these were usually granted. There had never been violence at No. 13 and never a death. A death can cast a shadow on a boarding house for many a year. She inspected perspective guests with a keen eye, almost like a horse trader buying a new mount. She looked at their posture, how they carried themselves, checked the glow of their skin and the condition of their teeth, just stopping sort of peering down their throats or putting an ear to their chests. She admitted only healthy specimens.

With winter begun it was important to have the right balance of actors and she felt this winter would prove a very good cast. A mixed lot. Two available women, three if she allowed Beatrice Platt to be considered now that Mary had made a friend of her; three available men, four if she counted Lionel Quill who she didn't believe for a minute had a wife in England, and on whom she must keep a close eye for she sensed something fishy about him. And there was gentle Mr. Elder who would keep her occasional company while the wintertime events unfolded. Yes, she had done well. They were all cheerful, civilized people, physically attractive, with the appearance of good health and balanced minds, not an unpleasant countenance among them.

In the interests of keeping her guests content she had decided to offer a proper Thanksgiving meal. That would make a nice change. She usually didn't "do" Thanksgiving dinners for her boarders as she preferred to concentrate on her own offering of thankfulness in a church, so in years past if anyone was staying in the house on that holiday, and not visiting with some far-flung family, they ate regular fare and gave their thanks, if they chose to, over beef stew or stuffed cabbages.

She always had a little Christmas party, of course; and sometimes guests would sit up in the parlor until midnight on New Years' Eve when she allowed each person a glass of wine; and she had hosted a special meal two years ago for Mr. Elder when he had retired from his teaching post at Harvard. They had all toasted him at the dinner and eaten a chocolate layer cake at the end of it. He had appeared outwardly embarrassed, but in the under-layer of his mind, where she knew his hidden feelings were kept, he had been pleased.

Proper food was essential to the smooth running of a good establishment. To be honest, she liked rich food herself and, as she ate her meals with the guests, they became beneficiaries. Of course well-fed guests offered fewer complaints and stayed for longer periods of time. In addition to breakfasts and dinners she occasionally offered tea with good sandwiches to one boarder or another in the dark afternoons of January or February, just to buck people up, because spirits flagged at that time of year and she preferred to see the household enlivened with happy people, as they were now. During these private teas she would sometimes nudge a guest towards or away from another, in subtle ways they did not even notice, rather like a good shepherdess, keeping the members of her flock moving in the right directions.

Mrs. Gill was particularly pleased with the idea of a Thanksgiving meal now that she had acquired the services of Beatrice Platt who could actually cook. The two girls who had occupied the position before her had been found wanting, and they had been swiftly dispatched elsewhere. Beatrice was a Godsend, but Maybelle feared she might lose her as the girl harbored thoughts above her station. Look at this alliance with Mary Prior as an example. It was the first time a guest had formed a friendship with a cook. She had allowed it in the interests of keeping Beatrice on and Mary content. Mrs. Gill also knew that the girl attended night school classes, often appearing with bleary eyes as she delivered the breakfast porridge.

Well, the challenge of a Thanksgiving feast would keep Beatrice busy. Mrs. Gill planned to ladle on the praise, maybe even part with a small bonus if everything at table was up to her standards. Sometimes money must be spent as an investment. And she would pray, of course. She would pray not to lose Beatrice Platt.

24.

"AND DAYS OF HANDS THAT LIFT AND DROP A QUESTION ON YOUR PLATE," said Lucille in her best teaching voice, speaking to the assembled boarders. "Whose hands? Days of hands? What question? Why is the question dropped on a plate?"

The poem was causing eyes to roll upwards in the parlor of No. 13. after the soporific effect it had had upon its landlady the week before.

Lucille Davenport had decided to read it aloud after dinner as a diversion. Usually those who were staying in for the evening would play card games or read. It had transpired that Mary Prior and Captain Arlington could both play the piano, so sometimes a duet was heard, or as the Captain played in a kind of seasick way, endured.

Lucille had, in past times, read out poetry that she was particularly fond of in the evenings, especially when there had been a more generous mix of intellectuals among the boarders, but troubled as she was by this poem, she had decided to try once again to elicit a conversation about it, Mrs. Gill's snores having offered Lucille no lasting comfort.

At her request, Himself had agreed to join them in the parlor after the dinner hour, which was very unusual for him. He had dropped his spoon into his cabbage and potato soup, making a small splash when she had first asked him to hear her read the poem aloud and offer up his thoughts.

"Do you mean the poem from the literary magazine you've been carrying about?" He asked, dabbing at a spot of soup that had escaped the bowl. "I've read it. I've heard you mentioning it at meals."

"You have read it?" Was reading poetry how he filled his solitary hours down in those basement rooms now that he was retired? She wondered. Lucille was aware, of course, that until recently he had taught literature and creative writing at Harvard but she had rather hoped, in a romantic way, that he might now be busy writing the great American novel.

"I recognized the poet," he continued. "On the cover of your magazine. He was a student of mine in years past, and I was curious. I do not have much appreciation for the poem."

"We are of like minds in that regard, Mr. Elder, but I do wish to understand it, if it is to be the coming thing."

"To understand the indecipherable?"

The other boarders appeared mildly interested in the interchange, not because it centered on poetry, but because these words were more than any of them had heard Mr. Elder say in their many meals together.

The salesmen had excused themselves immediately after dinner and departed for livelier amusements than poetry discussions or misshapen piano duets. A little piece of Lucille's mind had trailed along after them, wondering at their adventures, wishing that—oh never mind she thought—as her obsession with the poem caught her up once more.

Mrs. Gill had joined the guests with her knitting on her lap and soon appeared to nod off again. Mary and the Captain had quickly lost interest and were quietly talking of other matters in a far corner over the silent piano keys. Lionel Quill was listening, but shaking his head from side to side as she read out each line as if to say, no, no, I do not think much of any of this. Only Mr. Elder seemed truly interested, curiously anxious about the poem and desirous of knowing her understanding of it. Maybelle Gill, only pretending sleep, was displeased to see, through half closed eyes, that Beatrice Platt was standing in the parlor doorway, having crept in from the dining room, and was listening intently as Lucille tried to parse the poet's meaning.

"No," said Lionel. "No, I don't think this poem is sensible. Was this student of yours mad, Mr. Elder?"

"Not when I knew him, Mr. Quill, though I fear something fierce has taken hold of his faculties."

"Well, you have read it all the way through beautifully once, Miss Davenport," said Lionel, "and it certainly is a curiosity, but I dare say, I am not up for hearing it through this second time."

"Well that is understandable, I suppose, but do call me Lucille, she replied, with a shy smile, especially if I am to call you Lionel."

Maybelle Gill's eyebrows raised slightly, for it was clear to her that dear Lucille was, once again, barking up a wrong tree. Lionel Quill showed no real interest in her, only politeness. But had she noticed Winston Ward watching Lucille more closely than usual at dinners lately? Now *that* would be a devil of a thing.

"And thank you, Lucille, for trying to make a more cultured man of me," Lionel continued graciously, as he lifted himself from the straight-backed chair on which he had been delicately perched. "Goodnight, Ladies, Captain, Mr. Elder." With a polite little bow he left the room and quickly climbed the stairs.

"Perhaps we have all had enough poetry for this evening," said Mr. Elder, startling Lucille who was just warming up to what she had hoped would be a fruitful discussion. "I am sorry, Miss Davenport, but I suddenly feel the need for my evening perambulation. Perhaps we could continue with a discussion at another time?" And without another word he walked straight out of the house.

Something is troubling that man, thought Maybelle. Something deep. And she offered up a little prayer on behalf of Himself.

"A walk! What an excellent idea!" declared Mary Prior from the far corner. Some fresh air would do us both some good, don't you think so Captain Arlington? Will you wait for me on the front steps while I find my wrap?" And almost instantly they, too, were gone.

Lucille stood abandoned in the center of the room. She held onto the worn magazine like a child clutching a favorite blanket, slender arms falling gently to her side.

Our dear Lucille needs a little praying for, too, Maybelle Gill surmised. She waited until Lucille departed, listening as she trudged dispiritedly up the staircase, then she resumed her knitting with rested eyes and renewed energy.

She did not fail to notice that clever Beatrice Platt had slipped away from her place in the parlor doorway, and made her way down the back stairs to finish the after dinner chores alone in the kitchen.

Alone, except for the cat, who was dreaming of fish.

25.

TIME FOR YOU AND TIME FOR ME, mused Captain Arlington with satisfaction as he boldly took hold of Mary Prior's forearm to guide her carefully down the front steps of No. 13. She did not protest at the familiarity of his gesture for they were becoming friends. Friends! Who needed friends? He had friends enough in a dozen ports, on ships that still sailed, and in his seaside hometown should he ever have the nerve to return to it. What he wanted was a lover. A passionate lover, eager for his every look, his every touch, but how to turn this fresh, pretty girl into the lascivious wench of his imaginings? That was the overwhelming question.

And so he must be patient, take his time. He must walk slowly along the streets gazing idly into shop windows like a gentleman, and through the parks where flowers were to be admired. He must compare *her* to a delicate flower. He must not thrust her into the bushes and wrench apart her bodice, plunge his face between the two luscious pillows of her bosom, then reach down and drag up her skirts above that lovely slim waist and attend to the challenges that lay below the silks and ties in which women bound up their most delicious parts.

He must be politic, cautious. He must continue to chat in an interested manner about this and that—the soup at dinner, Lucille Davenport's annoying obsession with bad poetry, the unexpected presence of Himself in the parlor for the discussion of the Prufrock poem, and his abrupt, almost rude, departure. In the coming evenings he must continue to chop away at their piano duets, feeling the warmth of her body at his side, watching hungrily as her delicate fingers danced over the keys.

Due to his feelings of infatuation for Mary, Captain Arlington knew he was beginning to believe in life again. He thought that he might be able to allow his humiliation to slowly recede into the past, that his conscience might yet admit moments of happiness to arrive. He must not rush. He must not push. There will be time, he told himself. There will come a time.

26.

"AND TIME YET FOR A HUNDRED INDECISIONS," sighed Lionel Quill, for the blackness of night was now edging out the last gleam of day. Perhaps this evening, unlike the yellow cat, he should not prowl. He should step gracefully down the front stairs again and sit politely in the parlor and be content with the afterglow of his recent adventures. He should be kind to Mrs. Gill and keep her company, speak of women admiringly, in short, he should behave.

So far, he thought, this landlady was not suspicious of him, but behind her placid exterior she missed very little. He had often sensed her curious eyes upon him, and he knew if he kept on with his habit of creeping away on many a night that sooner or later, hearing the creaks as he descended down the back stairs, she would begin to speculate.

But no. He had no wish to dally with Mrs. Gill! He owed her nothing. She did not suspect him at present or he would have been told to vacate.

And if she did discover his difference, there were other boarding houses, other landladies to charm and fool and eventually shock. He heaved a sigh.

Lionel, as so often happened, was feeling the hollowness of his life this evening. Since leaving the Paris studio the previous year in order to follow his faithless lover, his life had become one of deception, fear, and the endless search for diversions that only momentarily staunched the wound of his broken heart. So again it would be the back stairs. He put on his woolen coat, preparing to join the murky darkness which had already shrouded the windows.

Now that November was here the nights were turning bitter, and soon there would be snow. People were beginning to muffle themselves up, look down at the sidewalks watching for patches of ice, and it would become ever more difficult to pass a sharp, knowing look to a man striding by in the dusk, a look revealing who he was, asking if they were brothers in ignominy. The winter would force him to enter into bars, risk recognition, perhaps take up with the wrong sort, be beaten. It had happened before. He shuddered. Perhaps it should be the front stairs after all?

But plump, grey, self-satisfied Maybelle Gill, now sitting alone with her knitting, would be too stultifying to be borne. Likely as not she would want to discuss God, a God whose existence he seriously doubted. Why, he had often asked himself, would God have created him as a man who could love only men, and then condemn him to this lowly, skulking existence? For what purpose would a benevolent deity conjure up a whole category of men only to despise them?

Because Lionel was to the manor born and the third son of his entrenched English family he had been expected to enter the church. Instead he had run for cover into an artist's life, and in so doing greatly dismayed his parents. Preaching to others about purity had been out of the question given his inclinations, not to mention his lack of belief. He might be a disappointment to some, but by his own standards it was an honorable decision. God was only an idea to Lionel, an empty concept, a tedious argument, and it was best not to argue with Maybelle Gill when it came to God!

So once again, full of hopeless hope and fearful need, he wrapped a cashmere scarf about his neck, buttoned up his coat, and glanced at his shoes to be sure they were well polished. Satisfied with his appearance, he descended the back stairs, as lightly as Eros.

27.

AND FOR A HUNDRED VISIONS AND REVISIONS, at last! He had the time to write!

Thomas Stearns Eliot sat alone at his desk in his shabby rented flat located in an ancient building on an unfashionable street in London, England, far from the concerns of all those he had left behind in America. The silence in his room was like a block of glistening white marble waiting to be carved.

Thank God for this time alone. His worrisome wife was away to visit her friends and then to spend some time with her mother, and oh, her mama was welcome to her! Vivienne, who never ceased complaining about her unsavory female maladies and uninteresting womanly sorrows. She interfered with his ability to write even as she professed a love for his poetry. It was maddening. He had known on their honeymoon that she wouldn't do. They were not compatible. They were not suited to one another. Why had he done it?

In truth he knew the reasons, knew them all. He could enumerate them. Foremost, he needed to demonstrate his adult independence, to oppose his dominating mother's plans for his life as a Harvard professor and, in the process, to confound his rigid father. *They* wanted him back. At home. In bloody Massachusetts, participating in their smug lives, back where *they* supposed he was supposed to be, at what *they* deemed to be his proper pursuits. How he hated them. How he loved them. The old people. That's how he thought of his parents, who were more like grandparents to him. They had been old before he was born. As he was learning to walk and talk his six elder siblings were growing up fast and disappearing off into the world, leaving his mother, bloated with expectation, to turn her full attention upon her final act of fecundity.

And his father! Solid as the brick company he managed, and deaf as a post, spending his days going over the company accounts, the family's genealogy and, in his leisure time, drawing cats. Why cats?

He had needed to make a clear statement, one that would distance himself further from them, and from the other old person who thought he knew what was best for him. His mentor, Professor Josiah Elder, always hovering with his unsettling glances, his expectations and illusions, and who had agreed with his parents about a Harvard career. Well, he had had the last word when it came to *that* man!

He had shocked them all. First with *Prufrock's* success, then with his sudden wedding to Vivienne Haigh-Wood. A married man must be thought of as grown, self-reliant. He could no longer be formulated, no longer be pinned up on the wall of their expectations like poor J. Alfred.

Unfortunately, he was now largely dependent on his wife's allowance and his friends' charity, and on public school teaching which he loathed, and lecturing which paid only a pittance. His pen tapped on the edge of the desk.

He knew himself to be, in a way he could not explain even to himself, a wrong sort of man. He was usually withdrawn, and was often preoccupied with sexual thoughts that were unacceptable in nature, so he had also married to appear normal, respectable, choosing a pretty English wife to bedazzle his friends and, more importantly, the prospective friends she could introduce him to; other writers, literary lights in the tight community beginning to form in Bloomsbury, and of which he wished to belong for the sake of his career, not for their company.

He had married to astound and befuddle his newest champion, the marvelously eccentric poet, Ezra Pound, far more modern in thought, in every way, than dotty old Professor Elder. Ezra was made exceedingly happy by the marriage, for it meant that he, Tom, would most likely remain in England for the foreseeable future. Was the future ever foreseeable?

And of course he had married for her money, although it was not old money, and not as much as he had imagined. In fact, it was very little. He wasn't entirely a cad he judged, as he had convinced himself that he was in love with Vivienne at the time of the proposal. Oh, not the syrupy romantic love of his youth that sweetened his memory of Emily Hale back in the States. Alas, it was not love at all that Vivienne Haigh-Wood had actually inspired, only an infatuation with her British differences, her out-going personality, her erratic pursuits of pleasure, so unlike his pompous Unitarian family. And so unlike himself.

He had known that he needed to rebound from his failure to capture the heart of Emily who had liked him well enough, maybe loved him, but not enough. What was ever enough? Maybe it was his physical oddities that had given her pause, the truss he wore for his congenital hernia, his weak heart, his bad teeth. These maladies were known within the family of course, and Emily was close with his sisters and cousins, so doubtless she knew all about him. Or perhaps she had simply sensed that he was peculiar. Vivienne was not bothered by his imperfections. She was too wrapped up in her own preoccupations to have much care for his manly difficulties.

And then there was the loss of Jean, whose memory he knew he must lay to rest. His heart began to beat in its irregular fashion.

His brief sojourn in France, just after leaving Harvard, had provided him with a soulmate, Jean Verdenal. Jean had loved him just as he was; cared for him man to man without conditions. Now Jean was missing in action, thought to be dead, a useless sacrifice to an ill-conceived battle of the horrid war now raging on the continent. Wasted.

When he had left Jean on the Continent at the outbreak of the hostilities, when he had abandoned him for the safety of England's shores, he had feared that he might never see the man again, this man he loved; and now he knew that what he had experienced with Jean, the truest form of spiritual communion, was gone forever from his life. Yet, somehow he could not conceive of Jean Verdenal as dead. He could not picture him as a lifeless body. He saw him only as animate, smiling, laughing, taking hold of life's challenges with his muscular arms and amazing intellect. How could all that vanish into nothingness? How could a man so vital be extinguished?

Now, with Jean gone, he might as well be married. Vivienne was, at least, considered pretty. He had thought she might be stimulating, but instead she had proved boring. Thankfully she drank, and she smoked, and she danced. He liked to dance. Somehow they must rub along together. The one place where they did not chaff was in the matter of his poetry. They both considered his need to write...his ability to use words to reveal ideas that entered the minds of others and thereby changed their lives and altered the world...to be of the utmost importance. Perhaps that would be enough. Perhaps he could learn to love her for loving his poems. But only if they were good! If she loved bad poems it would be a mockery.

He must write.

With *Prufrock* published and so well accepted he must now prove himself to be a poet of stature, a poet with stamina; not a one trick pony...such a trite phrase! Or a flash in the pan...worse! Deep in his heart he feared that he would never surpass *Prufrock* no matter how much his loquacious wife prattled on to everyone about his genius, and no matter how certain Professor Elder and Ezra Pound might be of his poetic genius. He trembled to think he might soon be recognized by everyone as an imposter if *Prufrock* proved to be a singular phenomenon. It was like living with a corpse buried in the garden.

Yes, he had kept on writing, but what he had produced of late had been, to his eye, second rate. To others he appeared confident, up and coming. Oh these tired clichés! They filled his ears. His mind fed him nothing but the well-worn phrases of others. He could find no words inside himself that were truly, uniquely original.

But maybe, he thought, just maybe with his wife safely stowed with her doting mother; in the blessed silence of her absence, perhaps new words would arrive and spill out upon the page where he could find their rhythms, arrange them and derange them into another meaningful poem.

He sighed. His fountain pen had made a glistening black pool of ink on the pristine white paper.

28.

BEFORE THE TAKING OF A TOAST AND TEA Mrs. Gill bent her head to say grace, then hesitated. The repast had been thoughtfully carried up to her sitting room by Beatrice. She was alone now, at the end of a long day, and deeply troubled because as Thanksgiving approached, God, as she had always known him, seemed suddenly absent. It had been some time since she had heard the murmur of His voice, felt the warmth of His presence, and in that unaccustomed void she felt—what did she feel? Chilled. Alone.

This can't be so, she admonished herself, wrapping a shawl around her shoulders. She was not alone. She was surrounded with people. Those who came and went from No. 13, but also those who stayed and cared. Lucille, Josiah.

Her private world was populated with saints and angels and Jesus and The Virgin Mary, all of whom she had prayed to at one time or another. Nevertheless, it was God the Almighty who had been her most constant and beloved companion. Now her assurance, her *knowledge* that God was always with her had vanished.

It had begun with a nightmare, a terrible dream in which she could not move. She was alone and lying on a table in a darkened room. She tried to get up but her body would not respond. She was paralyzed. Terrified, she attempted to call out, but no sound would come. She realized then that she was on a slab in a morgue, but she was still alive. What if they buried her alive!? Horrified, she tried again to move, to signal that she was not dead, but could not lift a finger or utter a sound. Suddenly a bright light flashed overhead and she awoke to sunlight streaming in from the window onto her still rigid body, cold with fear. She crept cautiously from the bed, relieved that she could move, and on bended knees began to thank God for another day as she had done every morning of her life, but the experience was utterly strange. Her words seemed to evaporate into nothingness. Was she still asleep? Was this a continuation of the nightmare? No. She was fully awake but for the first time in her life, she felt not the warm and understanding presence of God, but a dreadful absence.

Surely He must still be silently guiding her, keeping her healthy, keeping her comfortable in this uncomfortable world, she thought, but she could not find a means to contact Him. She had prayed fervently at every opportunity since the dream of course, but to no avail.

God had watched over Maybelle Gill all her life, just as Maybelle had watched over the souls that came and went from her rooms and where, when needs must, she had quietly, gently intervened in their lives, caring, protecting and disciplining them, just as God must do. She mulled over the small events and petty trials of the past few days and found nothing unusual that would explain His abrupt departure. The unyielding emptiness felt like the very opposite of grace.

Long ago in the early days of her marriage when her young husband, Mr. Leon Gill, had been struck down by a tree she had not doubted God's plan. He had preserved her through that difficult time, helped her to find this house at No. 13, the number, she felt, representing Christ and his twelve apostles.

So this evening, out of lifelong habit, she dutifully thanked God for the toast, and for the tea, and for the cozy room in which to enjoy it, while the air around her remained lifeless. Where was His warm appreciation for her gratitude? Where had He gone? Where, for that matter, *could* He go?

"This is quite ridiculous!" she declared aloud. "God doesn't go away." She knew He was everywhere so He must be right here. If he were here and she could not find him, there must be something wrong with *her*, which was a frightful idea. Perhaps something had gone seriously wrong with her brain. Have I had a stroke? she asked herself. Do I have a tumor? Am I becoming senile? She trembled. Her teacup rattled in the saucer. Oh, my nerves are bad tonight! she thought.

She heard a voice then, clearly in her mind. It was not God's familiar voice. It was unknown to her and it said: *There is no God.* The cold, harsh statement hit her with the force of a ship striking an iceberg and some tea spilled into her lap, but fortunately it did not scald her, and she made herself believe that God, in this small blessing, must surely still be taking care of her, even in this moment of appalling doubt.

No, it wasn't God, contradicted the voice, *the tea was tepid because you held onto it for a long time, and it cooled.* Struck broadside again she could only wonder at how she could be thinking such shameful things. It was blasphemy. She decided to pray.

To whom? There is no one to hear you. You are talking to yourself.

A terrifying idea formed unbidden in her mind: this new voice could only be the utterance of Satan. How could the prince of darkness have found a rip in the seamless fabric of her faith?

She looked around her, into the deepening shadows of the room. Perhaps something wicked had entered the house, eluding her careful watchfulness, sliding into her ear as she slept. She sensed evilness afoot within the walls of No. 13. What could it be? A person? A person secretly intending to do ill? Perhaps it had come in with the godless poetry that Lucille was always chanting nowadays like a heathen prayer. She dismissed the idea. Surely a silly poem was no match for God.

Perhaps I have gone mad, came the next alarming thought. I am hearing voices.

You didn't think you were mad when you imagined you were hearing God's pronouncements.

"I felt his presence, I sensed his meanings," she responded aloud. "That is an entirely different matter." She felt it was right to talk back, to fight back, against this vile, insistent voice.

She took a deep breath and tried to reassure herself. "I am Mrs. Maybelle Gill," she continued aloud, mopping up the tea with the linen napkin. "I love God, and He loves me. I am not mad."

Father Sweeney, in his sermons, had often warned against sudden doubt, but he had not prepared her for blasphemous conversations with the devil! This experience, this harboring of wickedness, was a terrible sin she realized with horror, but I will be forgiven, surely. She listened in silence, fully attentive. Nothing. Nothing. She heard only human voices, murmuring through the closed door, coming from the parlor.

She had no appetite for the toast now, or for the remains of the tea, or for anything in her life that she could think of. For what was life without God? The question was overwhelming.

29.

"IN THE ROOM THE WOMEN COME AND GO TALKING OF MICHELANGELO," read Winston Ward aloud to the walls of the room he shared with Reginald Sterling who was out on a sales mission regarding sinks for the new public bathrooms now under construction. The prospect of this large order was keeping them in Boston during the dreary winter months, and so here he was, reading this damnable poem all because of the stupid bet he had made with Sterling. He didn't really fancy her all that much, but if was going to seduce Lucille Davenport he had best learn a lick of her lingo, or at least this particular piece of nonsense with which she was so besotted.

Michelangelo indeed! What sort of women were these? Not his type. He could make no sense of the poem. It didn't even rhyme. He thought of an obscene limerick that he much preferred and chuckled. This Prufrock fellow needed a bit of fun. He was way too depressing. He threw down the magazine, stretched and yawned. The fire was burning warmly, his flask had provided him with a nice buzz, and he drifted off into a self-satisfied sleep.

30.

AND INDEED THERE WILL BE TIME, thought Mary Prior, polishing her nails to a satisfying gleam. Her fingernails took an awful beating as they banged along all day on the typewriter keyboard, but she maintained them well. She sat before her mirror in the cozy bedroom that she was beginning to think of as her home, admiring the fine features with which she had been blessed; dark hair, darker eyes, soft smooth skin covering high cheekbones. There will be plenty of time now that Reginald and his friend Winston were staying on for the winter to determine if there was any mutual interest. It was true she had hoped for someone up a rank two from commerce, but who was she, a typist without connections, to be so picky? Especially after The Terrible Thing that had happened which she would not think about.

Reginald was an attractive man. A modern man. He worked hard, he smoked, he drank, but not too much. She liked his sandy blond hair always falling over his forehead into his pale blue eyes and the automatic way he brushed it back, a gesture of which he seemed unaware. There was no mystery about Reginald Sterling. He liked money and women and having a good time. He would do. And she would do for him. They would make a handsome couple. Except for that damnable limp of his. She was not bold enough to ask what caused it. Well, she thought, no one was perfect.

Reginald seemed shy of her though, seldom spoke to her, even at meals. Had she put him off in some way? Mary wondered. She had never been sure of herself when it came to dealings with the all-important male sex. She had made serious errors in judgment in the past. Here at No. 13 she knew she had Captain Arlington under her spell, though she didn't fancy him in any serious way. He made a nice companion for the time being. Safe anyhow. She did wish he played the piano better.

That was the way of it; the men she was attracted to seemed not respond to her charms. The ones she captivated were not to her liking. Perhaps she had been broken by The Terrible Thing after all. Maybe others could sense something was intrinsically wrong about her.

She knew she must soon marry or end up like poor Lucille Davenport, going quietly mad at the top of the stairs.

31.

"To wonder. That is a necessity!" Josiah Elder said aloud, talking only to himself in his darkened room. "To wonder and to dare. How else can great poetry be conceived?"

He had believed this and taught it to a generation of writers; but Tom's poem was bereft of wonder, and it dared nothing. It was only a sordid little caricature. Of Himself! Tom had made fun of him, of his bald spot, and the careful way he dressed! What had he done to deserve such contempt?

"Well, I shall wonder, and I shall dare!" He declared.

What would his world be like, without Tom Eliot alive within it? he asked himself. The answer arose swiftly. It would be barren. It would be without color and joy. It would be a wasteland.

He was interrupted in his gloomy rumination by a soft knock at his sitting room door. He could not recall any time in the past when someone had summoned him in this way. Perhaps Mrs. Gill had some kind of emergency. Perhaps there was a problem in the kitchen.

He was therefore quite surprised when he opened the door to find Beatrice Platt standing outside with a determined look on her face.

"Is something the matter Miss Platt?"

She took a big breath as though she were about to jump from a high place and replied, her words tumbling out so fast they ran together in places: "Dear Mr. Elder, I was hoping you might help me to understand the poem you were discussing with Miss Davenport in the dining room some time ago the one called *The Love Song of J. Alfred Prufrock* by T. S. Eliot that I wish to explore and write about for my English paper and I really like it but don't understand it quite enough and I know you were a professor of English before you retired and you said the poet was a student of yours once and I expect you are too busy to help me and that I am out of place to bother you so I'm sorry but I thought it would do no harm to ask you if you don't mind terribly."

She gulped for a breath then. Josiah could see she was actually shaking.

His own mind was dealing with the ludicrous irony of the request, the juxtaposition of emotional events this young woman could not possibly imagine and he suddenly, quite unexpectedly, began to laugh. It began as a slow rumbly laugh deep in his shallow chest that just kept coming and coming and was soon out of his control, doubling him over, spilling tears down his weathered cheeks. His amusement was contagious and quickly infected Beatrice who tried, without success, to stifle a wave of laughter that bubbled up inside her. It mixed with the relief she felt at knowing she, at least, had not given offense.

After several minutes, when they both were able regain composure, Mr. Elder stood to his full height, which was an inch or two shorter than Beatrice's, wiped the wetness from his face, smiled, and replied, "I will be glad to be of use."

32.

Do I DARE? AND, DO I DARE? wondered Maybelle Gill who was standing in the side aisle of the church staring with trepidation at the confessional cabinet, a place which in the past she had viewed only with the anticipation of relief. Father Sweeney had always been so kind to her, so understanding of her small sins; like the time she coveted a brooch on the bosom of another woman, or the dream she once had of kissing a man who was wearing a woman's hat, or the time she had missed Mass simply out of a desire for extra sleep following a heavy cold. He had assured her that oversleeping was not quite up to the mark as qualification for the deadly sin of sloth. He had given her only a mild penance as always. She liked saying the "Hail Marys" and the "Our Fathers."

But this! How could she dare to tell him she had lost her faith? And on the very eve of Thanksgiving. She must confess, of course. She needed forgiveness, but how should she begin? She fretted and she dallied.

Finally, with no others before her, she took a breath so deep it made her cough and, with the greatest reluctance, she approached the confessional.

Father Sweeney sat within the enclosure yawning at a morning's worth of petty sins. He felt his eyes growing heavy. What next? he wondered. Through a crack in the curtains he could see the landlady of No. 13 approaching. She was a good old soul and he was thoroughly sick of good old souls. Why didn't the unexpected murderer ever pop in? And there wasn't much adultery of late. He was fascinated by adultery.

His parish was becoming entirely too Godly.

He took out his flask from a fold in his robes. Forgive me, Father, for I am about to sin, he thought, and drained the lot.

33.

TIME TO TURN BACK AND DESCEND THE STAIR decided the yellow cat as his sensitive nose detected the smell of turkey roasting in the kitchen. On his early rounds this morning people had not called him "Herekittykitty" but "Happythanksgiving" as they put down the scraps for him, and everywhere he had been given turkey of which he was very fond. And now, delightfully, there was to be turkey right in his own home. He pushed inwards on the kitchen door with his strong yellow paw, slipped under the work table, licked himself all over once, curled up, and fell asleep, waiting contentedly for dinner to wake him.

34.

WITH A BALD SPOT IN THE MIDDLE OF MY HAIR! Reginald eye's shot open in dismay. When had that happened? He held the hand mirror above his head, appalled at what he saw reflected in the dressing table mirror opposite. He had just been enjoying the morning assessment of his looks—handsome face, still unlined, good teeth, no sign of a double chin or puffiness around the eyes, and then…"oh my God!" he exclaimed aloud.

"What's the matter?" asked Winston without real interest from his bed on the far side of the room. There was still sleepiness in his voice, this being Thanksgiving morning with no need for an early rising.

"I'm going bald! Just as my father did."

"No you're not."

"Look, see for yourself." Reginald bowed in the direction of his friend's still reclining figure.

"I don't want to look at your head. Well, there is a spot, but it's very tiny. Push your hair around the other way. No one will notice."

"Beatrice will notice. She bends over my shoulder when she serves from the platters at dinner. She has probably noticed already. Oh, this is awful."

"Why look at you. You are indeed taken with her, aren't you? This is bad. I've just been jollying Lucille along for the fun of it and in order to win our bet. But I think you really like this girl Beatrice, so you must be careful or she'll have you. Besides, she's just the cook. Can't you set your sights a little higher? Mary Prior, for instance. She has her sights on *you,* I dare say, and she, at least may go up in the world."

"I don't want a wife that goes up in the world."

"Wife! Wife you say?" Winston sat up now. "You'd best stop such talk or it will be your goose that the pretty kitchen maid will be cooking."

"She is not a kitchen maid! And don't speak about her that way."

"Are we having our first fight? This is what women do to men when they get their claws in. They separate good men, one from the other."

"Oh do shut up Winston."

"No. You really need to hear this. A woman shouldn't be important to a man. Women are not complete people after all. They haven't brains as developed as men's brains. They don't think logically. The government understands this. They don't let them vote, or control property when they have a husband or father to manage it properly. Women are useful as objects of pleasure, I grant you. They produce children if you want them, and the one you have taken a fancy to can cook very well. But you must never let a member of the weaker sex assume dominion over your thoughts and your feelings."

Both men grew quiet then, neither wishing to prolong their argument. Sadly, Reginald thought Winston might be right. It was the camaraderie of men that mattered in this world. Look at how businesses are run, governments, hospitals, universities, the police, the church. Everything important in the world was organized and run by men. That was the natural order of things with men holding the most valued positions. Yet in his secret heart Beatrice had come to feel more important to him than Winston, or for that matter, anyone.

Winston got up and dressed, and Reginald went back to examining his hair, and soon the disagreement was forgiven and forgotten by both men as the house filled with the rich aromas of a Thanksgiving dinner that they would enjoy later in the day.

They made their way down to the dining room for breakfast, Reginald eager to see Beatrice, but still silently fretting about the bald spot, and Winston secretly pleased that it was Reginald, not he, who had discovered one.

35.

THEY WILL SAY I went mad, of course, thought Mr. Elder. They will say that I lost my mind, or that I became senile. Perhaps they will dredge up the old rumor that I was forward with Tom in an improper way, there in the halls of learning. It was not improper. I simply loved him. I never touched him in a wrong way. I never insinuated that I wished to; but he misunderstood. Misunderstood my shy demeanor, my hesitancy, and my pure and noble love for him. Mistook it for something base. I admit that I loved loving him. I loved his genius, his uniqueness, his extraordinary talent among so many smart young men. He stood out like the North Star. I wanted nothing but the best for him. I did my utmost. I taught, I mentored, I befriended. It is true, I was a little like Polonius with my cautions and concerns, and I was not afraid to mention love. But it was a selfless love! Sadly, someone must have whispered a vile thought into his ear, and he believed it of me.

Even with the shadow of such a disgrace upon me I loved him, longed for him when he left for Europe, then to England, hoping someone at Oxford or Cambridge would nurture him as once I had done.

And then, for gratitude, I read this mockery of myself. I did not imagine he could be so cruel.

Now, when he is murdered, they will say it was true all along, it was a crime of passion, and I will not speak to defend myself. There will be no running away, no alibi at all. I have decided. I will, like Clytemnestra, stand upon my act. I shall hold tight to the bloody knife or the poisoned cup and offer no word of remorse.

And he will lie upon the floor like a patient etherized upon a table, as he so revoltingly wrote, and he will not move again. Will not write again. Then I shall both weep and rejoice at so much ruined promise. Will there be a look of surprise in his eyes, just before he dies as he realizes that old Professor Prufrock has at last, like Hamlet, acted?

36.

How his hair is growing thin, thought Mary as she settled herself at the breakfast table, looking down upon Reginald who was already seated, as she did so. I had not noticed that bald spot before. Perhaps that is why he brushes his hair back into place so often. She imagined him in ten years' time, limping along with a shiny, sweating pate and in that moment, over their respective bowls of steaming porridge, her interest in Reginald Sterling died.

She knew it was a weakness in her character to care so much about outward appearances, but she was who she was, and she could not abide bald men. She felt her emotion slowly turning of its own accord, like an animal picking up a new scent, in the direction of the willing Captain Earnest Arlington with his neat appearance and his full head of silvered hair.

37.

My morning coat, my collar mounting firmly to the chin, my necktie rich and modest, but asserted by a simple pin. Captain Arlington had assessed himself thus, and he was pleased with his appearance this morning. He must look his best all the day long, he thought, if he was to make his offer to Mary Prior in the evening of this Thanksgiving Day.

His excitement left him no appetite for breakfast, but he was trying to work his way through a piece of buttered toast nevertheless. It was important to not be seen as anxious by the other boarders. His passion was not a show for others to enjoy. He suddenly loathed them all. He wanted to be far from here, alone in a ship's cabin with Mary, sailing on a cooperative sea with rapturous, but gentle, waves slapping at the hull pushing them further and further from any shore; her breast beneath his hungry lips. He bit down on the toast so decidedly that the others turned at the crunching sound.

He swallowed hard, the toast catching in his throat and he was suddenly unable to breathe. He tried to suck in air, but this only served to block his windpipe further. He stood up in alarm, knocking the chair to the floor with a crash, grasping at his throat with one hand, pointing frantically with the other, signaling his distress. This was unnatural, painful, worse than drowning. He flailed about while the others jumped to his aid, pounding him on the back to no avail, and slowly the room began to spin and grow dim as he collapsed onto Mrs. Gill's immaculate dining room floor.

He regained consciousness slowly, gasping and coughing but receiving just enough air for his vision to clear, though the world continued to spin. He was staring upwards into the wrinkled face of Mr. Elder of all people, and someone was, for some unfathomable reason sitting squarely on his chest. A crowd of concerned faces were peering down at him. Now what, he wondered, were all these boarders doing on this beach? He closed his eyes.

"He will be alright," said Josiah. You may get off his chest now Mary. Your quick response did the trick. I shall go and wipe the offending toast off my hands."

Eyes still closed Captain Arlington began to realize he was not on a beach. He had not been saved from drowning. He had choked, most stupidly, on a piece of greasy toast. Mr. Elder had reached down into his throat while Mary Prior had plopped herself onto his now aching chest, and as she did so the toast had dislodged itself into Josiah Elder's probing fingers. He could not think of anything more disgusting or humiliating. It was worse than the time when he had been pulled half dead, filled with sea water and shame from the ocean. He thought he might simply die of embarrassment. He wished that he would.

His dear Mary had helped to save his life it seemed, but what could she be thinking about this dreadful spectacle? Of this ridiculous old man unable to eat breakfast without choking? And on Thanksgiving morning, the very day he had planned to propose to her. He was mortified. His tender feelings fled. Suddenly the lines from the poem that had of late caused so much controversy in the house popped into his mind like the masticated toast had popped into Mr. Elder's hand:

> I have heard the mermaids singing, each to each.
> I do not think they will sing for me.

Slowly he righted himself and left the dining room, suffused with shame, not even trying to locate his dignity, as the others watched him stumble away without saying a word.

38.

THEY WILL SAY I am an imposter, thought Tom Eliot in despair. They will read this poem or that poem, and they will say it is not as good as the other poem, what was it called? The Love Song of J. Albert somebody. And I will be a has-been before I have really been anything at all.

He re-read the beginning of the newest poem. "Among the smoke and fog of a December afternoon…". This is quite pathetic he thought, crumpling the paper into a ball. I repeat my own imagery in the very first line.

Tom was alone in the bedroom again, so as no one was there to see him, he lay on his bed and allowed himself to be miserable. He had the flat to himself for a few hours, which was a blessing that did not comfort him. It seemed he could not write whether Vivienne was dithering about or thankfully absent. He was emotionally immobilized. His true love was most probably dead in the war, and his faith in the future had died in April when he had first heard the news. His talent had fled, his funds were low, his marriage a disaster, his family angry, his prospects bleak. His life was a desert of rock with no water.

Now what was it that old Professor Elder always said? One must wonder and dare, go deep, deep into oneself and find the overwhelming question. What was the question? How was he to go on? *That* was the question.

And the answer was clear and as black as night. He must swallow his pride and go home, return to Massachusetts where his parents now lived most of the year and beg for more funds, consider a return to Harvard with his tail between his legs and there, perhaps, to take up teaching as was expected of him.

To do so he must sail across the Atlantic Ocean yet again. The sea was daily more thick with the German U-Boats which might sink his ship as they had the *Lusitania*. He feared death by drowning. It must be horrible agony to breathe in icy water and feel yourself sinking, sinking out of sight forever. Fortunately, Vivienne was too frightened of the whole prospect to consider making the crossing with him, as Vivienne would strike his mother like the iceberg struck the *Titanic*. He must find his courage and sail across alone.

He must think of it as an adventure to travel during war, as Jean would do. And though he knew he was not a brave man, he felt that he had just enough courage to face the ordeal of the sea, which would be far less of an ordeal than that which awaited him when he went ashore. So much disapproval was lying in wait for him. But, he tried to reassure himself, his mother's love would be stronger than her disappointments. She would embrace him and in her arms he might find himself again.

There was staunch, once beloved Emily Hale to be faced down as well. He had fallen for her in the way of a first love, all fantasy and hesitation. Emily had not shown much reciprocity of affection back in the day, but her letters to him now were warm. There was something unfinished there, he was certain.

If that wasn't enough there was business with Professor Elder! He had received an unexpected letter from his old mentor asking for the opportunity to speak with him the next time he found himself in America, in order to set things to right between them. It was a very proper, very courteous letter, from a man he had once admired, learned from, and felt affection for; rather like son might feel towards a father who could actually hear him. Professor Elder had heard him, recognized him, of that he was sure. But Josiah's fondness had over-reached itself into… into…Tom gave himself a shake. All that had occurred was history. It had been a youthful error to let the man become so close. Lately he had been able to push Josiah far away from his thoughts, after assaulting him with the poem. Writing *Prufrock* had been cathartic at the time, but now that it was published and circulating, he had to admit it troubled him. Had he been too cruel? Could he face the man? Did he dare?

Then the unexpected had happened. In the letter Professor Elder had congratulated him on writing such an excellent poem! Yes, astoundingly he had said that he had recognized some characteristics of himself within it, but forgave Tom in the interests of literature; understanding that it may have been distress that inspired the poem to be written; said he had been amused at such a clever use of his phraseology once he saw past the caricature to the poem's greatness. Tom had not anticipated this response, not at all. This awareness coupled with forgiveness. It confused and troubled him. He would not apologize for the poem. He would not defend it. He stood by every line. But if he went to Boston he really should agree to meet with the old man, and grant him the respect of a civilized conversation. It was the gentlemanly thing to do.

Surely no harm could come of it.

39.

BUT HOW HIS ARMS AND LEGS ARE THIN, thought Maybelle Gill as she knelt and accepted the Communion wafer from Father Sweeney at the altar. She could see his skinny arms up the inside of his cassock sleeves and could imagine the rest of him. She shuddered. He had been reassuring in the confessional. He had told her that times of doubt came to many, often to the most devout, just as a gift of grace could arrive unbidden. There was no explanation beyond God's will as to when one felt his presence and when one languished in the dark night of the soul. It was God's way of testing her, he said, and he told her that she must pray with all her strength for the grace of God to descend upon her once again. Had she smelled alcohol in that small enclosed space? Sacramental wine, surely.

She had, long ago, admitted to an innocent infatuation with Father Sweeney, but she had never said a word to him about it, for she judged it a harmless fancy. They had spoken together, week after week, she with her confessions; he with his absolutions, never discussing their relationship. He occasionally came to tea at No. 13 and at those times they made awkward small talk together. That was all. The odd intimacy of the confessional and the brief acknowledgments of her personhood outside it had been enough to nourish the spark of interest that she felt for him, but now she knew it was over.

She saw, as he handed her the wafer, how old and spindly he seemed, and as the Host began to melt away in her mouth he seemed shorter, less attractive, insubstantial under his swishing robes, and all the while she should have been thinking only of Christ's incredible sacrifice.

"The blood of Christ."

But was it? This Thanksgiving morning it tasted only of cheap red wine, left out too long and turning slightly to vinegar. She would not have allowed such awful stuff in her own kitchen for the tenderizing of meat. Bitter blood.

What has happened to me? she asked herself, as she rose and returned to the pew. She knelt again, supposedly absolved of all sin and united with Christ through the sacrament, but still feeling full of wicked disbelief. Her whole body, here in this place in this posture, was now a lie. A shaft of light fell across her line of sight, but it was filled with dust. The woman next to her wore a damp coat that smelled of mothballs. Father Sweeney's prayerful pronouncements were grating on her nerves.

She got up then, and with aching knees, walked hurriedly from the church, noticing how dark and ugly it was for the first time.

From the altar Father Sweeney noted the abrupt departure of Mrs. Maybelle Gill, watching as she failed to cross herself with the holy water from the font, and he smiled inwardly. It was the first interesting thing she had ever done.

40.

Do I DARE DISTURB THE UNIVERSE? This, Mr. Elder knew was to be his own overwhelming question. And the answer would be yes.

His former protégé was supposedly destined for great things, but he, Professor Josiah Elder could, and would, put an end to all such prospects.

Bending over the library table he studied a lengthy chapter of the large encyclopedia using a magnifying glass. He had determined that this book had all the information he would require. Then, in his first act of criminality, he secured the volume in his briefcase and scuttled towards the library doors. No one paid him the slightest notice. He walked home as briskly as he was able, unable to keep from turning his head back occasionally, fully expecting to see an enraged librarian giving chase. But he made it down the steps of No. 13, unmolested and unnoticed but for the cat who showed no interest.

Now he could take his time and slowly ponder this book of poisons, ancient and modern. It was not so easy to determine what would be the right choice. The substance had to be easily obtainable for one thing, and something that would not reveal its nature to the taste if slipped into tea or whiskey. It had to work swiftly so there would be no time for an antidote, and because he was not by nature a sadist, it needed to be relatively painless. Common rat poison would not do.

And now, after risking disgrace for the thievery of the poisons book, he listened to Beatrice rattling around with platters and pots on the other side of his door and imagined an even more efficient alternative. He pictured himself stepping behind Tom for a moment, sliding a kitchen knife from out his sleeve. A swipe across the jugular would be fast and lethal, time for a look of surprise and then nothing more. Which should he choose? Both would render speech impossible. Tom would not produce another word. Justice!

Because he had realized that he would not care for his own fate after such a deed was accomplished, and in truth hoping he would be arrested, found guilty, and dispatched quickly by the powers of the law, either poison or throat cutting would do, because either could be done efficiently here in the convenience of his rooms.

However, his next thought gave him pause. What if Tom balked at meeting him in private rooms given his previous misunderstanding of Josiah's innocent behavior? And there was dear Mabel Gill to consider, too. A murder at No. 13 would be terrible for her future business.

No, his plan must be to execute Tom in another place. Where could it be done? The Harvard Yard perhaps. That would be fitting. There he could run a dagger through the heart of the treacherous Harvard man who had struck at him with those insidious words. In such a hallowed place there would be witnesses. Now that he thought of it, there *should* be witnesses. He *wanted* witnesses. Then every autumn his story would arise like Lazarus come from the dead. There, they would say, pointing to the spot to the newly arriving students, there is where a Professor Emeritus murdered a disappointing student!

What should it be? Poison, knife, dagger? He simply couldn't decide.

41.

"In a minute there is time for decisions and revisions which a minute will reverse," quoted Beatrice under her breath, as she fiddled with the decorations around the silver platter on which rested the warm, roasted turkey. She was surrounding it with cranberries, walnuts and figs, however she was not thinking of turkey decor, but of the paper she would present to Mr. Elder tomorrow in their scheduled meeting. He is such a kind man, she thought, so considerate to take his time to help her with the English literature paper, particularly as he was not fond of the poem.

She had written and rewritten the paper and felt ready to have his fine educated mind look it over. And that phrase stuck with her...decisions and revisions...going round and round in her mind much as a tune can play over and over in the brain, even when one wishes it would cease.

But for now she really must concentrate on the presentation of this bird and all its trimmings. Very soon she would hear the shuffling feet of the boarders overhead as they took their places in the dining room. There might be a little financial bonus for her if the dinner went well. Enough to pay for another class.

She paused in her work to put some stuffing and drippings down for the yellow cat who everyone called Tom, though she sensed it was not his actual name, stray that he was.

The cat was fond of Beatrice, who always called him "ThereYouGo." He knew the turkey scraps would come later but for now he tucked into the juicy dressing with pleasure. Life was good at No. 13.

42.

FOR I HAVE KNOWN THEM ALL ALREADY, KNOWN THEM ALL: HAVE KNOWN THE EVENINGS, MORNINGS, AFTERNOONS, I HAVE MEASURED OUT MY LIFE WITH COFFEE SPOONS.

And there it was staring her right in the face. Lucille Davenport could no longer deny it. The heart of the poem, described her own inner life. That was why the poem had so enthralled and enraged her. She was Prufrock in skirts...hesitant, absent-minded, self-critical...in short, afraid. The realization, kept at a distance for these many weeks had at last broken through into her consciousness, tumbled out of the verses and punched her in the heart.

All the while Winston Ward had been flirting with her. That was the word. Flirting. And she would not, could not, even smile in return. Winston was rude, a rake, not the kind of man she would ever fancy, but she was unable to even pretend at interest, as she knew women often did. Why she could not even look him in the eye of late, she stammered, she blushed, and she supposed he was secretly laughing at her discomfiture, talking behind her back to Reginald who she did rather like. It was humiliating.

Lucille fought back tears as she had trained herself to do. If she had cried as a child in the orphanage in which she had been raised, she would call attention to herself. This was never a good thing. The sisters, the brood of bullies who had raised her, didn't tolerate cry-babies or attention seekers of any kind and were quick with the hickory stick. Be quiet, stay in line, don't stand out, pride was a sin, envy was a sin, laziness was a sin, self-pity was a sin, *everything* was a sin.

She had emerged pale and shaking from her childhood and had gradually found stable footing as a teacher. Her love of poetry had been her secret childhood passion, and when she finally realized it was not an offense to God she made it her life's mission to know it and love it and teach it. The poetry of Shakespeare, Wordsworth, Byron, Keats, Shelley. She knew them all, all the romantic writers that had lifted her up during her long dark childhood. Good poetry. Poetry that offered beauty and promised life.

She remained a God-fearing woman, though she harbored doubts. She had not allowed herself frivolous attachments or adventure, hoping for marriage, and a proper life. She had survived the orphanage, flowered a little briefly in sunlight and freedom and then slowly, ever so slowly, withered. Mrs. Gill had made a friend of her, even mothered her at times, and kept her close to her religion, as life proceeded with its many stresses and distresses.

She hadn't fully realized until she read the poem by T. S. Eliot, the poem that offered no redemption, no hope of a better life, no moment of grace, only disappointment and death, just what had happened to her or, better said, what she had wrought. She had suffocated herself in decency. She could see it clearly now. She had begun life as an unwanted baby and had grown up to become an unloved old maid.

Here she sat, rigid and alone, on this park bench, in the middle of Boston Common on a cold Thanksgiving afternoon, while all the world was elsewhere, giving thanks, enjoying the warmth of their families.

This morning she had been late as usual, hoping to meet up with Mrs.

Gill in church in the chilly dark of early Mass, but had not found her in her usual pew. So after enduring the service she had walked to the Commons to sit in the sunlight. She had pulled out the now ragged copy of the poetry magazine and once more considered the poem, the poem which was, in its relentless way, her undoing.

She stood up then and straightened her shoulders, determined to get through the Thanksgiving meal with a calm demeanor. She must go and bathe herself, and pin her hair into place and put on a brave face to meet the faces she would meet across the dining room table. She would even try to smile at wretched Winston Ward, just to prove to herself that could, that she was still alive, and still a woman.

43.

I KNOW THE VOICES DYING WITH A DYING FALL BENEATH THE MUSIC OF A FARTHER ROOM…so drifted the thoughts of Captain Arlington as he listened to Mary playing a melancholy tune alone in the parlor below his quiet bedroom, and the muttering of guests as they began assembling for dinner. He lay unmoving, feeling sullen, alone on his bed, where he had reclined since the horrible choking experience at breakfast.

Sunk into melancholy, his treacherous mind floated to Benedict his first mate, Charlie the little cabin boy, Mike and Timothy the roguish twins, John who had been so young and strong, Pirate Pete who had played the fiddle in the evenings on quiet seas, Fighting Willie the pugnacious bosun, and Boris who spoke no English. Others, too, all swallowed by the waves but whose voices lived on in his mind. Sometimes he heard them going about the work of his ship, sometimes singing drunkenly as they returned from port, sometimes screaming as the ship foundered, broke apart, and sunk beneath their boots into the churning waters. His fault. His fault. He could blame no other. Yes, the sea had been rough, the winds catastrophic, but he had been their captain and he had failed them. He knew he would hear their voices until he died, and when he went to Hell, where surely he was destined, he would hear them forever as he burned, or more likely, boiled.

But today he must get up and get dressed and join the others over a Thanksgiving dinner. He had once again withstood the dreadful choking off of his life's breath. He had survived the ocean by God's will, and he had survived the toast because Mr. Elder had sprung into action and Mary Prior had sat on his chest. He didn't know which was worse.

44.

So how should I presume? asked Mrs. Gill of herself. How shall I presume to utter Grace when my faith has fled from me? Yet the guests, dressed in their best, were now all seated with cheerful expectant faces, and the bird, roasted to perfection, had been presented. She smiled at them weakly and bowed her head. Opened her mouth. Closed it. Lifted her head again. She knew the words, but could not speak them. The guests hesitantly raised their eyes, looked at her, then at one another. There was a nervous cough from Mr. Elder. Throats cleared. Feet shuffled under the table.

It was Lucille who came to her rescue. Gently laying her hand on that of Mrs. Gill she said the traditional, graceful words.

"Amen," chorused the assembly and everyone seemed to relax.

"Thank you, Miss Davenport," she whispered. "Mr. Elder, will you do the honors and carve the turkey?" She said, relieved to find her ability to speak again.

"I shall indeed be honored, Mrs. Gill," he replied, and set about with an artful flashing of the carving knife and long- pronged fork.

The meal began to proceed normally. Platters were passed, gravy spooned onto slices of turkey and mashed potatoes. Ruby red cranberry sauce decorated plates piled high with green and yellow vegetables. The meat was deemed delicious.

Only Maybelle found herself without appetite. Beatrice, who was keeping an eye on her whilst serving, removing, and replacing dishes, was worried that the dinner was in some way unsatisfying to her employer, but wondered how that could be as everyone else was eating heartily and were generous with words of praise.

It was Lucille again, leaning towards Mrs. Gill who whispered a word of concern. "Are you feeling all right, Mrs. Gill?"

"It's nothing," she replied, her voice a whisper. "Nothing at all," which was exactly the problem, she knew. For God was nothing at all.

"Are you feeling better?" asked Mary Prior of Captain Arlington, totally unaware of the embarrassment he felt regarding the morning's debacle. "I hope I did your poor chest no lasting harm."

His mouth flinched in acknowledgment, but failed at smiling. She seemed remote to him now, this woman to whom he had been prepared to offer his hand in marriage on this very day. He watched her as she enjoyed her dinner, talking with the other guests, laughing from time to time at something Winston or Lionel said. He remembered her bottom sitting heavily upon his chest, and her expression as she had peered down at him as he regained consciousness; not of concern, but of enjoyment at his confusion upon finding her there. He could excuse her, he supposed. She was young and flighty by nature, and by the time he had come to his senses it was apparent that he was going to be all right. Still, she had all but laughed in his face! It had been a daring thing for her to have done, plopping down on him as Mr. Elder cleared out his throat. Most unladylike. The two of them had likely saved his life. He did not feel grateful. Once or twice as the meal progressed he saw that Mary was smiling at him, a conspiratorial, flirtatious smile, but he felt not a flicker of interest in her anymore.

Josiah Elder, having taken smaller portions than the younger people, looked up from his empty plate to notice a startled, almost terrified look pass across the face of Lucille Davenport. She shifted slightly in her chair and lowered her head, but he could see that her cheeks were burning red. Mrs. Gill to Lucille's left seemed not to notice her discomfiture and stared off into some tangle of her own thoughts about which Josiah could not guess, but Winston Ward on her right was smiling covertly at Reginald Smith across the table. It could only mean one thing and it shocked Josiah. Winston must have put his hand on Lucille's knee under the table. He drew in a breath expecting Lucille's objection. Mrs. Gill would put Winston out on the street without pause and Thanksgiving dinner would be ruined. He leaned forward now, preparing for her outraged words and an abrupt ending to the felicitous meal, but Lucille held her tongue. Not only did she not object, but as the high color remained on her cheeks Josiah was sure he caught the flicker of a smile come and go across her features. She continued to eat quietly, not conversing with anyone. Whatever had occurred beneath the table seemed destined to remain there.

Determined to speak a harsh word to Winston himself when he next found him alone, Josiah shifted his attention to Mary Prior. He had noticed that something had changed in Mary's world. Neither of the men on whom she had been so diligently bestowing her attention as recently as this morning, were giving her the slightest notice. Reginald had never seemed interested in Mary, but what had happened to put the Captain off? He wondered. The choking situation at breakfast had called for immediate action or the man would have died, and the jolt to his chest that Mary's rump provided had dislodged the offending toast; and it now appeared to have dislodged Captain Arlington's affection for Mary as well. Oh my, he thought, how the slightest gesture can disturb the universe.

Reginald, for his part tried to enjoy his food, but those lovely arms of Beatrice Platt, white and bare to the elbow, kept appearing and disappearing from his vision as she served the meal. He had the terrifying thought that he might be compelled to turn and lick her wrist. He wouldn't. He knew he wouldn't. It was outside the bounds of civilized behavior. But what if he did? What if he couldn't help himself? He would be disgraced, reviled, turned out. So he concentrated as best he could on the squash and beans that remained on his plate, but tasted not a bite of them.

Winston had no such conflict. He had laid his open hand directly on Lucille's knee beneath the table, and when she neither moved away nor protested, he had begun to inch it up her leg. She had blushed, but not gasped. An unexpected communication was taking place out of sight of the others. Alas, he thought, for just as things were getting interesting she suddenly stood up, rather clumsily, scraping her chair backwards and lifting the glass of wine which had been given to them on this special occasion, she announced a toast to their landlady, Mrs. Maybelle Gill, and added her personal thanks for the warm home she provided for her, and so many others, for so many years.

"Here, here," they all chimed in. "To Mrs. Gill of No. 13." This certainly broke the lustful spell for Winston who now, his arm back upon the table, began to think of pumpkin pie with thick whipped cream, and just as he did so the desserts began to make their appearance.

Mr. Elder, continuing his perusal of the assembly, noted that Maybelle Gill looked pale, even as the wine glasses were cheerfully lifted in her honor, her smile was forced. Well, he thought, we all have our problems this Thanksgiving Day. Mine is how to arrange the murder of Thomas Stearns Eliot. Hers, no doubt, was no great matter. Still, he thought, he should step into her living room after dinner and offer a kind word. He had truly enjoyed the meal. The dreadful poem had not been mentioned even once as Lucille's thoughts seemed to be preoccupied in some new way. A slight tic was now jumping merrily below her right eye. A shame, he judged. She seemed to be going down a very wrong path with its attendant distress. He was fond of Lucille, but he knew he could not save her from Winston. Or herself.

Josiah Elder stretched out his arm in what he knew was called "a boarding house reach" and took, for the first time in his life, a second helping of pie.

45.

AND I HAVE KNOWN THE EYES ALREADY, KNOWN THEM ALL—THE EYES THAT FIX YOU IN A FORMULATED PHRASE. AND WHEN I AM FORMULATED, SPRAWLING ON A PIN, WHEN I AM PINNED AND WRIGGLING ON THE WALL, THEN HOW SHOULD I BEGIN TO SPIT OUT ALL THE BUTT-ENDS OF MY DAYS AND WAYS?

Those lines had gone into the mind of Lionel Quill and firmly lodged there as Lucille had obsessed over them and repeated them in the parlor, evening after evening, driving them all, earlier and earlier, to their rooms. The lines spoke to him all too pointedly. It was just a matter of time, he knew, before he would be formulated by this lot, pinned and catalogued as a deviant, and then sent packing from No. 13. He understood that this was the way of the world, but did not understand *why* it was the way. If he sat them all down after this warm Thanksgiving dinner and told them what his life was really like, of the loneliness, the fear, the deceptions and regrets with which he lived would it change the way they thought of him? Would they allow him his humanity or still see him as just a repulsive bug?

He wondered if the poet who wrote those trenchant lines was a secret homosexual. There was evidence for it in the estranged and tortured soul of J. Alfred Prufrock. There was the dread of women that ran through the poem, and a longing to belong.

Lionel pushed his plate away, now emptied of pie, and drummed his fingers on the edge of the table. He did it without thinking, releasing a little of the pent up tension he always felt around normal people.

As Mr. Elder proposed a toast to the cook, Lionel suddenly felt he could bear their company no longer and with a false smile and a little bow he began to stand up. Let them think I have indigestion. Let them think whatever they damn well please, he said to himself defiantly; but just then a gentle hand was placed on his shoulder, pushing him gently down, and Beatrice Platt, of all people, whispered an astonishing sentence into his ear. Lionel sank back down into his chair, astounded, as she withdrew, smiling at the glasses raised in her honor.

46.

"AND HOW SHOULD I PRESUME?" asked Tom Eliot.

"You can presume because you have written a poem for the ages," replied Vivienne Eliot as they lay on their backs next to one another on the narrow bed. "Where there is one great poem, there is another."

"But how should I presume to think that I, with just a pen and some trifling thoughts, can disturb the universe?"

"Oh don't be tedious, Tom."

"I shall stop these sorry attempts at poetry and get myself a proper job. A bank. I shall work in a bank and become respectable and wealthy."

"Do as you like, then. But don't forget we have that dinner party to attend on Friday night. The Woolfs will be there. You should read aloud. It is expected."

"I have nothing to read. Nothing good enough."

"Then write something new."

"What shall I write about?"

"It doesn't matter. Write about me. Write about us."

"I should rather hang myself."

"You are an impossible man."

"Married to an impossible woman. What shall we do? What shall we ever do?"

"Do just put your arms around me for once."

But Tom did not. He turned his head allowing only his eyes to traverse the landscape of her body, then returning his stare to the ceiling he lifted his arms up, up, up towards a damp stain, far above them, outside his grasp.

47.

AND I HAVE KNOWN THE ARMS ALREADY, KNOWN THEM ALL—mused the No. 13 cat, as the dish was placed before him. Arms that reach out to pet me, to hold me, to feed me, to do me harm. It was best always to remain at arm's length in the world of humans. In this home, however, arms were not a problem. Only two people were ever here in the lower floor, an old man who referred to him as Tom and never tried to touch him, and a cook who only patted his head gently when she put down food, just as she did now. She, too, had called him "happy thanksgiving" today. It was a nice enough name, he thought. Here, beneath the table in the kitchen that he had adopted as his home, he ate his turkey happily, and found a corner where nobody went, far back under the lower pantry shelf. He bathed, and curled up, and went to sleep dreaming of his girlfriend, a stray who was called Shoo Shoo by the neighbors, but he knew her real name, just as he knew his own which was, of course—but he fell asleep too quickly to think of it.

48.

ARMS THAT ARE BRACELETED AND WHITE AND BARE (BUT IN THE LAMPLIGHT, DOWNED WITH LIGHT BROWN HAIR!). Those were the arms preferred by Winston Ward, and he knew exactly where to find them. Trifling with silly Lucille Davenport was amusing, but now that he was well fed he desired the real thing. Reginald had declined to come with him to the brothel tonight, but surprisingly Captain Arlington had inquired if he might accompany him for it was common, if unspoken, knowledge as to where the salesmen headed off to in the evenings. Reginald had been downright strange since developing his attraction to Beatrice Platt, thought Winston. He was always worrying about his looks and hanging around No. 13 in the evenings hoping to cross paths with her. The cook! Well, at least she was a good one. The meals here were often very satisfying.

The Captain had seemed withdrawn throughout the dinner, so Winston was startled when the old chap had suggested he might join him tonight. He usually spent the evenings mooning over Mary Prior at the piano, and politely pretending to be interested in Lucille's obsessional prattling. The old lady had been odd too, having arranged the special meal for Thanksgiving, she had sat, pale as a ghost, eating almost nothing, saying nothing at all. Maybe she was ill. He didn't care one way or the other. It was not his problem. Being a loner, having no roots, being detached was his chosen lifestyle and it had its compensations.

Winston knew he had the ability to charm people for short periods of time; long enough to sell a stove, long enough to seduce a woman, not that they needed seducing here in the brothel, only money, of which he had plenty. He had never dreamed of marrying or having a family. He had grown up in an unhappy clan that had put him off the whole idea. He had never even engaged in a serious romance, finding women useful only to satisfy his fleshy desires, as his father had before him. His mother, when he thought of her, seemed to have spent his childhood years alternating between screaming and weeping and he hadn't been able to get out of his parents' home fast enough.

On his own since the age of sixteen he had found freedom, and pleasure, and brief companionships that served until replaced by another. It was a life that suited him. Whereas Reginald was always wondering if Beatrice liked him, Winston had never given a thought as to whether he was liked or disliked; unless of course he counted Lucille, who would have to be cajoled into liking him in order to win the bet.

49.

IS IT PERFUME FROM A DRESS THAT MAKES ME SO DIGRESS? wondered the Captain. It was his nature to quickly submerge any childhood memories that surfaced, for they always came wrapped in depression. Yet, here in this tawdry place, with this blousy woman, his long lost mother was occupying his mind like a conquering army, driving his normal thoughts and appetites into retreat. He took a large drink from the glass of watered down whiskey by the side of the bed.

"Where have you gone to?" asked his companion of the evening, a plump woman named Cherry blessed with a cheerful countenance whom he had enjoyed selecting from the number of available women, rather like choosing a sweet from a chocolate box.

"I was thinking about my mother."

"In such a place as this? she asked with mock astonishment in her voice. "You should not think of your Mama when you are with the likes of me." She placed his hand on her breast. The material was flimsy and he could feel the softness of her flesh, the hardness of her nipple beneath.

"She was a very beautiful woman."

"Do I remind you of her?"

"Not in the least. She was tall, thin, with beautiful straight hair, long and dark."

"You are not so young, Mr. Captain. Is she dead?"

"Very much dead. She drowned herself."

"No!" Cherry seemed genuinely shocked, her blue eyes opening wide beneath her soft blond curls. She laid a gentle hand on his arm. "Will you tell me this thing?"

Strangely he wanted to talk, needed to talk, and why not? Sweet Cherry would soon forget him, he knew, within minutes after he walked out of her room. He took another swallow of the whiskey.

"I was eleven. We were on the beach. I was doing what children do, wading along the shore, my trousers rolled, looking for shells and star-fish brought in by the waves. She was nearby, staring out to sea for a long time. Then she bent and kissed me on the top of my head. She said, 'Goodbye, my dearest one' and walked quietly into the water. Out she went, farther and farther. I stood still. I kept my eyes on her. I, of course, expected her to turn and come back at any moment, but she slowly disappeared beneath the surface of the waves and was gone."

"Oh, what a terrible thing you tell to me."

Could this woman care? He wondered. Even for a moment? She seemed to do so.

"Yes. It was terrible. In my grief I decided that she had become a mermaid and that someday I would find her, but it was a sad, childish idea, soon forgotten."

"And now; why do you think of her now? Here is where men come to forget their troubles, not to remember them."

"Because, my dear, she returns when *she* wills it, not when I do, and when she returns, she is always still leaving. I think, Cherry, that you wear a perfume like she once did, and that odor has summoned her."

"Oh yes, the scent is on my clothing from the spray of the cologne. I will take off my dress and then, perhaps we will find ways for you to be happier?"

"Though I have tried...tried many things...I have never been truly happy since that day on the shore, my dear Cherry, nor do I expect to be, but I am most willing for you to give it your best effort."

50.

"ARMS THAT LIE ALONG A TABLE, OR WRAP ABOUT A SHAWL," read Beatrice aloud. "The poet presents only parts of women seen through the eyes of Prufrock. The reader never gets to see a picture of a whole woman."

"A very keen observation, Miss Platt, and do you see other signs of misogyny?"

It was early morning, a week after Thanksgiving. Mr. Elder and Beatrice were seated together at the kitchen table. They were alone but for the cat, and were engaged in a close reading and discussion of the poem about which she was writing her mid-term paper.

Winter had enclosed No. 13 with blasts of cold wind and a blanket of thick snow, but the kitchen, as always, was snug and warm. The beef stew for dinner was simmering on the stove top and fresh bread was baking in the oven giving off a heavenly aroma. The cat slept in its favorite corner.

The irony of his situation continued to secretly amuse Josiah. Here he was bent over a poem about himself, while planning to murder its author, all the while smiling encouragingly at the young woman who was so determined to make sense of it. He had grown familiar with all the humiliations of the verse, nurturing a hardness in his heart each time he felt the scorn that had been heaped upon him—the bald spot, the hesitancies, the pretentiousness, and the foolishness. Beatrice, at the moment, was more interested in the poet's insubstantial view of women.

"He makes the women sound shallow, or patronizing, cruel even," she replied.

"Does he say so directly?"

"No. But he gives them no real substance, except to reject Prufrock."

"Or so Prufrock imagines. The women do speak of Michelangelo which means they are cultured."

"Yes, but Prufrock is the very opposite of a depiction by Michelangelo, so I think they are put there to mock him."

"We are not told how he feels about them. What do you think? Maybe they are just showing off to each other."

"I suppose it could be read that way," she admitted. "It does make them seem unappealing either way."

"Your assessment of the poet is that he is somewhat of a misogynist then. But of Prufrock, himself. What do you make of him? Is he intelligent?"

"He is curiously unreflective."

"But the whole poem is a self-reflection, is it not?"

"Oh no, I think it is a quarrel with himself, not a self-reflection. Once he has invited the reader to go along with him to the party he thinks of no one but himself, that is true; but he hesitates, obsesses, he anticipates, even looks back upon an imagined failure of his intended actions, but he never really asks himself why he is how he is."

"Perhaps he is afraid."

"Yes, he is filled with fear, but seems to think his life could be no other way."

Her remarks were unsettling. "Do you think he is a good man?"

"Yes, I do, except he is not good to himself, of course. If I met him, I think I would want to help him. Encourage him."

"You have a kind heart, Beatrice."

And so they hummed along warmly together, Beatrice thinking how generous Mr. Elder was to take this time to help and encourage her with the essay; Josiah eyeing the excellent carving knife that he enjoyed handling at Thanksgiving dinner now gleaming in its place on the knife rack.

"I keep wondering why should a young man like Prufrock be so determined to ask a woman to marry him." Beatrice mused. "I mean, if he isn't comfortable with women and is so frightened of proposing, and so certain of rejection? Does he fancy himself in love? That isn't at all clear."

"So you see Prufrock as a young man? What about that bald spot?"

"A young man can have one. Reginald Sterling does. I see it when I lean over to serve him at meals. Oh!" Her hand flew to cover her mouth. "I am so very sorry. I have made remark upon a guest. A terrible thing for a servant to do. For anyone to do."

"Never mind, my dear. I have a few thoughts of my own about the guests who come and go from here. Getting back to my question though, is Prufrock actually young?"

"He says he will grow old."

"No. He says, 'I grow old—' so perhaps he is an elderly man remembering the past, inviting the reader to share his memories, recalling his hesitation to act on some fateful day long ago, and mourning the resulting loss and loneliness that attached to that failure."

"I wouldn't have put that together. Oh dear, Mr. Elder, there are too many ways of looking at the thing."

"Is that not both the strength and the weakness of the poem? I myself read an earlier version of this piece several years ago when Mr. Eliot first came to Harvard. It was then a simpler poem; and, as you imagined, it was about a young, hesitant man approaching a woman with his overwhelming question: 'will you marry me?' It was quite splendid in the original, but he has layered it with so many meanings in the intervening years that it has become inscrutable and ill formed."

"Like when I over-work a dough. The bread will not rise properly."

"Just so. If you are determined to write about it, I would suggest you give emphasis to exactly who Prufrock *is*, for he speaks in many voices: man, woman, young, old, cat—"

"Lazarus, Polonius—"

"Is that enough for you to think about today? Enough to get you back to work?"

"Yes, it is more than enough. Thank you so very much, Mr. Elder."

"You are most welcome, Miss Platt. Do you have any marshmallows?"

"What?" Beatrice was surprised by the unexpected question. "Why yes, I just bought some to use on the Christmas pudding decorations."

"I find I have a desire for a marshmallow or two. I always enjoy a sweet after teaching."

As Beatrice hurried towards the pantry to comply with the request, thinking how much it pleased her to give sweets to the sweet, Josiah was wondering if arsenic could be injected into a marshmallow.

The cat continued to sleep.

51.

AND SHOULD I THEN PRESUME? fretted a troubled Lucille. Should I presume that Winston cares for me? And how have I myself come to have a care about the rogue? His attentions are always secretive, a wandering hand beneath the table, a small caress as we go up the stairs, once a glancing kiss upon my ear when we were the last to depart the dining room together following breakfast. Shocking behavior, but he has said nothing. My acquiescence is improper in every way, and yet I wait upon his smile, his seemingly innocent nearness. If anyone saw, oh, if they guessed! How dreadful that I feel this way towards a man to whom I am not married, not even engaged. Why I hardly know him and what I know I do not much like. And yet I dream of him every night. In my dreams I feel his weight upon my naked body, smell his manly scent, enjoy the movements of his muscles, and I drown in a pleasure in my deepest place that I have never felt before. I awaken full of joy before the terrible shame comes over me, mortifies me. Does he have a care for me? Do I care for him? Do I care if he cares? I dream only of his exploring hand, that finds its destination in my dreams.

Lucille was walking through the snowdrifts of Boston, the park covered in a mantle of whiteness, her thoughts becoming more and more confused in the night's wind. She knew she should seek refuge in the church, but how could she enter such a sacred place with these impure thoughts, these ungodly longings? She could never go to confession again. She could never speak these words aloud to Father Sweeney, or to anyone, so never again could she take Communion. What would the priest make of it? What would Maybelle Gill think of what was in her mind, of what went on below her dining room table? And of her dreams, which she could not control?

Oh, surely she was a lost soul, she thought. She would be damned, and she knew it would not be for any sin of commission; only for her feelings, only for her desires. And the worst of it all was that a small, beastly part of herself did not care if only the dreams would come again. Or the man himself. Should she tell him to come to her? Did she dare? She could never dare.

For years she had read romantic poetry; poetry that spoke of love and longing; but not this. This was lust and it was sin. She felt sensations of which poetry did not speak, for these feelings were not about the breaking of a heart or the longing of a soul, but an aching in her most private parts, an animal desire so base there could be no poetry in it. Only unspeakable want. She wanted sex. Loveless, unrelenting, unrepentant sex. She swallowed frigid air into her lungs, but did not feel cooled.

It was snowing steadily and, as she wandered into the night, so did her thoughts wander over her shrouded life. Who was Lucille Davenport anyway? Even her name was a fiction given to her by the nuns, meaning what? Light, they told her. Lucille meant the bearer of light, but so did the name Lucifer. They told her that, too. And Davenport! She had been discovered on one, in the entrance hall of the nunnery. Why had she been abandoned there when she was only a few hours old? Was there something in her first cries that foretold depravity? Was she marked for sin from birth?

Upon leaving the orphanage at eighteen, she had, until now, clung to propriety as if to a life raft. She knew exactly how to behave having learned it well to avoid the fury of the nuns, her keepers, and her knowledge served her as a way to navigate the society she entered outside the cloistered walls. Her awareness of how to conform to society's rules had enabled her to find a place that nurtured her and rooms in which she could hold her head up high. She had become a respected teacher, a loving friend to Mrs. Gill and Mr. Elder, a responsible member of the household in which she lived with its ever changeable parts, a church-goer; she had been a good woman, living a life within clearly drawn limits.

And then the poem had arrived, the poem that told her that she was failing to thrive. Instead she was cringing from life, refusing excitement, anticipating censure, and always dreading the moment when she would be found wanting. Under all her appropriate behavior there was nothing but fear; the fear of God, and the judgment of others. Then, just as she had begun to examine the choices which had led to the moments of loneliness so stark that she sometimes wanted to die, Winston Ward's hand had begun the ascent of her thigh. And she hadn't stopped him. She had felt no wish to stop him. The beliefs that had held her together all these years now lay, like shattered ice, in a pile of confusing shards.

In spite of the darkness and drifts she found the bench in the Commons that she most preferred. Today it looked like a large, plump sofa engulfed as it was in untouched snow. It would be obscene to sit down on it she thought, sinful to disturb its virginal white cushion, so she stood next to it, and shivered, and started slowly to freeze. Her racing thoughts became calmer and cooler. The snow, heavier now, began to cover her as well, but she no longer had the will to move. She heard the cry of Prufrock repeated, over and over, in her numbing mind: "Do I dare? Do I dare?"

When Lucille at last lost consciousness it arrived as relief. She collapsed quietly, into a unrecognizable heap next to the pristine bench. The snow continued to fall.

52.

AND HOW SHOULD I BEGIN? Mr. Elder stood on the threshold of the parlor, reluctant to enter with his dreadful news. All the others were there, warmed by the fire against the unseasonable cold, awaiting word on Lucille Davenport who had gone missing now for a night and a day.

At last he stepped forward and spoke. "I have been to the hospital," he said gravely. "Miss Davenport is not expected to survive, and if she does it will be a long recovery and she may be disfigured from frostbite. She was found in the Boston Commons, and taken for dead, but she still lives. Barely. The physicians are doing all they can. And we can but pray."

Each of those present took in this news in their own way. Maybelle Gill was the most visibly distressed for she loved Lucille, in her fashion, but how could she pray? Instead she wept silently, her head bowed; then arose and walked haltingly into her rooms. Mr. Elder was quick to support her, his hand beneath her elbow, as she departed.

Captain Arlington, Mary Prior, and Lionel Quill began to talk quietly to one another, saying the reassuring things that people say in such circumstances; how Lucille was strong, how skilled the doctors were these days; and wondering what she had been doing outside alone on such a night.

Only Winston Ward and Reginald Sterling were silent, for they knew. They had enjoyed their bet, wondering if Winston would succeed in his seduction without noticing, or perhaps not caring, about the decline in Lucille, until now, when it was too late. As they thought back over the previous two weeks it was clear she had been thrown into an alarming conflict between her morals and her desires, causing her faculties to fail. She had grown pale, suddenly flushing to red if spoken to; her eye often ticked; she had begun to stutter. And the poem, the blasted poem had seemed to devour her. She spoke of little else, for the arising of her sexual feelings were for her, no doubt, unspeakable. She had wandered off into the blizzard after a dinner and they hadn't even noticed her go.

Winston wiped his hand over his sweaty brow. The room was suddenly too warm. He bolted for his room and tried to shut the door against his conscience, a conscience he had not known he even possessed. Reginald sat staring into the fire. He had not laid hands on Lucille Davenport but felt as if he had, laughing with Winston about her on evenings past, thinking of her body and the desire Winston was clearly arousing in her. His hands felt dirty and he wanted to wash them, but he did not want to follow Winston to their room. He was afraid he might hit him. Hitting Winston would not, he knew, relieve his guilt.

Excusing himself, Reginald walked into the dining room and down the stairs into the kitchen, something he had never done before though he had often imagined doing so. Beatrice would be there. Seeing Beatrice would help him through this dreadful, shame-filled evening. But Beatrice had left for the night. Oh where was she when he needed her most? Only the cat prowled around the edges of the kitchen, sensing his distress and giving him a wide berth.

Reginald sat down alone at the table just as tears began to cloud his vision. He hadn't cried since he was a child, but in this shameful moment he gave into the relief of tears. He wept for Lucille, a fragile woman who had never done anyone a moment's harm. He wept for his complicity in Winston's callous treatment of her. He wept for the meaningless life that he was leading, of money-making and loveless sex. He wept because he was in love with Beatrice and was afraid to speak of his feelings.

Later, when Mr. Elder entered the kitchen after consoling Maybelle Gill, he saw Reginald, his arms dangling, his head resting on the table top, snoring gently as he slept. The cat had joined him, curling around his balding head like a golden crown.

53.

"SHALL I SAY, I HAVE GONE AT DUSK THROUGH NARROW STREETS, AND WATCHED THE SMOKE THAT RISES FROM THE PIPES OF LONELY MEN IN SHIRT-SLEEVES, LEANING OUT OF WINDOWS?"

"What is that she is saying?" asked the matron, peering at the prone figure of Lucille Davenport, who had been brought in barely clinging to life two nights before.

"She utters only nonsense," replied the nursing sister, "although sometimes it rhymes."

"Her brain has been affected by the experience. Report to me if she says anything sensible. How are her vital signs?"

"Improving."

"Then she is a fortunate woman."

"Would it have been worth it?" cried out Lucille from her painful delirium.

54.

I SHOULD HAVE BEEN A PAIR OF RAGGED CLAWS SCUTTLING ACROSS THE FLOORS OF SILENT SEAS and, but for an unkind twist of fate, I would be so, thought Captain Arlington. Or perhaps I would be transformed into a coral fan, or pearls in the shell of an oyster. Had I drowned it would be so. I would have decomposed and become part of the oceans. Instead, here I am, a man shuffling around on dry land as best I can; a creature without purpose, an embodiment of disgrace. When I fancied myself in love with Mary then life was not so bad, it lifted my depressions, but now each footstep over the unyielding earth, the unmoving cobbles, is more intolerable than the last.

The sea completed me in a way I did not fully appreciate, he thought, and now that I know this truth about myself I can no longer run from it, as I once believed. I must find a way to return to the waters. I could never captain another ship for my shame is too great, but there are other possibilities, perhaps working as a crew member on a freighter, or by purchasing a small fishing vessel. I have considerable savings. If all else fails I can do as my mother did and simply walk into the sea.

His thoughts returned to Mary. I have done poorly by her, he judged. With her I have again failed to be admirable. She clearly doesn't deserve my coldness. Being a woman she cannot fathom male pride, of which I have no reserves. Pride went down with my ship. I cannot abide the smallest slight, the minutest embarrassment. Me, a man who has withstood all the violence of typhoons, has become weak as a jellyfish. I have tried to grow a carapace, like a crab or a lobster, but my efforts all fail. I am as vulnerable as a mussel that has been slid from its shell.

And now, at fifty-six I know I must run away to sea again. Somehow. As soon as the ice breaks up in the harbor, I will go.

55.

Aɴᴅ ᴛʜᴇ ᴀꜰᴛᴇʀɴᴏᴏɴ, ᴛʜᴇ ᴇᴠᴇɴɪɴɢ, ꜱʟᴇᴇᴘꜱ ꜱᴏ ᴘᴇᴀᴄᴇꜰᴜʟʟʏ, mused Maybelle Gill watching the snow fall, and fall again, through her parlor window. A god looking down at No. 13 would not see else but calm, yet below the quiet appearance of normality there is so much suffering, and no peace for anyone at all.

Mrs. Gill had been crying off and on since hearing of Lucille's condition. Why had the foolish woman, whom she had come to care for, been so careless with her precious self? What could have possessed her to walk about in a blizzard? And now she might die, leaving us all to mourn through what is sure to be a long, harsh winter.

She thought now that she should not have allowed the salesmen to stay on. Something, she knew not what, had occurred between Winston and Lucille. She had seen no evidence of misbehavior, but Lucille had begun to moon at Winston whenever she wasn't raving about Prufrock. And now Reginald Sterling had been found sleeping in the kitchen! What was that about? His explanation of needing a glass of milk to settle an upset stomach did not sound plausible to her. Had he been bothering Beatrice? She didn't need her cook to be upset on top of everything else. Or worse, to run off with the likes of Reginald Sterling!

Now, on top of everything, there was the Captain, of whom she was so fond, acting strangely, pointedly ignoring Mary Prior who showed every sign of becoming depressed as a result. And there was something distinctly odd about Lionel Quill sneaking out into the dark, down the backstairs even on the coldest nights. Is he a burglar? She wondered. A pickpocket operating under the cover of darkness? Surely he is up to some mischief. Her mood grew ever darker.

"This was not what I meant to have happen when I chose these guests for an interesting season, not what I meant at all," she said aloud, although there was no one to hear her.

Not even God. Perhaps all these upsetting things were occurring because she had lost her faith. It seemed to her that God had abandoned her for good, as well as all those who resided at No. 13, leaving them to their own vices and devices.

Well, she thought, I am still a decent woman and tomorrow, if the snow allows, I will visit what is left of Lucille. She shuddered. It would be hard going without the assurance of God at her back.

56.

SMOOTHED BY LONG FINGERS, her dark hair let down for the night, Mary Prior gently brushed it for one hundred strokes as she had once been advised by her mother. She sat again before the mirror, looking into her reflection, trying to find the reason why men turned away from her. It can't be my hair, or my face, or my age, she thought, and she peered closer, searching for lines, but found none. Her face was still young, her smile was still pleasing; at least to herself.

Nothing she did had bewitched Reginald or Lionel; and the Captain, though enchanted for a while, was now merely polite and had clearly lost all interest. That left Winston, but she didn't like him. There was something callous in his nature that disturbed and distanced her. The way Winston looked at her reminded her of The Terrible Thing. That must be it, of course. They all somehow knew.

She had begun to feel lonely here. Without Lucille to talk to, she sought out Beatrice from time to time for company, but Beatrice, like Lucille, had become involved with the same ridiculous poem and she could sense she was intruding on the time Beatrice needed to cook or to write.

Mary considered that perhaps she should just abandon No. 13 altogether, but she had paid several months ahead when her end of the year bonus had been larger than expected, and her prospects among the boarders had seemed brighter. Now she felt cruelly stuck here until April.

Well, she would make the best of it. She would improve herself, polish her accomplishments, few as there were. She would practice the piano more and learn to recite some verses...*not* Prufrock...so when she took herself to a new rooming house she would be even more attractive than she was at present. This lot of males was just her luck. Bad luck.

57.

"ASLEEP...TIRED...OR IT MALINGERS," said the nurse, speaking of Lucille's semi-comatose condition. She says things out loud from time to time, but they make no sense.

Mr. Elder and Mrs. Gill stood beside the bedside. The nurse had assumed they were Lucille's parents and spoke kindly to them of her prospects for recovery which, gladly, improved with each passing day.

"But will she regain her senses?" asked Mr. Elder.

"We must wait and see," said the nurse. "We are doing all that we can to insure her physical recovery. We hope no infection will arise in her injuries, but it often occurs in frostbitten fingers and toes. And, as you see, her poor nose has suffered."

Mrs. Gill had brought her unfinished, misshapen knitted blanket to the hospital and tucked it around Lucille who did not respond.

"Oh, you have made that with love," said the nurse, smiling inwardly at the clashing colors and uneven stitching. "I am sure it will comfort her when she awakens."

Josiah Elder sighed. Lucille's decline had begun with the arrival of the poetry magazine and its evil poem. It had taken hold of her and made her unhappy with her life. Now look at her, he thought, both a physical and mental wreck. He squared his shoulders, finding support for his decision. There before him lay another valid reason to rid the world of Tom Eliot.

58.

STRETCHED ON THE FLOOR the yellow cat felt too full and too lazy to go out for a prowl around the neighborhood, but he might miss his chance to meet up and spend the night with Shoo Shoo, so he yawned and stretched and sat by the kitchen door expectantly. He had trained the nice woman well and she soon came to let him out. She sometimes left the kitchen at the same time as he departed, but tonight she hesitated at the opened door where the snow had tumbled down the steps into heaps well over his head and up to her knees. "Are you sure?" she asked, which he did not understand. Had she given him a new name? He decided to ignore her and jumped gingerly upwards through the snow, eager for adventure. She followed him up slowly, holding tight to the railing so as not to slip on the icy steps, and at the top they went their separate ways into the winter's night, each to each.

59.

"HERE BESIDE YOU AND ME I see a dark shape. What is that dark shape?" asked Lucille. "It frightens me."

"There is no dark shape that I can see, my child," said Father Sweeney. "It is true the sky is dark outside the window. Perhaps that is what you see?"

"No. I think it is death come for me."

"It cannot be death, my child, for death comes to us as light. We walk into the light."

"Are you a doctor? Am I a patient etherized upon a table?"

"You are a patient in a hospital bed. I am Father Sweeney sent here by your kind friend Mrs. Gill to give you comfort."

"Did you bring any coffee spoons? If I am not going to die I needs must have more coffee spoons. For that is how I measure my life."

"I don't quite take your meaning, Lucille, and it is still possible that you *might* die."

"Then I won't need the spoons."

"But perhaps you would like to receive the last rites?"

"That is an overwhelming question."

"Just to be on the safe side. The safe side of God's forgiveness?"

"Actually, I would like some sex."

Father Sweeney's eyes widened and he felt himself reddening. This was not the first time such an unexpected thing had been requested of him by a lady, but it had always been within the protected confines of a confessional booth. Before he could think of a proper response, Lucille spoke again from her deranged inner world.

"Is Hell as hot as they say, Father? I might like a nice, warm place. I have been very cold of late."

Father Sweeney had to admit to himself that he was at a loss regarding what he should do for poor Lucille Davenport. For the Holy sacrament of last rites to be given most effectively the person receiving them should be in their right mind. He had come here on this frigid night at the request of a faithful parishioner to insure that another soul who lived under his watchful eye *not* go to Hell, but rather enter the gates of Heaven in peace, absolved of her sins. And what a unpleasant request it had been! Mrs. Gill had actually said to him: "With all due respect, Father, I don't believe in your rites and rituals anymore, but Lucille still retains her faith."

"I will go and make the visit," he had promised, deciding he would deal with Mrs. Gill's apostasy at another time.

Well, he had come to the hospital only to find that Lucille had rallied that afternoon, or so the pretty young nurse had informed him, and the medical staff now believed she would, most likely, live. So here he stood by the bedside ready with any help she might need, be it his anointing oils or his prayers and reassurances, while she talked a lot of mumbo jumbo, and seemed to not want anything but coffee spoons!

He puzzled over what he should do.

She spoke again. "The women who come and go. Who are they?"

"Why they are your nurses, Lucille. They are helping you to recover."

"They talk a lot about Michelangelo."

Father Sweeney decided that he would leave Lucille to rest in the care of the doctors and he would continue to pray for her. That would be the proper course to take. Hopefully, her mind would recover along with her body. He would go back into the cold, and when he was safely returned to the rectory he would warm himself with a hot cup of tea. No. He was quite shaken. With wine.

60.

SHOULD I, AFTER TEA AND CAKES AND ICES, HAVE THE STRENGTH TO FORCE THE MOMENT TO ITS CRISIS? Over and over Josiah returned to this particular question, fully aware he was using the poem's phrasing.

Tom Eliot had replied to his disingenuous seductive letter, informing him that, yes, he planned to again make a crossing to America on the first available steamer in the Spring, most likely in April. He would be coming alone as his wife was afraid of the U-boat attacks. And yes, he would have tea with Professor Elder as requested. Tom had suggested the Parker House near The Commons and mentioned his desire for the taste of a Boston Creme Pie. So that is where the murder of T. S. Eliot would occur. Over a tea table in the Parker House dining room.

If, and it truly was an if, Josiah could summons the courage to do the deed.

In his earlier fantasies, in the heat of his initial outrage, the moment of his imagined revenge had posed no difficulty. But as this deadly winter had worn on, the act of killing another man, especially one who had once been so beloved, had begun to seem beyond his powers.

Not long ago he had put on his best suit, a clean collar, a silk tie and gone to the Parker House to survey the intended setting. He had tried to imagine the two of them sitting there together, talking, sipping the tea, eating the sweets, appearing to resolve their differences as gentlemen, while Josiah, having found the strength, slipped the poison into the cup. He pictured Tom suddenly becoming frightened as the toxin began to act and as he realized something was dreadfully wrong, staring at Josiah Elder in horror as he grasped what had happened, then dying swiftly before nearby diners were even aware of his distress.

It was a perfect plan.

But Josiah could not with certainty visualize what he would then do. His imagination failed him at Tom's last breath. Would he run away? Or stand and declare his guilt? Would he simply return home and await the arrival of the police outside his door? And, later, after the trials and the verdict, as I am led off to the hangman, will it have been worthwhile?

In this January morning, taking advantage of an unexpected thaw, he had walked his familiar route, then repeated his steps over the icy cobbles, wandering too long, too far, like King Lear upon the heath, and all the while asking himself his overwhelming question: Have I the courage to do the murder?

As he returned to No. 13, now quite exhausted, he saw the yellow cat waiting in a sunny spot on the steps. With the cat was a skittish companion who backed away as Josiah came closer.

"Scaredy cat," he said. "Don't be such a scaredy cat," and opened the kitchen door. Both cats slipped into the warmth of the room and were quickly out of sight beneath the table. Beatrice was nowhere to be seen.

Josiah entered his rooms, upbraiding himself. Advice I gave to the new cat I must take unto myself, he thought. If I allow fear to stay my hand, if I cannot find the will to revenge myself after being so betrayed, so publicly smeared, then I am indeed as Prufrock is portrayed in the poem, a spineless creature, who only goes about whinging and whining to himself about the difficulties of life.

No. Tom and I have an appointment with fate. He wrote his death sentence with his own pen.

Josiah had never before thought of himself as a man of action. He was a man of the book and gown, grown in the dimness of a library, in love with literature and with poetry, but never with life as others led it. Tom had stepped into his classroom with a halting step and timid smile, and Josiah had known in an instant that every book he had ever read was informing the moment when their eyes met. Love had merely been a word. Now it was a living creature and that creature was himself. He had given no outward sign, nor had he changed his outward appearance or habits in any discernible way, but inside he was forever changed.

And now, having lived the drama of great love, love that had heroically endured both loss and betrayal, could he become instead, the embodiment of tragedy?

In short, Professor Josiah Elder was afraid.

61.

Bᴜᴛ ᴛʜᴏᴜɢʜ I ʜᴀᴠᴇ ᴡᴇᴘᴛ ᴀɴᴅ ғᴀsᴛᴇᴅ, ᴡᴇᴘᴛ ᴀɴᴅ ᴘʀᴀʏᴇᴅ, nothing I do has brought God back to me, ruminated Maybelle Gill as she polished the furniture in the empty parlor. Christmas day at No. 13 had been a bleak affair without Him, really quite pointless and especially with Lucille still recovering in hospital.

Now, however, Lucille had arrived after her long, prone, stay. She was weak, but her nose was intact, somewhat changed in shape; her mind was still disordered with a strange malady the doctors called hysteria.

She was finding a changed house. In the month she had been gone much had occurred at No. 13. Winston Ward had stolen away the night after her hospitalization leaving no forwarding address, and his bill unpaid. Reginald had assumed the debt, without argument. The report of Winston's behavior had confirmed her suspicions about him. He had been up to something that was wrong all along, though she knew not what. It might be hoped that with Winston gone from the premises, God might agree to return.

Lionel Quill had paid up as well and departed cheerfully, on good terms with her and with the other boarders. She found herself somewhat relieved in regards to Lionel, although he had caused no harm whilst he stayed. She couldn't blame him for going. Lucille's madness had changed the pleasant atmosphere of the house, darkening and disturbing it.

And wonders never ceasing, Reginald Sterling and Beatrice Platt had done the unthinkable. They had eloped! Maybelle had been caught completely off-guard in respect to their attachment. She supposed it had taken place largely out of her sight below stairs, and something told her that although they had acted impulsively, they might just make a lasting match. She had, of course, reemployed Beatrice when she had returned to No. 13 after only three days away, for Beatrice had thoughtfully arranged a temporary replacement in the kitchen so as not to leave Mrs. Gill entirely in the lurch. On her return she apologized for the sudden absence, and tried her best to look shame-faced, but Maybelle had seen the happiness lurking behind the contrition. She did not resent the girl's success on achieving a husband who had survived the honeymoon, and only felt relief that delicious meals would continue to be served.

At first she hadn't known where to put the two of them. Beatrice was a servant, Reginald a guest, and of course they must stay together. The answer had soon arrived in her mind. She moved them into Lucille's rooms at the top of the house, moved the Captain into the salesmen's old room with the fireplace which pleased him, and put Lucille in the spare bedroom of her own apartment where she could nurse her back to what she hoped would be full health. Only Mary Prior remained in her previous room, but glumly. Maybelle expected her to bolt, taking her disappointments with her, at the first sign of Spring.

There had been occasions in years past when running the boarding house had not gone as expected. It was quite natural, she thought, as it was a place of comings and goings, but it had been disconcerting to Maybelle whenever there was such an unexpected sea change. She did not like unpredictable events, especially as she had anticipated a quiet winter with compatible tenants and only entertaining interactions amongst them; not insanity, tragedy, and abandonments. The unforeseen marriage was all right, she supposed.

To save her own sanity she had begun Spring cleaning early, prayer no longer being an option. Cleanliness was the next best thing she dutifully believed, and the shifting of tenants had given her cause to sweep, and mop, and wash, and polish, filling her days with purpose. While working in Lucille's old room she came across the poetry magazine that had so unhinged the woman, and she took pleasure in tearing it to shreds.

These exertions had helped her during the daylight hours, but as the light drained from the day she found the evenings were long without the habit of attending Mass. Mr. Elder stopped in occasionally, though his mind seemed to be elsewhere, preoccupied with some troubles of his own.

Then, just as she was about to slide into a melancholy, one without her god to comfort her, The Reverend Ian Davies, had knocked on her door.

There he stood. He was tall, attired in a dark double-breasted suit, a handsome man of retirement age, smiling, and offering Maybelle Gill a white envelope containing his references, which were as spotless as the linen paper on which they were written. She had taken one look at the Reverend Ian Davies and her newly acquired faithlessness had begun to wobble.

62.

THOUGH I HAVE SEEN MY HEAD (GROWN SLIGHTLY BALD) in the mirror each morning, I can hardly believe it is me, always smiling, always cheerful, and gifted with all this sudden good fortune, thought Reginald Sterling. Love, he was sure, was making him grow more handsome by the hour. Marital happiness had saved him from a meaningless life more efficiently than an act of grace could have done. Though Beatrice, it seemed to him, was a walking act of grace.

It was only after Winston had bolted that Reginald realized how oppressive the man had been in his life, how badly he had influenced him. Winston Ward was a man without dignity. Reginald had shaken off his friendly feelings for Winston as he had once shaken off the dog that had bitten and injured his leg, a painful, necessary action. Beatrice took no mind of his former associations, or his limp or his bald spot. Beatrice, pleasing them both, simply loved him. She was a miracle.

Beatrice had found him asleep in her kitchen when she arrived in the morning following the news of the disaster that had befallen Lucille. She had come in early to prepare and serve the breakfast having failed to arrange it the night before. And there he was. He had proclaimed his love for her before he was fully awake, pouring out his affection for her from a dreamlike state which made his words almost poetic. She was not surprised, which surprised *him*, but he had since learned that not much got past Beatrice. Amazingly, she had been receptive, quietly returning his affection. Their romance was breathtaking in its speed. Beatrice had told him that she feared hesitation, something he had never considered before, but he had taken her cue and proposed. She had smiled and accepted.

Perhaps, he thought, knowing that Lucille might die had given them both a glimpse of the preciousness of life, and they had decided to seize their moment.

When Maybelle Gill agreed to let them stay on they had settled into a haze of bliss. Beatrice cooked. He worked, and for the first time his efforts had value for him. They saved their money in order to afford a place of their own someday. In the meantime Beatrice continued her studies. She had been commended for her paper on Prufrock and her determination to continue with her education was something Reginald failed to fully understand, but was determined, given his new lease on life, to fully accept.

He had quit smoking and drinking at her first request. It hadn't even been difficult. The combination of love and sexuality that he experienced with Beatrice made his previous encounters with women seem like caricatures of the real thing. There would be no need to ever set foot in a brothel again. Winston had feared the effect of women upon men and now Reginald understood why. Beatrice was a force to be reckoned with, and love was a drug of such power that it sometimes frightened him.

The most wonderful surprise about it all was that he could make Beatrice happy, and in doing so he was also made happy. It was so simple. Why had he never been told this? He had been led astray in a society that fed a man's ego on money and power. No wonder the supposedly successful men he had known were so often lonely and mostly wretched. Happiness lay in the lap of a satisfied woman.

63.

Brought in upon a platter was how his whole new life felt to Lionel Quill, and in a way it had been brought to him in just that way. Beatrice had been holding the dessert tray, a great oval platter, when she had gently pressed him back into his chair at that fateful Thanksgiving dinner. She had whispered into his ear, startling him with what she knew and accepted about him, and then astonished him with what she had offered: "I would like you to meet someone; someone who is dear to me, who is like you. He needs a worthy man in his life, and I think you may need one as well."

Her brother, Augustus Platt, was a beautiful man, the twin to Beatrice and as handsome as she was pretty. Tall and well-built he was an accomplished architect designing many new buildings as Boston was spreading itself in every direction. Lionel and Augustus had begun, as two men of their kind often do, as lovers, but in a very short time they had they had become friends, and Lionel thought they might be friends for life.

Growing up Augustus and Beatrice had lived in a modest house in outlying Quincy, the Platt home for three generations, and where they had been well loved. The Platt family were outsiders, defiant Protestants in a Irish Catholic enclave who believed that with education anything was possible, even for women. Their mother was a poet of some renown, hence their romantic given names. Their father had been a respected civil servant who taught English voluntarily to newly arrived immigrants. They stuck together, the Platts.

Augustus soon told Lionel how he learned early in life to maintain a low profile in his neighborhood after being beaten up by the local Catholic lads a number of times, but he had, nevertheless, thrived in the classroom where he stood out in both art and academics. To his relief he had then been sent to a private school, at great sacrifice to the rest of the family. This ability to live unobtrusively had served him well when he discovered his true nature. Unlike Lionel he was not ashamed of his homosexuality, though he was very careful for his personal preferences to remain undisclosed.

Lionel now lived in a small annex to the original Platt home, which Augustus had designed for the convenience of his widowed mother. It had a private back porch for sitting, a fine large bathroom with indoor plumbing and no stairs to navigate. When she died he began renting the apartment, giving the money to Beatrice for her night school courses, and now it was Lionel's to enjoy.

There was, of course, a connecting door.

They lived discreetly. They lived happily. And the coincidence of Beatrice and Reginald's whirlwind romance and marriage had pleased them greatly.

"It often happens with Beatrice and I," Augustus had told him over a cup of hot chocolate before the fireplace in the main house. "As twins we seem to live parallel lives."

There had been some discussion as to whether the annex should go to the newly married couple, but Beatrice and Reggie, as he was now called, seemed happy to stay at No. 13, so there Lionel remained; in privacy, in love, and in gratitude. His nightly excursions were unnecessary now, the longing for his lost love in England was fading fast in the mix of excitement and contentment he now felt whenever he looked at Augustus. In this atmosphere he felt the first stirrings of his creativity returning. When he mentioned a desire to paint again Augustus was delighted at the prospect.

Mrs. Gill had once told him that she prayed for all her boarders. Perhaps her prayers for him, without her knowing what she prayed for, had brought Augustus to him, for he felt his new life was a blessing. He hoped that back at No. 13 her prayers would continue on his behalf, for so much good fortune, so suddenly arrived, unnerved him. Did someone such as himself deserve so much happiness?

64.

I AM NO PROPHET, but I know exactly what will happen if and when I go back to America, obsessed Tom Eliot. My great and powerful mother will, as always, attempt to take charge of my future, hectoring and prodding. My father, in so far as he can hear her, will back her up. They will insist, especially with the war growing like a cancer in Europe, that I remain in Boston, that I defend my doctorate, that I teach at Harvard, and that I annul this loveless marriage to Vivienne. The last, he thought, would not be so bad.

He was beginning to hear the thrum of a new poem, not an ordinary poem, and a whisper in his mind that said: *I may yet have greatness in me.* Vivienne's insistent belief in him was having an an influence, he acknowledged reluctantly.

Ezra Pound said emphatically that he should not go, not when a magnificent new poem might be born. Ezra, here in London, was the perfect mentor, the perfect editor, and the perfect friend. He knew that he didn't love Ezra. Who could tolerate the rogue long enough to love him? But he respected him, as much as he had once respected Professor Elder.

Mother. Father. Josiah. Emily. Vivienne. Ezra. Many voices. Could he use them? No. Maybe. At present they were a cacophony, drowning out the true voice of his poem. Shakespeare, Dante, Buddha, Marlow, Ecclesiastes, Baudelaire, Spencer, Marvell, Verlaine, Balzac. His head was stuffed with the past. He needed to hear his own muse, now, as it called out to him; it was still the cry of a faint and distant voice, often indistinct, dark, hopeless, heartless, but it was his, and his alone. If he could hear it more often, if it grew louder, if it were louder and more forceful, he would be able write it down. He could create what might be an epic poem, for now it only drummed in his mind with its new rhythms, rhythms that pleaded for his words.

If he could listen, if the words would come, the poem might arrive. His father would be able to read it, if not hear it. His mother would be shocked and disapproving and nevertheless, proud. Vivienne would applaud it, Emily Hale would not understand it, and Professor Elder would be satisfied that he, T. S. Eliot, had at last fulfilled his early promise. Would the voice survive the voyage across the Atlantic? Would he?

He had sent a cable informing them all that he was coming, but as April relentlessly approached he could feel his dread increase. Oh, how the nightmares of the turbulent sea terrified him, waking and sleeping! He hesitated to cancel the journey; he hesitated to make ready to go. He must protect the rhythms, encourage the voice. He did must not let it drown so young, before the words were made manifest, before they were allowed to change the world.

65.

AND HERE'S NO GREAT MATTER judged Father Sweeney as he listened to Maybelle Gill explicate her guilt through the confessional window. A lonely widow in love with him was an ordinary occurrence, also single women and sometimes, more enjoyably, wives. It was part of the priesthood. He was a handsome man and the enclosed intimacy of the confessional combined with expectations of forgiveness were powerful aphrodisiacs. In another life he might have been a lady-killer. But in this life his morals in regards to the ladies, were adamantine. Whatever he felt, he was first a priest.

What Maybelle Gill was confessing to him in the same breath, however, was *both* her passion and her loss of interest in him, which at least had the pleasing tang of the new. He would go lightly on her penance in gratitude for such an unusual moment, and off she would go with her rosary and her prayers. At least she was back in the fold. The collection plate would be a little heavier.

He was left to ponder what remarkable roles God devised for his children. Here he sat, quite alone and often lonely himself, while women with anxious voices detailed their lusty thoughts about him through a tiny grate and he issued bead-counting and knee bending and recitations of ancient supplications in response; then he put crackers in their mouths having judged them pure enough to eat the flesh of a man who had died two thousand years ago. Good Lord!

It was no wonder that Mrs. Gill, raised in such a faith, had the imagination to doubt it and then to conceive the idea that an angel had come to her door, bringing back her faith and stealing her heart (from him!) at the same time.

Father Sweeney had never been thrown over for an angel before. It was all really quite amusing, especially as she had not quite realized what had happened to her. Bless her. Just for a moment he allowed himself to imagine she was right, that God had sent a heavenly messenger to Mrs. Gill in the unlikely form of the Protestant minister, Ian Davies. He sighed softly. Alas, the age of miracles had passed.

Perhaps, he thought, with two batty women and an angel in residence, it might be time for him to make a pastoral visit to No. 13. It sounded like a steadying hand might be in order, and the tea cakes were always delicious there.

66.

I HAVE SEEN THE MOMENT OF MY GREATNESS FLICKER thought Captain Earnest Arlington, remembering how he had stood on the bridge on his ship, the Serena, a freighter out of Argentina, dressed in Captain's whites for the first time and overflowing with pride for his accomplishment at so young an age. Had he the powers to foresee the future he would have jumped ship, lived out his life in the South American jungles, and never looked at an ocean again. But we cannot peer into the future, he mused. There is a wall as opaque as marble, always one second in front of us, pushed back only by time itself, moment by moment, revealing its wonders and its terrors. We can regret what has happened, we can worry about what may come, but we will always live incarcerated in the ignorant, unrelenting present, our noses pressed against the unknown.

The ship on which he had stood in his youthful moment of triumph had sailed towards an unseen and unimagined future, and when it arrived, years later at that fateful moment in time, it had gone down.

He took a breath and tried to enjoy the moment he was in. A *sadhu* he had once met in Bombay had told him that breathing mindfully was what he needed to do in order to end all his suffering. The *sadhu* had been naked and covered in ashes. Not surprisingly this advice proved insufficient for Earnest Arlington's own clean and well-dressed woes. He had tried prayer as well. And drink. And wanton women, all to no avail. His depression had overwhelmed him, blotting out all his thoughts for a new start, and he had come to the conclusion that he had no right to happiness, or to live at all, for had he been a good enough boy his mother could not have left him to the whims of motherless time.

So now he stood at the end of the pier, large waves crashing into the pilings beneath, preparing himself to return to the sea, this time forever, to the watery depths where he could not breathe if he tried.

He concentrated on an inhalation, perhaps his last. Only he could decide. The sea air was intoxicating in the way it had once been in his childhood; on that day on the beach when she gazed out upon the waves, before she became a mermaid. Before she became dead. Had she felt as he did now as she stood in the sand and considered what she was about to do? Had she loved her last breath?

The swirling March wind slapped him first on one cheek, then on the other. One more breath, he thought, then I will join her at last. Do I dare?

He filled his lungs, crossed himself (just in case), and readied himself for the sudden leap, only to feel a firm but gentle grasp lay hold upon his shoulder.

"Don't, please," said a mellifluous voice behind him. He recognized the voice of the new boarder from No. 13. Ian Davies. They had been introduced and had spoken only briefly during the week since his arrival. They had talked of simple things, music, Beatrice's puddings, nothing personal. Yet here the man stood, in this most personal of all moments, as though ordained, as though he had a right to be there.

How dare he? thought Captain Arlington and whirled around angrily to face the intruder, expecting self-righteousness, expecting judgment; but the man was weeping. Tears in salty rivulets glistened on his handsome face, his shoulders shook with sobs. Completely taken aback, the Captain found himself reaching out, making the same gesture, placing his hand upon the man's shoulder, saying the same words, "Please, don't." And then he, too, suddenly and shockingly began to weep himself.

There they stood at the edge of the pier, two grown men, seemingly motionless, perfectly attired, looking for all the world to simply be engaged in a gentlemen's conversation, while both allowed themselves to experience all the sadness of their beings, all at once. Nothing like this had ever occurred in Captain Arlington's long life and he soon found himself fighting for outward control.

As he slowly began to collect himself, he felt his face begin to flush with shame, as if he had engaged in some act of perversion for all to see with this relative stranger.

"Please, don't," Ian said again. "Please don't jump and please don't return to your life of regret. You've been living there far too long. I have watched you. And I know your story. I know about the wreck of your life upon the rocks."

"How could you possibly know that?"

"I sought you out to bring a message from my brother Willie. He was aboard. He saw you go down bravely, with the ship, after doing all in your power to save it. And although the ship was lost, he was not, and you were not. The sea refused you both."

As the words were spoken, almost too fast to be taken in, the Captain, already weakened from his flood of tears, began to shake. He lowered himself slowly to a bench at the end of the pier in order to avoid collapsing. Ian knelt beside him. "Willie died not long ago, after a long and painful illness that had nothing to do with the shipwreck. He asked me to find you, to tell you that you are forgiven, by him, by your crew, the living and the dead, and to please remember him all of your days."

"Willie? With the red hair and the red temper? We called him Fighting Willie. I never sailed without him."

"Yes. That Willie. My brother, your boson. He told me no man could have saved that ship in that place in that storm. You did your best. No other Captain could have done more or better."

"You are kind to tell me this. Very kind."

"And now you must be kind, as well. Willie's last wish was that you remember him, as he was at his best in life. At sea with you and ashore with his mates. Fisticuffs and all. If you drown yourself then those memories will be lost."

Captain Arlington, a man who had been long in service, recognized duty when it called. Slowly he pulled his mind back from the depths. He became aware of the rough boards beneath his feet and the rougher water below. "I will live", he said. "I will grow old. It is the honorable thing to do for your brother and my boson, Fighting Willie."

"For them all, Captain," added Ian, helping him up to his feet, and the two men, strangers in the morning, returned to No. 13 in the afternoon, as friends.

67.

"And I have seen the eternal Footman hold my coat, and snicker, and in short, I was afraid," quoted Lucille.

"Oh, do be quiet, dear," said Maybelle Gill with a sigh, "just for a moment, please." Her tone was unusually sharp. She needed to think about No. 13 for a few minutes without Lucille's constant prattle.

The guests appeared to be settling in well to the new room arrangements, as she had hoped. Everyone was stacked up neatly again; the newlyweds, Reginald and Beatrice, at the top where Lucille had been; on the second floor Mary Prior still in the front room next to Captain Arlington, now with a fireplace, and in the back the Reverend Davies made comfortable in the room with the private stairs. Lucille was in Maybelle's extra room on the ground floor where she could be carefully looked after, and Mr. Elder, as always, was there beneath them all. She took a satisfied breath.

Maybelle had surprisingly asked the guests to assemble in the parlor for a few minutes after breakfast. She needed them. Or more, correctly, Lucille did.

Now she sat next to the benighted woman, who was murmuring softly beside her while the others tried not to stare at Lucille's changed face with the slightly askew nose.

Somehow, observed Mr. Elder, it made her prettier, though he did not say so.

"I must ask you all for help," said Maybelle. "I know it is an unusual request for a landlady to make of her guests, so please forgive me, but Lucille is having difficulty re-joining us, and we are all she has for family.

When she speaks she only recites lines from that wretched poem about a man who prattles on about bald spots and mermaids; Pruman, or Putlock, or something."

"Prufrock," corrected Mr. Elder. "It is a poem about hesitation."

"Well, it's a dreadful piece of nonsense whatever it is called! It has invaded her mind and played havoc with her sensibilities."

They all sat quietly in long agreement.

Maybelle continued. "Lucille, seems hesitant to live fully among us again, unwilling to return completely to reality. Rev. Davies, you did not know this woman before her misadventure, but she was a sweet, caring soul, a very proper lady with a set of good manners, a healthy brain, a belief in God, who was engaged in responsible employment. She sometimes misplaced things or forgot appointments but I think her mind was simply busy in those moments with thoughts of her work, with poetry and the like. She took great care for her students' education. Now, as you can see, her mind is quite confused, wandering about in the clutches of that one particular poem."

She noticed a dark shadow cross the solemn features of Mr. Elder as she spoke. The others bowed or shook their heads in sad accord.

"Beatrice, I hear that you have written about this poem yourself, although why I cannot comprehend. Do you have any idea how to help her find her way back to us? Help her to—"

"—Will be time, there will be time—" interrupted Lucille.

"Perhaps if we took turns, reading her other poems, different verses, that might help," suggested Beatrice.

"I could make a selection," offered Mr. Elder. "She loved…loves…the English poets, all the Romantics."

"For I have known them all already, known them all," interjected Lucille.

"I could take her out to the shops with me," volunteered Mary, "now that the worst of winter is passing. Perhaps the fresh air and different sights would be a tonic."

"That is a kind thought," replied Maybelle, but I fear she might bolt. She often talks of going through half deserted streets, as if she is looking for something, or someone."

"She is. She is looking for Winston," said Reginald, reddening as he spoke. "Winston Ward. He was attempting to seduce her." All heads turned towards Reginald whose own head hung down with embarrassment. "He told me before he left."

Horrified, Mrs. Gill's hands flew to cover her face. "Right here! Under my own roof, where she should have been most protected? Oh, this is an outrage. A betrayal."

"Do I dare? Do I dare?" screamed Lucille, clawing at the air above her head as if trying to drag down God himself for help.

The sight of the deranged woman set into furious motion at the mention of Winston's advances, was upsetting to them all, and they looked from one to another, at a loss as to what might calm her.

"The poem is a love song," said Ian Davies in a quiet resonant voice. At the mention of the word "love" Lucille's hands floated gently down and rested on her bosom. "It is entitled a love song, though the word love is never mentioned in the verses. It reminds us of those for which we have longed, and for those we have loved and lost a while."

"Love," repeated Lucille, as if the word was magical.

Ian continued. "In my experience only thwarted desire can so unnerve a lady. I believe her heart has been broken, whether by a lover or by a longing I do not know. Now it needs must have time to mend."

It was Mary Prior who boldly asked the question that was in everyone's mind. "And what experience, have you in such matters, Mr. Davies?"

"A great deal, Miss Prior, a great deal," he replied with a rueful expression, but he did not elaborate.

"And how shall I begin?" Lucille asked suddenly, still speaking from within the poem.

"Why you must begin with yourself," replied Ian. "You must decide to find out who you really are, Lucille, broken heart and all."

"'...As if a magic lantern threw the nerves in patterns on a screen...'"

"Yes. Exactly. And if you do, then you will need to go about accepting yourself. And more. If you can find a way to love that truest self your heart will mend."

"Myself. My Self. My *true* self," she seemed to marvel at the words.

All eyes were on Lucille who remained sitting quietly, deep in thought, and soon she began to look about her in a curious way, as if seeing the room full of well-wishers for the first time. She smiled a little shyly.

"I would enjoy very much going to the shops with you, Mary," she said in a normal voice. "I...I myself...I would...*love* to go."

Eyes widened and expressions of surprise turned hopeful as she looked at each person in turn. Though tentative, it was clear that she was back among them, back with the living. "You are indeed like the family I never had growing up," she added.

"Then I will accompany you and Mary to the shops," said Captain Arlington. "I shall keep you both under a watchful eye, and bring you safely back to No. 13."

Lucille seemed to light up at the suggestion, but Mary looked startled. She had quite given up hope when it came to the Captain, and had of late turned her curiosity in the direction of Ian Davies. Had the Captain now taken an interest in Lucille? No. As he spoke he had looked and smiled directly at her. As she met his eyes her heart began to warm again.

"Thank you, Rev. Davies," said Mrs. Gill. "Your understanding is clearly appreciated by Lucille and most certainly by me."

It wasn't just his words, thought Maybelle. It is the way he listens, and the way he speaks with such assurance, but also with such tenderness. He is mesmerizing. She felt a little faint.

"Perhaps a rest then, dear?" she suggested, as much for herself as Lucille. "Before you attempt such an outing? Thankfully the weather has become milder."

"Yes, please," replied the docile, but now fully alert, woman. "Yes, a rest, and then some shops, and then perhaps some poetry this evening?"

Looks of alarm passed among the guests, but she continued, "Byron? Keats?" All heads nodded in relief as she was led by Maybelle back to their rooms. At the door of her chambers Mrs. Gill looked back over her shoulder into the eyes of Ian Davies. Heavenly, she thought. He held her gaze until she, blushing, turned away with Lucille in tow.

"That was something," declared the Captain, breaking the silence. "That was, indeed, something." He, too, looked at Ian appreciatively, and then smiled at Mary, who began to blush in a most charming manner.

Beatrice put an arm around Reginald, who still looked quite forlorn. She had known, of course, about his part in the bet, though she had felt it was his place, not hers, to speak up about the matter. He had confessed his sadness, and his remorse to her on the same morning he had declared his love. She had known then, and knew now, that he was both a faithful and a truthful man at heart, and a good woman was all that was needed to encourage that heart to grow. Today, tea and a piece of cake would

help restore his spirits. With a nod, the couple left for the kitchen.
Josiah Elder sat without moving. A love song, he thought. A love song.
"Hesitation," said Ian Davies, addressing Mr. Elder, "is not *always* a
bad thing."

68.

AND WOULD IT HAVE BEEN WORTH IT, AFTER ALL? wondered Winston
Ward far away in freezing Chicago. Would it have been worth it to have
toughed it out, played innocent, stayed in Boston? Reginald wouldn't
have said anything about their bet, and loony Lucille wouldn't have been
believed if she dared to speak of his indiscretions. He had lost a lot of
commissions by bolting, and Chicago was harsh, the gusts coming in
relentlessly off the lake.

He didn't like to admit it, but he missed the friendly partnership of
Reginald Sterling with their nights together on the town, and he missed
the food at No. 13, missed even the seductive adventure with Lucille.
He hadn't deliberately meant to hurt her; just have a bit of fun, not that
any of it mattered. Well, he had sinks to sell in the morning, a brothel
to visit tonight.

He pulled his coat collar up against the night wind, pushed his hat a
little lower on his head, and walked on alone, deeper into the darkened
city, shivering with the cold.

69.

AFTER THE CUPS, THE MARMALADE, THE TEA, and a big kiss Beatrice
sent Reginald off to his day's work. He wasn't as eager in his work life as
he had been when he shared it with a partner, she knew, but it was only
temporary, until he found something else that he would really enjoy. He
spoke of working with his hands, doing something practical like install-
ing the newfangled electrical lights in peoples' houses. It was a pleasant
thought, her husband brightening the lives of others. He had brightened
hers. It was his simplicity, she thought. He simply loved her and wanted
to be a loyal husband.

As she washed up the breakfast dishes she considered what she might next do with her own changed life. Their marriage had been so hasty they really hadn't taken the time to think about the future.

He did not object to her studies as some men might, even trying to see the point of poetry and novels and art, though progress was slow in that regard. She knew his faults, and she didn't care. He loved her romantically, passionately, and the experience of being loved brought to life all the literature she had been reading, made sense of the poetry, the flights of ecstasy that had once been interesting in only an intellectual way. Now she felt the pulse of the poets, heard their heated breath in the chosen lyrics. Even poor Prufrock had loved, thwarted only by himself, never uttering the word but he had loved nonetheless.

Well, they had all had quite enough of Mr. T. S. Eliot's poem! No one dared to even mention it at meals or in the parlor for fear of setting Lucille off again into despair. Beatrice, cherished as she now was, thought she understood. Lucille had been thwarted in a similar way to Prufrock. She had not been loved as a child, had entertained no suitors as an adult, and was, as Lucille must surely know, the only one who had stood in her own way, buttoned into the tough corset of respectability. When she had been toyed with by Winston his advances had awakened her, shattering the small pride she had taken in her high-minded choices.

Beatrice was glad to be a witness to her recovery and only hoped it would endure. But what could Lucille do now? She knew nothing of the world except what she had read about it. She still professed her Catholic faith even as it tried to shame her for perfectly normal feelings. Lucille's road into the future would be far more difficult than Beatrice's, because Beatrice had Reggie and Lucille had no one.

70.

Among the porcelain objects in Mrs. Gill's display cabinet there stood the figure of an angel. It was definably female, with predictable white wings and a halo over its benign face. It looked nothing like the Rev. Ian Davies who was without wings, and whose face was a perfect masculine face, or so it seemed to Maybelle Gill, with his square jaw,

cloudy blue-gray eyes like the sky on a hazy day. He appeared as a gentleman, one who was kind and smiled often. However, she was quite
sure, from the first moment she saw him, that he was an angel, sent by
God to return her to the one true faith. How curious that he should
arrive disguised as a Protestant minister.

Well, the Lord doth work in mysterious ways his wonders to perform,
she thought, and sighed happily.

He had explained that although he was recently retired, there was
work for him to do in Boston, but he was unspecific as to what exactly
that work might be. He dressed modestly in well-cut suits and wore
immaculately polished shoes, so she guessed his responsibilities might
be of some importance. Did she dare to ask?

She could not help but compare him, a tad unfavorably, to Mr. Elder
who had seemed to grow smaller and dimmer with age, even more so of
late, whereas this man seemed to glow. Maybelle Gill was not yet ready
to accept that she had fallen deeply in love.

71.

"Among some talk of you and me," Captain Arlington asked gently,
"perhaps you will allow me to explain?"

Mary nodded her assent, while keeping her expression cool even
though the Captain was back in her fold, she was certain.

"I have found again my affection for you Mary, and I ask you, with all
my heart, to forgive me for my lapse which was entirely occasioned by
my own foolishness."

Now she allowed herself to smile.

"Of course I will forgive you, Earnest," replied Mary Prior. "At the
time you withdrew from me, I was deeply troubled, but I believe you
now when you say your reasons were your own and not something
ill-natured in me."

The Captain and Mary had taken Lucille under their wing. During
the long walks with her, the meals taken together in cozy restaurants,
they had found a way to renew their affections. They believed Lucille to
be the perfect chaperone.

Both had changed during their estrangement; observing each other covertly, avoiding eye contact and piano duets they had been forced to listen more subtly, one to the other.

The Captain had soon realized that Mary, rather than being insensitive to his humiliations, simply hadn't imagined him to be vulnerable in such a way. She saw him as a complete, strong, decent man, just as he wished he could actually be. He began to imagine what it would be like to have a woman at his side who believed in him. A woman who would have no cause to abandon him.

Mary, for her part, realized it was not some flaw or unattractiveness of her person that had caused his sudden change of heart on the morning when he choked on the toast in the breakfast room, but the arising of unimagined conflicts in his soul that left little room for her whilst he came to terms with himself. How strong he had seemed to her, when he was actually fragile. She hadn't known men could be so sensitive, raised as she had been among robust farmers who did not discuss their feelings. Mary had then begun to imagine what his life was like, what it was to be a man who had lost his life's purpose. And later, when they were reuniting and he had spoken of it, what it would be like to be a child whose mother had walked away from him into the sea. She saw now that he was easily wounded, quick to view himself in an unfavorable light. An unexpected desire to be of help to him arose in Mary. It surprised her. She had always judged men by what they might offer her, not what she might offer them.

In response to Mary's kindness a warmth had grown in Captain Arlington that he had not felt for a woman before. He was no longer in love with her. The blinding rush of lustful passion he once had felt was not to be recovered, but he felt safe with her, happy for her acceptance and friendship. If he was going to live as long as he could, as he had promised he would to Ian Davies in order to remember and honor his shipmate Willie and all the others, he thought it best not to live alone. And once again he began to think of proposing to Mary Prior.

Mary, faced daily with the sight of poor, lost Lucille thought marriage to the Captain would not be the worst thing to consider should he find the courage to ask. She would be an asset to him, she knew, and though he was much older and quite lost in his own way, he was what the world was offering up to her. If he proposed she knew she would accept, and then she would never again have to fear becoming an old maid.

Lucille watched the tender affection grow between her two friends. It was what she had always imagined she wanted for herself. But it was not what she wanted anymore; not what she wanted at all.

72.

"WOULD IT HAVE BEEN WORTH WHILE TO HAVE BITTEN OFF THE MATTER WITH A SMILE, TO HAVE SQUEEZED THE UNIVERSE INTO A BALL TO ROLL IT TOWARDS SOME OVERWHELMING QUESTION—" As Mr. Elder pondered these lines, speaking only to himself, alone in his room, he thought, yes, right here in the heart of the poem Tom had portrayed him absolutely correctly. Tom had jumped from his own mind into his. He had imagined what was going on inside of me on that fateful afternoon, in that moment between the two of us when I struggled to find the right words, when I got everything wrong. In the poem he had gotten that right.

It *was* a love poem. And it conveyed the warning that one must not hesitate in matters of love. It was not the love song of Professor Josiah Elder dressed up in the verses as J. Alfred Prufrock mooning about some unnamed woman; but a love song that was being sung between T. S. Eliot and Himself! Why had he not seen this before? Now he could see it no other way.

Why else would Tom have spent so much time and effort, worked so hard to rewrite this poem, unless he too, deep down, had cared for his mentor in ways about which he dared not speak? All the conflict of his being was written there. Love and hate and fear and hesitation and disguise and hope and despair and dissimulation. Everything the heart must bear.

And how had the Rev. Davies sensed his personal interest in the poem? He wondered. And who the hell was Ian Davies anyway? The man had been damned chary when it came to revealing anything specific about his own life, except that he was recently retired from a Presbyterian congregation in some Godforsaken town in Ohio. Mr. Elder had to admit there was a kind of magnetic power emanating from the man. Mrs. Gill and Lucille Davenport were both clearly smitten, and the others listened to Ian with a great deal of respect. It had been a fine thing to see Lucille respond and return to reality after he had spoken of unrequited love, and of finding her true self. Yes, there was something in his manner, present yet contained, that beguiled; something in those misty eyes. He had probably been a persuasive preacher.

Ian had turned and said exactly the words to Himself that had sent his mind spinning, sent his thoughts in an entirely new direction and now required him to reevaluate everything. A love song. And it sings to me.

73.

To say there was a change occurring in Lucille would be an understatement, everyone agreed. She had not come in to breakfast on this particular morning, nor had Mrs. Gill, so their absence gave the others a chance to wonder openly about her transformation as they enjoyed their warm biscuits and tart homemade marmalade.

"They say there can be a personality change after a severe illness," offered Mary.

"But who are those who say this?" queried Himself.

"My friend in the typing pool told me. She read about it in a women's magazine. They are knowledgeable doctors who write these articles."

"Doctors writing in a women's magazine? I dare say that sounds questionable to me." He raised an eyebrow.

"It is quite true," said Beatrice, who now sat with the others after bringing up the meals. "We discussed this in my psychology class last year."

"Lucille will still be Lucille though, won't she?" asked Reginald, looking concerned. "I quite liked her as she was."

"She almost died, Reginald. In that state she may have hallucinated or had haunting dreams," suggested the Captain. "When I was drowning I thought I heard music, women's voices singing. I thought they were mermaids. I believe it has to do with oxygen deprivation, but it seemed quite real to me at the time."

"I sometimes hear those voices, and I am not drowning," said Ian Davies.

"You hear mermaids singing?"

"Angels, I think. Yes, most definitely angels."

Everyone was quiet now, keeping their reactions private, though Beatrice and Reginald looked at each, sharing their amused surprise without the need for words.

Ian leaned forward and addressed them all, as if they were a class of attentive students, or a congregation. "Some people have particular sensitivities to sounds, or colors, or smells. Some believe they can talk with the departed. Some are certain they can see into the future. My only claim to special sensitivity is to sound. I often hear music when others do not. I prefer to believe they are angels though a doctor would probably say it is an affliction of the ears." He smiled. "Or the mind."

"Do you hear them now?" It was Beatrice inquiring.

"Yes. If I am quiet I can hear them."

"What do they sing to you?"

"Love songs."

74.

"I AM LAZARUS, COME FROM THE DEAD, COME BACK TO TELL YOU ALL, I SHALL TELL YOU ALL," cried the voice in Tom's nightmare; wrenching a line from his own poem.

He awoke shivering in the cold of his flat, Vivienne snoring softly next to him. While he slept it had not been Prufrock who cried out to him, but Jean Verdenal. Jean, *mon ami*, he thought with an ache in his heart. He was now confirmed dead among those corrupting bodies washed onto the beaches of Turkey in this wretched, bloody war. But Jean, like Prufrock, revealed nothing of the beyond to him; nothing about how to live, or how to die, or what comes after death; he simply screamed and wept at his fate. Was he warning Tom? Or was he calling to him? Was he saying that he, too, would endure death by water if he got aboard that ship?

Should he go? That was the overwhelming question. His parents expected him. His friends in Boston and Cambridge were eager to see him. Emily Hale wrote that she longed to walk and talk with him again as they had done in happier days in the sweet-smelling hyacinth garden, and along beaches of Cape Cod. Might her eagerness offer more? Might her interest give him the strength to ask Vivienne for an annulment?

Harvard awaited him, too, waiting to swallow him up like a great whale, it's mouth agape. And, of course there was Professor Elder. Oh damn Professor Elder!

It would be wonderful to put an ocean between himself and his wife, the mistake of his life. She would say she would miss him, but in truth she would waste no time in her affair with Bertie Russell, and Russell would continue to support them financially. It was embarrassing. It was emasculating. It was necessary.

Except for establishing the relationship with Ezra Pound who was a far more modern and far-seeing mentor than Josiah Elder could ever be, Tom felt he had made a right mess of his life in England. He found no comfort here. Yet, now there was the voice emanating from his soul that was beginning to be heard, crying out in his dreams, whispering in his waking hours…but what then was it saying to him? Europe had become barren without Jean. England, cloying. America, demanding.

His thoughts spun around and around and around, encircling him in fear. The German U-boats, the unforgiving depths of the sea, his own imagery coming back to haunt him…those claws forever scuttling across the silent seabed, the warning cries in the night from Jean. "Do I dare?" and "Do I dare?" he asked himself, over and over. His mind revolved and dipped over the horrors of life. It stopped only long enough for him to wonder if he might be going mad.

75.

If one had to give up roaming the alleys and stick to a chosen place, this kitchen was not a bad choice, thought the yellow cat. Shoo Shoo loved it here. The room was always warm. The food was plentiful, but two nights ago a swarm of tiny yellow cats surrounded her in his favorite spot in the pantry. She licked and cuddled with them, too busy for him it seemed, so a stroll through the darkened streets felt like the right choice for tonight. Perhaps the little man behind the restaurant would bring him some chicken and rice. He trotted up the kitchen stairs towards the door that now had a hole in it with a flap that the humans had made. He didn't know why they had put the hole there, but he found it very convenient for coming and going. On the top step he paused, listening to the soft mewling sounds coming from the pantry below. Hesitating, he sat on the curb and licked his paw. It was very cold. He turned and descended the stairs. He walked back to Shoo Shoo who was still covered in little cats. She was adorable. Yes, he thought, this is the best place to be. He nudged the pile of furry little beasts aside, curled up beside her, and went contentedly to sleep.

76.

SETTLING A PILLOW BY HER HEAD, Lucille Davenport, who now insisted on being referred to as Luci Dee, plotted her escape from No. 13. She could hear the endless clicking of knitting needles on the other side of the closed bedroom door. She had once believed that she owed it to Maybelle, who had always been so kind, to stay by her side whatever came, but a month at such stultifying close quarters had cured her of that idea. And, besides, Maybelle now had a new interest in her life that did not concern Lucille in the person of Rev. Ian Davies.

How she herself felt about Ian was unclear. He was nice. At times she found him attractive, at times intimidating, and at others merely amusing. He was like a big gentle cat, watching over the dinner table as if to pounce. Perhaps it was his stillness that was intriguing; or the fact that when he spoke what he said often changed the way a person felt about something, as it had done with her.

She could not picture him without his clothes. The Captain, yes. Reginald, yes. Not Mr. Elder as he was just too old. She still sometimes dreamed of Winston, imagining he might return, though knowing Mrs. Gill would not let him past the threshold. And she rather missed Lionel Quill who she knew was a homosexual, in the way that women knew such things nowadays. Rumor had it that he was living with Beatrice Platt's brother, Augustus. She could never quite picture what homosexuals actually did together, even though she had tried.

It had not been easy to get hold of the erotic postcards on sale from under the counter at the newsstand, and she had failed completely to purchase anything that showed what it was that men did with other men. The owner of the stall had drawn the line firmly and refused her money in that regard. But between the illicit French postcards and naughty magazines, and the carefully monitored hygiene books in the library, she had acquired a considerable knowledge of heterosexual activity. And she was determined to have some for herself.

Of course, she had hidden her erotic fascination from Mrs. Gill and the others, but they had not failed to notice her change of attire to brighter colored dresses with higher hemlines, her daring use of a little make-up, and the lighter color of her hair which she now rinsed with lemon juice. She knew they thought it was a reaction to her changed face, but she actually liked her face better now with its smaller nose.

However, she could not deny the unpleasant fact any longer; if she was going to pursue a life considered by many, including her former self, as sinful, No. 13 could no longer be her home. With the arrival of Ian, Maybelle had returned to the church with a vengeance. She now attended dutifully on the arm of the most willing Reverend Davies. They did make a nice pair, thought Luci. Come to think of it, she hated the word "nice!" Well, there were other boarding houses with less stringent rules. She would find a comfortable room, find a not so nice man, and invite him to visit. She would lose her virginity as swiftly as possible, then embark on many adventures, making up for lost time.

The high school where she had labored to teach poetry had replaced her during her long convalescence, but there were other ways to earn a living. No girl who grew up in an orphanage could be ignorant of the ways of the world as regarded women's employment. There were the well-spoken of choices: marriage, of course; but until that happy event occurred there was teaching, nursing, sewing, cooking, caring for other people's homes and children, or for some who were gifted with a vocation, the religious life, all highly valued; even certain kinds of office situations were now considered acceptable. But there were also the whispered choices: dancer, actress, mistress, worse.

In her youth the fearful Lucille had chosen the approved road, and what had it gotten her? A good reputation in the eyes of the local churchgoers; two small rooms with a bookcase full of second hand poetry books, and days spent in dreary classrooms filled with restless adolescents. She would be happy to never see another overgrown boy or budding girl again. She was through with the judgments of nuns and priests and the watchful eyes of middle-class matrons.

There was a new life waiting for her just outside the door of No. 13.

So what would it be? She arose from the narrow bed, stretched, gave her recently bobbed hair a toss, and smiled at her reflection in the mirror.

It was time for Luci Dee to disturb the universe.

77.

"SHOULD SAY *what*?" asked Augustus with asperity. "Should say that it's good, when I think it's not?"

"Well, you could be a little less critical!" replied Lionel Quill. "I am just beginning to paint again. I need support, not criticism."

"Support is it? You talk to an architect about support? A roof needs support. What you need is practice."

They were having their first fight. For Lionel it was exhilarating. He was arguing with a man he loved, about something he loved in a home that he loved. He was not listening to boring dinner table conversation at the No. 13s of the world, or having an soul-emptying encounter with a stranger. He and Augustus were figuring out how they would be with each other in the future. He didn't care greatly how the argument resolved, though Augustus's criticism of his most recent painting had stung a bit. There had been truth in what he had said. The painting, he knew, was rather ordinary.

"How about kindness then? Or silence?"

"How about better paintings?"

There was a reason Augustus was so successful. He demanded competence of himself and all those with whom he worked. Beatrice was like that, too, in both her cooking and her scholarly studies. Lionel had landed with people who asked the best of themselves, and now of him.

"Alright," he said. "Better paintings," and returned to his easel, outwardly sulking; but inside, he was smiling.

78.

"THAT IS NOT WHAT I MEANT AT ALL," said Mr. Elder to his mirror, as he practiced every imaginable conversation he could conceivably have with Tom Eliot at the Park Lane Hotel.

But if he faced the truth, it was exactly what he had meant. He had placed a hand on the young student's shoulder and said: "I love you, Thomas Stearns Eliot." And the boy had gone white, then reddened, had reached up and removed the offending hand from his person, none to gently. Then he had turned on his heel and never spoken to his former mentor again. Until the poem.

Josiah could deny it no longer. He hadn't just felt paternal affection, he had been hopelessly in love in a far more daring way. Thoughts of the flesh had come to him. He had suffered first in silence, and then, because he had dared to speak out he had been spurned, and had lived the rest of his days alone in the pain of longing.

Tom had left for Europe shortly after their encounter. Rumors had reached Josiah of his relationship with a young French man, Jean, whom he had met at the Sorbonne, followed to Germany, and left at war's outbreak. Had they been lovers? His sources on the academic grapevine said they did not know. Mr. Elder thought they knew, thought *he* knew. He had seen the horror in Tom's countenance as he recognized his true nature and then vehemently rejected it in their last terrible, intimate moment.

And now that Tom was promising to return, agreeing to meet, how should he presume? How should he begin to set matters right between them?

Murdering him had seemed challenging, but daring to speak with him intimately was far worse! Tom was a fully grown man now, and he had felt and reciprocated the love of another man while overseas. Perhaps they could both be at peace with their feelings for one another now. Josiah hoped he could bring about a simple acknowledgment of mutual affection. He desired this more than any physical satisfaction. He wished for their estrangement to be repaired and a reconciliation to occur. He desired this more than life itself.

But what if, once again, he had gotten it all wrong? If his current inter-pretation of Tom's poem is not what was meant at all; if Tom rejected Josiah again? What would he then do? This overwhelming question had a simple answer. He would turn the kitchen knife on himself.

79.

"That is not it, at all," declared Maybelle Gill. I have not the least idea what you are on about."

"Oh yes, you do!" declared Lucille. You are in love with Ian Davies, and I say that it is excellent turn of events."

"He is a *boarder*, Lucille. A fine one, I will give you that. Clean, quiet, well-spoken, religious in his way—"

"—and a hell of a good looker, too."

"Lucille! Language! It is true, he has fine features, but my feelings for him are quite respectable."

"Love is respectable."

"I do not love Ian Davies. And I will hear no more about it." Maybelle was not happy to find that her attraction to Ian was so apparent, and she didn't like prevaricating in regards to her private feelings. She had hoped her infatuation…and that is all it was!…would remain between her and Father Sweeney, to whom she had confessed it, but it had clearly been noticed by Lucille and had aroused her in a most unbecoming way.

"'The lady doth protest too much, methinks.'"

"Whatever has gotten into you, Lucille? Let the matter rest! Are you trying to upset me? For what reason? I have been nothing but kind to you all these many years."

"Yes, we have been a pair, but that is all about to change. Do you mind if I smoke?"

"*What?* Of course I mind. We do not smoke tobacco in No. 13. You know that perfectly well. And ladies do not smoke anywhere. It is most unseemly!"

"Mrs. Crofts allows smoking at No. 21."

"And how would you know that deplorable fact?"

"The truth is, Maybelle dearest, I have been looking for a room elsewhere. I have imposed on your great kindness far too long, staying down here in your extra bedroom. When I had my own rooms upstairs it was different. And to be honest, I find I have needs that cannot be enclosed within No. 13. Now that you have Ian, I feel that it is time for me to depart the scene."

The scene, indeed! The words had tumbled out of Lucille, but no words came to Maybelle Gill. She was shocked. She was deeply hurt. She was angry. She was silent; for a very long time.

When at last she spoke, her words carried no emotion at all. Her tone was flat, as if talking to a stranger about nothing of importance.

"Then pack your bags, Lucille. I will pray for you. Now I must go and speak with Beatrice about next week's dinner menus."

Maybelle Gill got up and left the room with as much quiet dignity as she could muster.

Luci, having been left so abruptly and without the argument and the forgiveness she had anticipated, suddenly felt unsure of her decision. She flushed and felt a little dizzy. Was she doing the right thing after all? Should she call back Mrs. Gill? Apologize? Perhaps she had been too hasty, too unkind. Maybe the decision to forsake this home she knew so well was all wrong?

And there she was, the old Lucille, full of hesitation, and trembling in the wake of another's disappointment.

"Not anymore!" she declared to herself aloud.

Lucille went to her room and picked up her bag which was already packed. Her books were still in the boxes from the move downstairs and they would be delivered to her at No. 21 as arranged. She placed a carefully worded letter to Mrs. Gill on the mantelpiece. She had written it earlier, just in case. It expressed all the gratitude and affection she had been unable to speak aloud as she awkwardly, belligerently, informed the kind old woman that she was leaving. She did feel some remorse about how hard it had sounded, even to her own ears. She really couldn't have made her announcement more unpleasantly if she had tried, but what was said could not be unsaid. Perhaps the note which was heartfelt and gracious would prove a balm when it was later read by Maybelle. She hoped so.

Had she forgotten anything? Probably.

Lucille left the overheated room and opened the front door. She paused on the threshold to look behind her, up the staircase she had ascended and descended a thousand times, then turned to face the world. The fresh air, heavy with the scents of early Spring, filled her lungs like cold water after a long thirst. If this was a mistake, she thought, then she hoped to make many more that would feel this satisfying.

Lucille Davenport quietly closed the door to No. 13.

Luci Dee stepped down the three front steps into the bright Boston afternoon.

80.

"AND WOULD IT HAVE BEEN WORTH IT, AFTER ALL?" asked Josiah as he tried to comfort Mrs. Gill who was weeping quietly. "It sounds as though Lucille's mind was fully made up before she even spoke to you. Begging her to stay would have been most unseemly. You are the landlady, she but a tenant."

"I should have tried to stop her," protested Maybelle between sobs. "I'm not sure she is yet in her right mind...to treat me so, to depart without kindness. After all these years. It's not like the Lucille I know in the least."

They were in the kitchen together, alone but for the cats. This was perhaps the first time in all their years of friendship that they found themselves together in this place. Maybelle, feeling miserable, had made her way down the stairs for tea and the comfort of cake but, not finding Beatrice, she had knocked at his door. It was a measure of her distress that she had done so, and he was quick to emerge from his room and guide her to the table. Now the tea kettle was whistling, and he rose to bring her a cup, strong and black.

"People change," he said, setting down the porcelain cup before her. "Sometimes they change for the good; sometimes for the bad. We must let them go their own way."

"Something is amiss in this house," she declared. "It has turned against me. Perhaps it is a punishment."

"Whatever for, dear Mrs. Gill?"

"I lost track of what was going on under my own roof. I didn't know what that sinful Mr. Ward was up to with Lucille, and you wouldn't understand this, Mr. Elder, for you are not an attentive Catholic, but it all went wrong at about the same time I lost my faith. I lost my love of God. It was only for a while, but I think He may be punishing me for my lapse."

"I may not, as you say, be an attentive Catholic, but I do understand. We all lose faith in what we love now and then. We doubt ourselves, we doubt one another. We are faithless creatures, and who can blame us in such a trying world? I'm sure God does not." He handed her an immaculate handkerchief from his breast pocket, one that Beatrice had been kind enough to iron for him. He continued, "and this idea that the house has turned against you. My. My. You know that cannot be so. I think it is a very different matter altogether."

"What is it that you think, dear Mr. Elder?" she sniffed, wiping at her tears.

"You have enclosed yourself inside this house as if it was the whole world. And choosing to insulate yourself in this way has protected you, but it has also given you the impression that everything that happens, happens here. You have made yourself content with only your guests and your God, but there is more going on, dear Mrs. Gill, than what happens inside these walls. In fact, it is the world *outside* of No. 13 that is changing for the worse.

"This war in Europe seems far away, but it casts a long shadow. Our upstanding American boys will die in it, no matter what the President may say about American neutrality at the moment. Mark my word. Rev. Davies, Captain Arlington and myself are too old to be called up, and I think Reginald's limp might save him from the military, but many will not be so fortunate. That is the evil you feel, and it is certainly man's doing, not God's."

"Why would America go to war so far away? For what possible reason? Europe's problems are not ours."

"Reasons will be found. And there is money to be made. Our ties to England will require it, I suspect."

"One wonders why we fought the War of Independence then," she said shaking her head slowly. "These great matters are beyond my ken, Mr. Elder, I have only the knowledge it takes to run this house. With Lucille gone, it will seem very different."

"I daresay it will." He sighed. "Nevertheless we must take into account that she is thirty years younger than we are. Please forgive me for refer-ring to a lady's age," he added, then continued. "She has been living her life as if she were our contemporary. It may well be a healthy thing for her to strike out, find some companions her own age, live a more youth-ful life."

Maybelle nodded, taking his point. "But I shall miss her so!"

"We all shall miss her. And although she does not yet know it, she will miss us as well."

"But I will not miss her dreadful obsessions." Maybelle said, managing the hint of a conspiratorial smile in spite of her distress. "Her poetry has cast quite a pall of late."

He smiled in return. "Her recitations will not be missed. Now dry up your tears. You still have a full house to attend to, and I won't leave you. Of that you can be sure."

"You are a great comfort to me, Mr. Elder. A great comfort. One would think that life would become easier as we grow older, now wouldn't you? We are more experienced, and wiser than in our youth. Still, life keeps on confounding us. It is just as difficult as ever it was to be alive, maybe more so."

He nodded in agreement.

They sat together drinking their tea companionably for a while, watching the kittens play, chasing a stray marshmallow.

81.

WOULD IT HAVE BEEN wise to let a room to this strange woman? wondered Mrs. Crofts of No. 21. Luci Dee had come without references, but was known to have stayed for many years at No. 13, a commendable house. The neighborhood grapevine could not supply the details of her departure, and the woman's statement that she needed a change told her little.

She looked well put together, a little flighty perhaps, and she was willing to pay three months in advance which gave an advantage.

We shall see, thought Mrs. Crofts, we shall see; and she lit a cigarette.

82.

"WORTH WHILE, yes, I would say Chicago was very worthwhile. I've been to Dallas, too, and St. Louis. That was the most lucrative," pronounced Winston Ward. "But I could not pass through Boston without saying hello to my old friend, Reginald. Married, I hear, and to the pretty cook. I almost couldn't believe it. Fast work, my boy, fast work." He patted Reginald on the back, with a little more strength than was necessary.

They sat together in a small cafe, Reginald having turned down an offer to meet in a bar. It was a gray, wet day. Rivulets of rain trickled down the outside of the window panes. Reginald cupped his coffee, not so much to warm his hands as to steady his nerves. He was fairly certain that his old sales partner was up to no good. Why else ask to meet? They were no longer friends. He had been left holding both the bill and the embarrassment at No. 13 when the scoundrel had bolted. Reginald had been quite surprised to know that Winston was even in Boston.

"The thing I don't get is why you stayed on there," said Winston. "The place is a mausoleum, a memorial to the past. The old lady is decent enough, but she needs to get with the times...let go of those outdated rules...no smokin', no drinkin', no nothin'. At least her protection of all things old-fashioned kept those insufferable suffragettes out of the house. Bunch of banshees. They would boil your balls for broth given the chance. The women there were okay. That's all I can say to the credit of Landlady Gill."

"My wife and I are both fond of Mrs. Gill, and it is convenient for Beatrice who is getting on well in her night classes at Pine Manor College. She has her eye on Radcliffe in the Fall, which is the women's answer to Harvard. It's expensive so we both work, and No. 13 is affordable."

"So the convenience is for Beatrice, and the money you make goes to her education?" Winston raised an eyebrow.

"My education, as well." replied Reginald defensively, "I'm becoming an electrician."

"Is there much money in that? Probably some, it being the coming thing, but I'll tell you what you should do, Reginald. You should come with me to Haiti?"

"Haiti! What on earth are you talking about? Isn't that some godforsaken French island off in the Caribbean? Why in the world should I go there? Why, for that matter, should you?"

"It was Frenchie a while ago, but got itself independence. Big mistake. The natives have made a right mess of things and so President Wilson sent the Marines in to install some order, in the interests of the good old U. S. of A., of course. The big banks saw there was opportunity there and wanted their interest protected. They put him up to it, I reckon. Smart man, that Wilson. He saw a chance and he took it, just as I'm going to do. We'd make a strong team. There is a lot of money to be made in Haiti, in sugar mostly, but gold, too; cheap labor, slave labor really; the Marines keep order well enough among the natives, I can tell you." He was talking very fast, as if giving a sales pitch to Reginald.

Reginald swallowed some of his lukewarm coffee. "So you want me to abandon my wife, run off with you to Haiti, live on a sugar plantation and keep slaves?"

"Well, put like that…maybe mining's the thing."

"Perhaps you really are an evil man, Winston. I thought at the beginning of our association that you were a decent sort, a little rough around the edges maybe, until that business with Lucille. You haven't even asked about her. You know she almost died."

"You were as keen as I to have some fun at her expense."

"To my eternal shame."

"Oh, the women have got hold of you for sure, Reginald. I see that now. They've got hold of your manhood and will squeeze 'til it hurts. You should make a break for it while you still can walk."

"You may think what you like, Winston. But while you are sweating away in that hell hole of an island, cracking a whip over another man's back, I shall be building a respectable life and a loving family. Frankly, I think there is more 'manhood', as you call it, in that."

"Well, we have concluded our business then. You disappoint me, Reginald. I'm leaving on a steamer out of Boston Harbor tomorrow. There is still time for you to change your mind and join me, but I can guess that you won't. I shall miss you. Actually, I shall miss the Reginald you were before Beatrice made a roast goose out of you. Here's a wedding present, by the way."

Winston stood up and slapped a small rectangular package down onto the table next to the unpaid check. Without a handshake or a backward glance he walked out of the diner into the rain.

Reginald sat for a while, hoping he had seen the last of Winston. He stared at the package without any desire to open it, wondering how he had ever been friends with such a bad sort. He was pleased with the way he had dared to stand up against Winston's bullying. Marriage had made him more of a man, not less.

83.

After the sunsets and the dooryards and the sprinkled streets the cat was always eager to return to Shoo Shoo who the food woman now called Mama, and the little cats who all looked like him, only smaller. They were all named NaughtyKitty. He continued to be content in his chosen home, but he still enjoyed the occasional wander of an evening, especially as the weather was warmer now. The people on his route now called him WhereHaveYouBeen. They were nice enough, but his own kitchen was best. Mama Shoo Shoo, after cuddling the NaughtyKittys for quite a long time, was again showing interest in having sex with him. Sex in his own home! It was very convenient.

84.

After the novels, after the teacups, after the poetry and the chatter, Tom Eliot was finally beginning to believe he had been accepted into the Bloomsbury literary set as he had so wished to be. Vivienne, with her rather too close association to Bertie Russell, had been his ticket into this magical circle of intellectual movers and shakers. Here he stood in the home of Leonard and Virginia Woolf, along with Vanessa and Clive Bell, Lytton Strachey, Maynard Keynes, Duncan Grant; it was a deliciously rich environment and almost made the marriage worthwhile.

The rooms were not large. Nothing in England had the spaciousness that Americans take for granted and expect, but they were inviting, hung with Vanessa's modern paintings on the walls, and close arrange-ments of comfortable furniture, if a little shabby, around the fireplaces in order to encourage intense conversations. He hung back on most of these occasions, watching, gathering words, and being as strange as he could naturally be, for these people adored everything strange.

He could feel the new poem beginning to grow within him like a tuber starting its journey upwards as the hard soil of winter loosens and gives way to Spring. He had created lesser poems since Prufrock, but now he felt the pulse of something strong and disturbing and, yes, ground-breaking.

Virginia Woolf seemed to like him, and that was important, although she was strange herself, fickle, flighty, a lady of situations. In some ways she seemed an even more difficult personality than Vivienne. Oh these fragile English women! How they must be treated so, and so, or their nerves go bad. What about *his* nerves! His nerves were bad tonight. He had read out a short poem earlier in the evening and the group had been amused, but he had sensed a mild disappointment as well, which ate at him. He was glad his part in the evening's entertainment was behind him. Now he sat alone by a window in the darkened dining room with a brandy in his hand, wishing to be left to his thoughts.

He gazed out into the dense fog of a London night listening with one ear to Leonard Woolf in the nearby drawing room read an excerpt from yet another of his pedestrian books. Outside the city appeared unreal, blackened, still, and hunkered down against the approach of zeppelins.

Inside, the war had been shut out. There was candlelight and talk of Shakespeare. Soon someone would put a record on the Victrola and everyone would dance about like clowns to the new ragtime rhythms. He actually like to dance, but not here in these stuffy smoke-filled rooms. He preferred a hotel ballroom where there was an order to things, and elegance, and space to move his awkward, truss-enclosed body around with some semblance of grace.

Nevertheless, he was grateful to be here experiencing the acceptance he had desired, that he actually needed, if he was to become recognized and well-known. If he was honest with himself he wasn't enjoying the experience. He asked himself when he had last enjoyed anything in life and the answer came hurtling towards him almost before the question had fully formed…with Jean in Paris, and in the mountains of Germany, before the war took him. In the cafes of the left bank he had been happy, drinking and talking; and hiking in the mountains, strong Jean was always ahead of him, looking back with a smile, their shadows coming to meet them as the sun, the heart of light, set slowly over what would be their last times together. Only memories now, fleeting, broken images.

What would Jean think of him suffering here for the sake of success in these unimpressive rooms, huddling against the war with these insufferable self-important people? Why he would laugh out loud. He would take hold of his arm and lead him out through the broken city, over London Bridge to the best pub to be found and they would eat and drink and laugh together until the publican announced it was time for them to close up.

Leonard, he noticed, had ceased to drone, and Virginia called out from a farther room. "Tom, Tom Eliot, where have you gotten to? Are you alive or not? Come and speak to me. Tell me what are you thinking?"

"I am coming," he answered reluctantly, turning stiffly towards her call. "I am just here in your lovely dining room."

I am just here in rat's alley, he thought.

85.

AFTER THE SKIRTS THAT TRAIL ALONG THE FLOOR and the voluminous bloomers, and the tightened stays of the foundation garments worn since childhood, Luci Dee felt she was able to breathe for the first time in her life. She was delighted with the modern, looser styles now seen even on the best of streets, the higher hemlines that made walking easier, a bra instead of the dreadful corsets that squeezed the life out of a woman, and to top everything off, the smaller more colorful hats that made dressing a delight.

She was less pleased with her room at No. 21, which was smaller and not as clean as she was accustomed to, but she had chosen it for privacy. It was upstairs in the back of the house with only a mudroom and a closet underneath, so the footsteps of her comings and goings would not be easily overheard by nosy boarders or by Mrs. Crofts. It would do. As yet she had only a nodding acquaintance with the other residents and she hoped to keep it that way.

She had quickly found a number of students in the neighborhood, faltering in English grammar, whom she could tutor one-on-one so money was not a pressing worry, but she needed to keep her personal life private so she guarded it carefully. This allowed her to maintain an aura of respectability and continue to be welcomed into suitable, middle class homes.

She was not, however, quite respectable anymore and it wasn't always easy to keep her parallel lives running smoothly side by side. So far she had managed. At home and at work she was as nearly like the Lucille of old as she could tolerate, although better dressed. In the evenings she was the new found Luci Dee, enjoying the restaurants and dance-halls and watering holes of the better sort. She smoked. She drank. She danced. And frequently she had entertained a man in her room. Mrs. Crofts had seemed to look the other way at first, (unthinkable to Mrs. Gill) but the damnable woman had raised her rent just enough to make a statement. Her behavior had been noted and would be tolerated, at a price, as long as she was discreet.

Luci was discreet, but did not wish to be. Sex, she had discovered, was better than she could have imagined. How can this be wrong? she had asked herself the first time a man's arms enclosed her naked body. We are adults. It feels wonderful, it pleases both of us, and if we are wise enough to avoid an illness or an unwanted child, it harms no one. She felt regret, of course, for all the years she had denied herself this enjoyment, but she was bound and determined to make up for lost time. If Mrs. Crofts became unreasonable there were other houses. She could keep moving down a notch until she found the right level of acceptance.

She admitted to herself that she sometimes felt qualms about her illicit adventures. She had been raised by sexless nuns, and gone faithfully to church for too many years not to have doubts about her startling new choices. And there were still times of loneliness, when the man she had enjoyed in the night was gone in the morning. It was a different kind of loneliness than she had felt when she had been living the proscribed and restricted life of a spinster. Now it was simply a desire for prolonged physical experience.

In her previous life she had imagined marriage as a way to secure respectability. As a liberated woman she thought of it as a way to insure regular satisfaction, but something would always be missing in a marital bed, something that she felt gave sex its charge…illegitimacy. She had realized that much of what she enjoyed in a sexual encounter was its forbidden nature, its secrecy, its very wickedness in the judgment of others. The experience of doing something that felt so right which was, at the same time, considered so wrong, fascinated her.

Luci now thought about sex the way she had once thought about poetry, which was most of the time and in great detail. She was a woman who did not do things by halves, neither decency nor wantonness.

86.

AND THIS, AND to this place alone, has life carried me, mused Ian Davies. His brother Willie's death had left him without immediate family. He had hunted down Captain Earnest Arlington to tell him of Willie's last request, and by sheer chance of circumstance had saved the man's life. When he pondered this it made him feel a little uneasy. He was not a God and had not asked for any such responsibility, but his life and the Captain's now seemed bound together in some indefinable way. Willie and fate had entwined their lives.

He missed his elder brother. Willie's birth had been difficult and he was born a firebrand requiring the lion's share of his mother's available energy, so when Ian came along within the year in an easy birth, he had slipped into life with a placid nature. He had matured into a man with a calm personality, generally relaxed and, until very recently, content with his life. People thought of him as kind, and he supposed he was. He certainly had no desire to hurt anyone. He simply avoided those who were not to his liking.

Willie, on the other hand had fought his way through school and run away to sea at the first opportunity, living an adventurous life that caused Ian to smile whenever he listened to Willie's tales, or received a postcard from someplace he had never heard of before. No doubt his brother had fought the waves that wanted him when his ship was sunk, just as he had fought the chest sickness that had finally killed him.

Ian's nature had taken him along a gentler path into the ministry where he could be of help to others and remain largely unknown. He only occasionally believed in God, though fortunately at the time he had taken his vows, he did. His growing agnosticism he kept to himself. He did believe in a goodness, perhaps a godliness, embedded in mankind, often buried too deep to be seen, but present nevertheless.

Too humble to model his life on Christ, he had taken the example of the good Samaritan as his way forward. He had tried to help his parishioners when they came to him with their homely troubles year in, year out. Now in retirement he walked daily, alert to be helpful to those he could, a penny biscuit for a hungry child, a talk with a lonely person in need of company on a park bench, a helpful arm across the street for a hesitant pedestrian. Sometimes a smile to a fretful passerby was all he could offer. He considered this his work.

Although his voice was resonant and his delivery pleasant, he had not made the best of preachers because he was by nature a listener. As a child he would creep out of bed and tiptoe halfway down the stairs to hear his parents' nightly arguments and conversations. Later in life he had found that people needed to be listened to so he had put this particular pleasure to work. He had heard it all; the kindness of which people were capable, and the cruelty. Over the course of his life he had garnered a little wisdom. He knew that nothing in a person's life lasts forever except the person's wish for his life to last forever. He tried to help them to understand that the present moment, the one they were in, was all the eternity they were likely to get. This had made him few friends among the heaven-seekers, but had enriched the lives of the thoughtful.

He had decided, shortly after arriving at No. 13, to stay on there into the Spring. He liked the collection of people he found in residence; different ages, sexes, walks of life, and no bad apples that he could see, so perhaps a little dull, but comfortable. No one had any children. Probably that was true of most boardinghouse ensembles. They were all the last of their families, at least for the present, as was he. Every generation before him had been the survivors, going all the way back to the tiniest dots swimming around in primordial seas, to those who crawled out onto the land and up into the trees and back down to the land again, walking at last on two feet; but his line would end with him, an unmarried male.

Still, there were other ways to procreate, he knew. He had counseled couples to mend their marriages and children had resulted; he had helped suicidal souls find hope and love and babies had arrived as their lives mended; he had supported terrified unwed mothers through their pregnancies as their children had been accepted or adopted. None would carry his name or know to love him, but they were *almost* his.

A bachelor by choice but not childless in spirit, he had gone forward contentedly into retirement. In the emptiness that followed he had eagerly sought out Captain Arlington on behalf of brother Willie. He had enjoyed a bit of detective work tracking him to No. 13, and as the place looked respectable, and had a vacancy, he decided to stay on, waiting for the right moment to talk with the man, and surely there couldn't have been a better one!

Suddenly, with that mission accomplished, he found himself at sixes and sevens, without a clue as to what to do next. His mind returned to those minutes at the end of the pier with Earnest Arlington; the biting salt air, the insistent waves, the unsparing sunlight, the shrieking gulls, the passionate Captain, with his death only a footfall away. He saw himself, too, merely a messenger; rational, calm, grieving for his lost brother, the direct opposite of the distressed man and those turbulent surroundings. He sighed. In comparison, he was not an interesting man.

Today he had returned from his daily stroll to find Mrs. Gill all a flutter. She had just heard the neighborhood rumor that a previous boarder, one she had cared for, had fallen into wicked ways. He had listened carefully, recognizing the woman in question as Lucille Davenport, the lady he had helped to feel understood, and who had left the house soon thereafter. He doubted that she was in the devil's clutches, but perhaps in those of a man or two. He could not say he disapproved. Ian had never been able to believe that God would give humans the pleasures of sexuality and then write down some impossibly complicated rule book about how and when to go about it. Men had done that, and as far as he could make out they had done it to control their women.

He had calmed down Mrs. Gill over a cup of tea, and promised to accompany her, as had now become their habit, to her Catholic church the next morning; this so she could pray for the soul of dear Lucille. Ian found Catholics interesting and did not mind attending Mass because he liked the look of the church filled with the color and imagery that Presbyterians couldn't abide. The Holy Roman Catholic Church had certainly understood the importance of a soul's need for beauty and for confession and for repentance. It had certainly profited by it, which amused him. The rest of their rigamarole was passable theater. Maybelle Gill always said she would be forever grateful for his company.

Thus he had settled into his life at No. 13; not much different from what he had done when ministering to the concerns of his congregation back in Ohio; listening as best he could, trying to be helpful, though he found the New England accents a challenge. It was not a bad way to live he thought, though he imagined Willie's voice prodding, chuckling, challenging...telling him life offered more...and asking if surely he did not wish for excitement, romance, and—

87.

So much more? "I don't know," said Ian Davies, answering his departed brother aloud. "It is true that there is much more to be had in life, but do I need it?"

I think you are partial to the old dame. I'll bet she still has some life in her. Give her a bounce or two before she dies. It would do you both some good.

"Willie, you are shameless."

I led a robust life, Ian. I lived a life of high adventure, while you just idled away your time on earth tending to a flock of tame sheep.

"And now you are dead, which means, Willie, that I get the last word!"

The last word, is it? May I point out that you are now talking to yourself? Get yourself some real excitement, Brother, while you still got some time.

Ian had to admit that the idea of a more intimate relationship with Maybelle had a certain enlivening appeal. Yes, they were both past the bloom of youth, but he did find her charming, nevertheless. There was a lingering prettiness to her features, and she had not become shapeless like many older women, just slightly more profound in certain places. Her competence appealed to him, and her decency. Such were the attractions of age. Perhaps he would court the good Mrs. Gill and see what might develop beyond their current friendship.

In his mind he heard music, not the singing of mermaids or of angels. It was Willie mischievously whistling the wedding march.

88.

"It is impossible to say just what I mean!" complained Maybelle.

She was hosting Father Sweeney in the parlor. Tea had been served along with some delicious scones that had been added to an array of sandwiches arranged on the best silver platter.

"What I mean to say is that nothing…nothing improper has occurred between us…nothing real. I mean many real things, but not wrong real things, but my feelings are quite strong and—"

"Having feelings are not in themselves a sin," Father Sweeney interrupted, brushing a few stray crumbs from his cassock.

"But there are impure thoughts, too. Surely those are sinful. I was taught so in catechism classes as a young girl, oh so long ago now, but I do remember. I am not a married person. Mr. Davies…Rev. Davies…is not my husband, and I imagine—"

"You seem bound and determined to see yourself as sinful, Mrs. Gill," the priest again interrupted, "This is not a healthy preoccupation. I beg you to desist. You are a good woman, shaken perhaps by the recent, and as I may confirm, *very* brief lapse of faith, but that is now well behind you. I can assure you that no one who serves such a fine tea to a man of the cloth will end up in the hellfires."

Father Sweeney smiled and helped himself to another scone with strawberry jam. He had actually come to check up on the errant Lucille Davenport, but it seemed he was too late. She had flown the coop. Maybelle Gill's moral fastidiousness was growing tiresome.

"It's all right then, Father? All right to think about being with… being…close to Rev. Davies?"

"So long as you keep your clothes on."

"Father Sweeney!" She exclaimed. Her hand flew to her mouth, and she blushed to the roots of her very fine white hair.

This gave the priest much amusement, though he kept on a solemn face. "Forgive me, dear Mrs. Gill, but I must make a point of what I am saying in such a way as you will remember it. God knows our most forbidden thoughts, our deepest feelings, and forgives us all. That is the point, as you know, of Christ's life here among us, his cruel death and his resurrection. But we *are* responsible for our actions, for what we actually choose to do. Now please tell me where I might find our lost lamb, Lucille, who no longer comes to Mass."

"She stays with Mrs. Crofts of No. 21 and I fear she has come under the sway of bad influences."

"Ha, yes. Hortense Crofts, something of an atheist, I believe. He shook his head sadly. Well, as there are no shortages of heathens about, or bad influences neither, all we can do is pray. Our prayers for Lucille were answered before, and if God so desires, He will answer them again."

Without a moment's pause Mrs. Gill dropped heavily to her knees. Father Sweeney sighed and did likewise, wondering how she could be so bendable at her age. His own knees protested and he promised

himself another scone, with even more strawberry jam, as a reward for
his efforts.

89.

B ut as if a magic lantern threw the nerves in patterns on a
screen Earnest Arlington could see, in his mind's eye, exactly what he
must do, and how to do it properly.

He took Mary's warm left hand in his own, and bending his knee
slightly, just enough to suggest the right sort of posture, Captain
Arlington proposed.

In his right hand he held his mother's ring, a single perfect diamond
in a setting of purest gold. She had left it on his pillow the morning
of her death. He had found it when he had returned from the beach,
holding a policeman's large hand, unable to fully comprehend what had
just happened to him.

Mary, who was sitting comfortably in the parlor chair, where they had
been talking pleasantly, suddenly appeared stricken. Her hand clenched
hard upon his own and she turned her head away, as if to hide an expression of purest misery.

"Whatever is the matter, my dear Mary? Have I misread your affection for me? Did I dare to presume too much?"

"Oh, Earnest, I'm so sorry. I should have spoken before, told you I
am not worthy of your love, but I could not find the courage. But now I
must. Oh, it is too horrible." She withdrew her hand and hid her face as
she began to weep.

"What, Mary? What is it?" He was terribly distressed by her sudden
change of demeanor, his confusion as to what he had done to occasion
such a fearful response. He had only wished to make her happy, and
instead she appeared distraught.

"Oh, do not ask what is it!"

"But how can you think yourself unworthy? I love you, Mary, with a
fine, steady love and nothing you say will change my feelings for you.
Please tell me. Have I done something wrong?"

"No, no." Her sudden tears had made speaking difficult, but the words
came out at last. "You have done nothing wrong. Nothing at all. Another

man did. And I am a ruined woman. It was back in Pennsylvania, before I ran away to Boston. I thought he cared for me, loved me, but that was not it, not it at all."

"Ruined? How ruined?"

"He took advantage of me. Against my will. I fought against him, but he was too powerful. It was a terrible thing. And I am a terrible person to have pretended to be pure, to have presented myself to you as an innocent. I am not the maiden you have believed me to be."

Her sobs were more violent now and he arose, and though shaken by her revelation, he put his arms gently around her shoulders.

"Mary, dearest," he said in his most tender voice, "I am a man of the world. I know the ways of good men and bad men, good women and bad women. You are among the good women. You cannot have been ruined by the action of another. I am only sorry, so sorry, that you have carried the secret of this terrible thing for so long, all alone, and felt it as something shameful. The shame is the man's shame, not yours, and it is you, Mary, beautiful, un-ruined you, that I wish to be my wife."

She was still trembling, but had grown calmer as he spoke. "Others would not think as you do," she murmured.

"Others will never know of it. And I can be no other than myself."

He felt her shift in his arms as she began to relax, and her tears lessened. Her breathing was now more regular, her heartbeat steadier.

"You do love me still? After the terrible thing that I have told you?"

"Believe me."

Then, hesitant, with the smallest of voices she said, "Then I will marry you, Captain Earnest Arlington, and think of myself as the most fortunate of women." She watched as he slipped the ring onto her finger.

For Mary, it was as if her years of unhappiness, shame, and fear had vanished into the sparkling stone.

For Earnest, it was as if decades of loneliness and grief had dissolved into her salty tears.

90.

WOULD IT HAVE BEEN kinder? wondered Augustus Platt, kinder to simply praise Lionel's latest paintings? He had not been raised to be false. He had been brought up to be excellent, to push himself one step further than he thought he was capable, and this had brought him success in his work, but less so in his private life where people found him difficult when he should be easy-going, unyielding when he should be understanding.

His sister had somehow managed achievement in both regards. Beatrice was proficient at whatever she turned her hand to from cake to scholarship to romance, and she was more tolerant of other people's weaknesses. He was happy for her, and he liked her choice of Reggie who, for all his efforts of adjustment, was not entirely comfortable among the hard-driving Platts. And it was asking a lot, he knew, of a normal man to be at ease around men of his persuasion, for he and Lionel did not hide their relationship when they were at home.

The truth was that Lionel was a deeply gifted artist who had let his talent diminish in his year of nomadic life. Augustus was not about to do other than what he knew to be right. He would push and prod him towards greatness. The world did not need any more bad paintings, but there would always be room for fine art.

Augustus believed that it was the artists, the intellectuals, the men of highest competence who should lead the way into this new era. The centuries of religious dominance were receding into the past, leaving a few magnificent cathedrals behind in their wake, buildings he had to acknowledge were marvels; but young enlightened minds would build the cities of the future, educate the young, liberate the society. America was indeed a land of promise, but not for the second rate, or so his parents had told him. In return for his best efforts at school and at college, and during in his long apprenticeship, he could expect success. He would expect no less of Lionel.

Now he sat as motionless as possible before the fireplace in his own comfortable parlor. He heard only the occasional ember fall into the grate and the rasping sound of Lionel's pencil against the drawing paper as he sought to capture Augustus' image. He was thinking of his most recent architectural project and except for the decorations on the facade of the building he was satisfied. It was a solid residential structure. It would have modern plumbing and electric lights. The client had asked for stonework ornamentation of intertwining ivy and flowers encircling the exterior walls which seemed to him, too ordinary. He wanted grander images that would be more vital, lions with wings perhaps, or swooping birds. The house faced the sea, so perhaps it should be adorned with mermaids.

"Thank you for being so patient," said Lionel as he finished up the drawing, clearly pleased with his effort.

The light flickering on his lover's handsome face was divine, thought Augustus. Lionel looked to him like a Greek God.

Yes, he thought, there is the answer. The facade would present to the world a pantheon of Greek Gods. He watched Lionel a moment longer. Naked Greek Gods.

91.

Worth while, thought Beatrice, my life would have been worthwhile but for this. If it had happened in two years hence, or three, then I would have been delighted, but now, just as I have been accepted into Radcliffe? A baby.

She was alone in the kitchen and had not yet told Reggie, who she knew would be overjoyed for both of them. He would not have to pause his life, carry the child inside, suffer the pains of labor, and risk death if the birth went wrong. He would not have to nurse and diaper and coddle away his days for years and years to come. She sighed and felt a shudder go down her spine.

When she was growing up she had envied her twin brother. Although she had been born first, Augustus was the most prized by virtue of his gender. Their parents had been unusual in encouraging her education as well as his, but he had been the one sent away to the fine academy whereas she had struggled along at the neighborhood school and at home. Her mind was as good as his, maybe better, but along with her studies her mother had insisted she take the time to learn cooking and sewing and homemaking. She had loved her mother, but thought of her as a thwarted woman, stuck with the housework and the rearing of children when her loves had been art and literature and, most of all, poetry. Had she chosen to have children or had the two of them just arrived with their endless demands which had to be put before her own? She would never know. Now she faced a future much like that of her mother. There were no alternatives.

This baby erased her own choices in life, and might actually take her life. Women died at an alarming rate from childbed fever even now. I have a competent doctor she thought, trying to reassure herself; he knows about sepsis and sanitary hands.

She took a steadying breath and squared her shoulders. The baby would be born alive or dead; she would survive the ordeal or not; and if they both lived she would love the child without question. So now she must rethink the future that once held so many possibilities, and she must tell her husband, and begin to make baby clothes, and mourn what was to be her education at Radcliffe.

She put a roast into the oven and sat watching pensively as the mother cat, without thought or grievance, nursed her kittens.

92.

IF ONE, SETTLING A PILLOW OR THROWING OFF A SHAWL could be more beautiful than his fiancée Captain Arlington could not imagine who or what it could be. He watched Mary as she moved about the parlor gently stroking the Tom cat that had gained entry surreptitiously, slipping up the stairs from the kitchen its nose alert to crumbs or mice, though the Captain knew in this spotless house its search was doomed to failure.

He knew he must think of finding and preparing a home for Mary and himself, the sooner the better. But he had liked it here at No. 13. He had enjoyed the cleanliness and quiet. The other guests had all been acceptable during the course of his stay with the exception of the odious Winston Ward. True, he had at first been uncomfortable around Lionel Quill who he sensed, and now knew, was deviant, but he was a likable fellow in his fashion. Beatrice, Reginald, Lionel and Augustus were all companionable when they gathered for cards in the parlor from time to time. Lucille's strange fixation on the Prufrock poem had been amusing and annoying by turns, and her crisis and transformation had proved to him that people could recover from injury, change their lives, go on in spite of the calamities suffered in their past. He missed her. He worried a bit about Mr. Elder, who seemed to be aging, growing more fragile, and more silent as time passed. The old man seemed to be brooding, as he had once done himself, but on what he could not imagine. Occasionally he said something that did not make a great deal of sense. Always kind, though.

Yes, No. 13 had been a fine dry-dock as it turned out.

Mary was slowly pacing and he knew she was thinking of the wedding, and he was drowsy with happiness as he imagined what would come after.

93.

AND TURNING TOWARD THE WINDOW, her back to Ian, Maybelle Gill finally found the courage to speak of her feelings. They had enjoyed a quiet evening together in her sitting room, leaving the parlor to the others. They had talked and laughed as they so often did and then, as the evening gentled, and the embers glowed in the fireplace, he had spoken of his growing affection for her, and she knew what Ian was going to do before he did it, before he had asked for her hand in marriage. She had come to the moment prepared.

"Dear Mr. Davies," she had replied, "you do so honor me with what you have proposed and I, in turn, confide that I feel a corresponding affection for you, but friends we must remain, only loving friends."

It was then that she had freed her hand from his, had arisen, and turned her back, walked away to the window.

"I am a Catholic woman," she continued, turning to face him. "You do not adhere to the true faith, in fact, although a Christian, you are a minister of another, dare I say, heretical religion altogether, so friends we must be, and nothing more."

He was listening attentively as he always did and she loved him for that quality among so many others.

"At first I believed you to be an angel," she continued, "so kind to those you meet, bringing love to me so unexpectedly, at this stage of my life, but angel you are not. You lure me, without realizing that you do so, from my religion, and yes, I admit that I am tempted. I feel the temptation to follow you into a life that would be sinful, for a marriage outside the church would be so. God has ordained that marriage is a holy sacrament, to be entered into only by two persons of the true faith.

You are a wonderful man and I have been alone for a long, long time, but as much as I might wish it, I would be wrong to marry you, and that I have not the power to change. So, no, dearest Ian, I cannot marry you."

Ian Davies bowed his head in acknowledgment, aware of the emotional difficulty Maybelle must be feeling as she delivered her decision. He was not entirely surprised by what she said as he had paid close attention on their Sundays in church together, knowing he could never in all honesty convert to her faith. And he was an honest man.

Among his own mixed feelings he recognized a faint sense of relief. He had learned to care for Maybelle in the wintry months of his residence. His brother Willie's remembered voice had prodded him, and perhaps the Captain's brave engagement to Mary had emboldened him, but in truth the experience of marriage was not *exactly* what he was seeking in his life, though he was not sure what it was that he wanted. Still, he had believed they could have made a success of it, from affection alone, and he was saddened to see how tightly the corset of Catholicism imprisoned Maybelle's soul.

Now that the anxious minutes of proposal and denial were passed, and Ian had accepted her exceedingly thorough answer, he thought that their immediate future at No. 13 might now be more relaxed. They would stay as friends, with nothing unspoken between them, until he figured himself out.

Somewhere, in her heart of hearts Maybelle knew she had not spoken the deepest truth in her carefully rehearsed speech. It was not only her religion that kept them apart, it was her age. She was old. She had grown used to her ways and was not eager to discard them. She had suffered the changes in her physical body as all women do, transforming over the years from pretty to pleasant to unappealing. The thought of a man, even one who loved her, *especially* one who loved her, laying eyes on her body as it looked now was intolerable. But for this pride, which she knew to be sinful yet could not put aside, she might have pleaded with Ian to convert, or even weakened in her own resolve to maintain her piety. Life had brought them together in the right place, but at the wrong time.

Maybelle and Ian smiled wistfully at one another and she turned back to the window again to watch the rain that seemed to sprinkle gentle tears upon the sidewalk in front of No. 13.

94.

Should he write again, beg Tom not to come? The newspapers spoke only of frightful dangers, of submarines crawling along the ocean's floor like scuttling crabs, then firing deathly missiles up into the bowels of harmless ships, killing innocent passengers. What if that were to be the fate of Tom? The world would lose a poet and he would lose the love of his life. And it would be partly his fault. He should never have written, asking to meet, in the first place.

Josiah Elder knew that his mind was not in order. He had too much time to himself nowadays. Ian Davies was monopolizing Mrs. Gill. Beatrice had not taken any literature courses this semester and so did not require his tutoring. He spent too many hours watching the feet of men and women as they walked by his windows. He took too many walks himself along his familiar route, but was so distracted that twice he had gotten lost. He tried to tell himself that it was the stress and worry about Tom that was causing his confusions, but he knew all the signs of senility, knew them all, and feared that this wretched time of life had come upon him as it had to his grandfather and father and all his uncles.

He remembered vividly the torments of their dementia and had always worried that the family curse would one day be visited upon him. Soon he would be sitting in a corner mumbling nonsense. He would drool. He would see and fear things that were not there in reality. These thoughts terrified him for there was no one to take care of him. Dear Tom had attempted to convey the distress of aging in two poignant lines of his poem: "I grow old, I grow old, I shall wear my trousers rolled." But such a young man could not imagine the true nightmare of those who faced senility. His own trousers would soon need hemming up yet again, but they were the least of his worries as he grew older and thinner and shorter and balder, here, alone in the sunless basement of No. 13.

95.

"Say, that is not it at all!" yelled Winston Ward, slamming his fist upon the desk. That is not what we agreed upon at all! You said if I put in the money and came down to manage the natives that I would have half ownership in this mine. Now that it is paying off you are sending me packing? I'll have your damnable head for this."

"Four of our workers have died in a month. That is hardly competent management. It's you who have broken the agreement," sneered the man who was so like his drunken father, slovenly, and mean to the core, with a fly crawling across his forehead. He squashed it without notice as he stared at Winston through narrowed eyes.

"I'll sue you," declared Winston.

"Hah. Sure. I suppose all your fancy banker and politician friends will come rolling up in limousine cars and take me off to prison. This is Haiti, Bub, not the USA. You are lucky I don't shoot you and roll you into the mineshaft. I've done it before. Now get the hell outta my office."

Winston knew from the beginning that it might be foolish to deal with this man, but just how foolish he hadn't realized until now. He had no friends in high places and if he did they wouldn't be here in this hell hole. Winston knew when he was beaten. The whole enterprise had been a disaster from the start; the days of seasickness on the way from Boston to Haiti, the terrifying lawlessness of the island, wildly beautiful as it was. He hadn't felt safe for a moment among the black, brutalized workers who clearly hated the sight of him, and he had quickly become as beastly as the other white men who thrived here.

The heat was unbearable, the living conditions sordid, and the men who held power, and with whom he had been forced to deal, were thieves and worse.

Hot and angry, he walked down the dirt road away from the mining office. He stopped at a ramshackle hut that served as a bar and bought himself a beer, warm, of course, and sat wondering about his next move. It was time to admit failure and return to the states.

A picture of No. 13 in Boston arose in his mind. Clean, cozy with that excellent chow that Reginald's wife turned out; Lucille descending the stairs both frightened and eager, but looking in his mind's eye damned fetching. Of course, the battle-ax that ran the place wouldn't have him back. He had burned that bridge. He remembered the warm women in the Nightingale Brothel down by the harbor, and the bars with the cold, cold beer.

With that, Winston counted what was left of his money, gathered his few belongings from the bunkhouse, and made his way down to the dock. A freighter was leaving the next day for the States, and he would be on it.

96.

"T HAT IS NOT WHAT I MEANT, AT ALL," declared Mrs. Crofts, her face red and her hands placed firmly on her ample hips. It was a classroom stance Lucille had once adopted herself when reprimanding recalcitrant children. She straightened her back.

"I never gave you permission to entertain men in your room," the landlady continued. "God knows who these strangers are. We might all be murdered in our beds."

"But you said gentlemen callers were allowed," Lucille protested.

"Is that what you call 'em? They don't look like no gentlemen to me, and a different one every time. People will say as I'm running a house of ill repute. Now, I tell you, Miss Luci Dee, you either change your ways or pack up your bags and make yourself scarce!"

"Yes, Mrs. Crofts. I am terribly sorry to have upset you. It will not happen again," replied Luci, letting her back soften and her voice lower, as she saw there was no other way out of this unpleasant confrontation. She could pretend repentant submission. She had had a lifetime's practice.

Mrs. Crofts waddled back down the stairs into her sitting room where Lucille was sure the old harridan drank herself into a stupor every night. It was only good luck that she hadn't yet burned the place down with a misplaced cigarette.

Hortense Crofts was necessarily concerned with keeping up appearances, not because she cared about the morals of her boarders, but for purely financial reasons. Within the boarding community one had to be thought of as running a decent establishment in order to receive referrals from other houses. It might be easier to run a brothel, she mused, looking around for a new bottle. She had met a few prostitutes in her day and had liked them all. She judged they were hard-working women trying to get by as best they could in a man's world, just as she herself must do.

Hortense had outlived two husbands and outstayed a third who had run off with a younger woman; but not before she had insisted that No. 21 be put into her name, a right to own uninherited property only recently having been granted to women. This feat had been accomplished because the abandoning husband was also a thief and she had the goods on him, as the police would say. He agreed to the signing over of the property in return for her silence, though looking back she felt lucky he hadn't just killed her. What a brute! She was glad to have seen the last of him.

She had also enjoyed some lovers along the way. They had been a pleasure so she actually felt sympathy for Luci Dee, but she needed to put on a memorable show of indignation to insure the woman's continued discretion. Mrs. Crofts, satisfied with her performance, sucked at the butt end of her cigarette, and poured herself another gin.

Luci had actually been trying to act discreetly. She had not come in with a man until after the other boarders had retired for the night, and she required her bedfellows to depart before dawn. She had kept herself to herself as much as possible at No. 21, taking her meals elsewhere, excepting breakfasts on the rare mornings she was up in time to eat them. These damn landladies! Putting their fat noses in everywhere! What's it to them if a girl has a bit of fun? This was the kind of slang she had picked up in the speakeasies and she liked it. Modern. Jazzy. In more straightforward words Luci believed her private parts were, indeed, private, and who she chose to share them with was her own business, not that of nuns, landladies, priests, polite society matrons, or anyone else on God's green earth.

Luci knew she would have to be even more circumspect in the nights ahead. The alternative was to abandon No. 21, because if Mrs. Crofts starting complaining about her, word would spread quickly, her reputation would be soiled, she would lose the students she tutored, and thereby her income. It was difficult, this newly liberated life, but it *was* life, not the stale non-existence she had led for so many years, the life of perfect conformity that had left her dry and starving inside, vulnerable to a man like Winston Ward whose attentions had ignited a moral conflict so intense she had been driven into temporary insanity. Or had it been the poem?

Both.

From time to time she still dreamed of Winston's hot, exploring hand, and the lines and rhythms of *Prufrock* still echoed in her mind. Prufrock himself also arrived in dreams, looking strangely like Mr. Elder and warning her against hesitation. The Eternal Footman haunted her when she was alone for too long, but the confusion, along with the delusions that had characterized her madness were gone. Others might say her recent choices were deranged, but what others might say was no longer of interest to her.

Eager to escape No. 21 for the evening, she slipped into a new frock. She brushed her hair which was now fashioned into short stylish curls, she added makeup and earrings and smart shoes. She spent a few minutes adjusting her hat as the damnable hatpin was bent for all eternity. Thus adorned she started down the stairs, realized she had forgotten her evening bag, and went back to retrieve it.

Emerging onto the stoop of No. 21, Luci smiled at the moonlight, making its way down through the trees. The sight of the moon always lifted her spirits. It seemed to appear in order to remind her how insignificant she was in the infinite, godless universe; how what she did or didn't do was of no great matter except to herself and a scattering of others. It was a relieving thought and she departed for the romance of the night with a light step.

Oh, she thought, this is so much better than going to Holy Mass.

97.

"No! I am not Prince Hamlet, nor was meant to be; am an attendant lord," he read aloud. Augustus looked up from the term paper Beatrice had aced in her previous literature class. "You know this poem isn't half bad," he acknowledged. "I can see why you chose it. And I can see why this paper got you into Radcliffe. Well done, Sis."

But Beatrice could not bring herself to smile. She looked at Augustus, his lover, and her husband; the three men sitting companionably together in her brother's living room, sipping brandy and talking before the fire. She was warmed by the thought that they cared enough about her to have asked to read her term paper. Augustus was, as always, reading carefully and critically as their mother had taught them. Her husband, a bit lost in her world of literature and poetry was trying his best to keep up, and Lionel was so grateful to her for making the match that he unfailingly approved of everything she did.

She knew she was fortunate to be surrounded with three such fine men, all of whom loved her, but tonight she did not feel so. Men did not share the trials of women. Men, if they could avoid war, led easier, more interesting lives, she thought. She did not like feeling petulant for there was no choosing of one's gender. She tried to concentrate on her knitting.

"You know," continued Augustus, "I have had the strangest notion."

"Tell us," said Lionel, as he continued doodling on a small sketchpad, trying to cajole his muse into suggesting a new painting.

"Well, the other night when we were all at No. 13 to play cards, that old man, Mr. Elder, the one that everyone calls Himself wandered in looking quite lost."

"I remember he passed through the parlor," said Beatrice. "You know he is the dear man who helped me write that Prufrock paper. Now that you mention it, he did seem distracted. More than usual."

"Well, as I was reading your paper, it occurred to me that Himself might actually *be* Prufrock; that he might be the man J. Alfred Prufrock is modeled on. Didn't you say he knew the poet?"

"T. S. Eliot was one of his students at Harvard."

"It was the gentleman's timidity when he came into the parlor," continued Augustus, "his hesitancy. As if he almost had no right to be there. When I began reading your term paper he came right into my mind, and now that I'm reading the poem it is as if he is being brought to life within it."

"But surely he would have said something," interjected Reginald," all those times when Lucille was obsessed with the poem, and when he was helping Beatrice."

"If it were true, he might not even know it, might not have recognized himself," suggested Lionel.

"It's not a flattering portrait and he might not want to admit it to himself," said Augustus.

"Or to others, if he did," said Beatrice, thoughtfully. "He certainly gave no hint of anything like that to me. No. That's not entirely true. I never knew why he had that laughing fit when I asked him to help me.

Might that have been the reason?"

"If it were true, perhaps he laughed because he couldn't cry," said Reggie.

"It is just a silly idea, I suppose," admitted Augustus. "Poets make things up."

"Not always," replied Lionel. "Poets, like artists observe, then they think, then they recreate reality as they want others to see it."

"Prose writers, the same," added Augustus. "It's a fine writing effort, Beatrice."

"Well, it makes no difference if it is fine or not," declared Beatrice.

"Whatever do you mean? asked Reginald, aware of the sudden strain in her voice, her distressed expression.

She took a deep breath and spoke. "There will be no Radcliffe."

All three stared at her, startled.

"Because—?" queried Augustus gently, asking for all of them.

"I had planned to tell Reggie this when we were alone, but here you all are so I shall get the words out to the three of you at once. There will be a baby among us in the new year, and a baby will need my full attention."

She had delivered such joyful news to them with such a woeful expression that the astonished Reginald found no words to respond, but he did know how to attend to her sadness and rushed to hold his wife in his arms, where she began to cry quietly.

Augustus and Lionel looked at each other, and an understanding passed between them. It was Lionel who spoke, finally seeing a way to repay her for saving him from himself.

"Dear Beatrice, you shall have your child and Radcliffe, too. Look at us. Three men who adore you, right here to help you. Certainly three men giving it our combined best effort can do almost as well for a baby as one woman can."

Beatrice stayed in Reginald's arms. Could it be so? She felt her husband nodding in agreement with the other two men. The right husband, she thought, and the right brothers, for Lionel had felt like a brother to her for some time now. Beatrice, in a flood of relief, could only nod dumbly. She had no words.

"But you must promise us one thing," said Augustus, sounding frightfully serious.

"Whatever is it? She asked, her mind awhirl with a flood of unlikely possibilities. "I think I will promise anything."

"You and I have suffered all our lives because our mother gifted us with such pompous poetic names."

Beatrice smiled as she caught her brother's meaning. "I promise," she declared, "if it is a boy he shall not be named Jay, Alfred, or Prufrock!"

"Oh, but I want a daughter," said Reginald, finding his tongue at last, and the evening became one of the kind that only loving families can create.

98.

ONE THAT WILL DO TO SWELL A PROGRESS, START A SCENE OR TWO, thought Tom. Yes, that idea will do. The thoughts were coming now.

He paced back and forth in the corridor outside the classroom. He had been hired to teach literature to the young men seated within, which was surely a waste of his time and theirs. He knew, even if they did not, that most of them would die in this dreadful war that grew and grew, determined as it was to suck an entire generation into its stomach of death. They would die and they would just be dead to those who survived. If there was an afterlife, the living did not know of it, only hoped for it.

The war. The ruin. The earth filling up with dead soldiers, the sea with drowned sailors. The waste, he thought, the waste of it all.

But he would not be counted among the dead. He was exempt from service here in England, and his decision was made at last. He would not go to America. He would not sail. He would stay alive on dry land. He would live to tell those who survived this present massacre about what had been done in their name, and what they had been left with. His masterpiece would be written. He would tell them all.

99.

"ADVISE me, Luci," said Mary, "the white or the cream?"

"The white, of course," replied Luci. "It declares your innocence."

"Oh, but you know I am not," whispered Mary. Since the acceptance of the Terrible Thing by the Captain, Mary had found the courage to share what had happened to her with Luci but her friend wasn't abiding it. Instead she was stalwart in defending Mary against any shame or guilt.

Earnest and Mary had decided on a simple wedding in the parlor of No. 13. At first Mrs. Gill had been against this, thinking as one would expect, that people should be wed in a church, a Roman Catholic church, but her better judgment was soon undermined by her warm feelings for them all and at last had allowed it. Now she felt only the anticipation of such a happy occurrence, followed by a reception right in her own house. It would bring renown to No. 13 as a very good boarding house for young single women to try their luck in life.

After a brief honeymoon the couple would sail away to the Caribbean where the Captain had taken a half share in a yacht, and which they planned to put to use as a pleasure boat, booking cruises for wealthy vacationers and sailing among the islands.

Mary had never imagined a life at sea, certainly not hosting well-heeled couples at leisure, but at the end of this harsh Boston winter it appeared in her imagination as exotic, exciting and, most of all, warm.

At the moment, however, the selection of a bridal gown was the matter at hand. They were all so lovely, but it had come down to two. She was glad she had brought Luci along as she preferred the white, a slender, silky garment over the lacier creme, and now she made the decision.

"The white," she told the clerk and all three women smiled.

"Shall we go for tea, Lucille? I mean Luci." she asked.

"I should rather a drink."

"That's awfully daring, isn't it? Two ladies unaccompanied, as we are in the middle of the afternoon?"

"Getting married is what's daring if you ask me," replied Luci. I know a place where no one will look askance and we won't be bothered unless we wish to be. Come along."

Having first made an appointment for a fitting of the gown, Mary gathered up her things and followed Luci to a cafe on the waterfront. Indeed it appeared quite respectable, ladies were being served cocktails, and the gin and tonics that Luci ordered for them, and which were a first for Mary, tasted delicious.

"You will have to learn all about cocktails for your pleasure boat business," remarked Luci. "I expected it will be you who will be mixing and serving them to the rich and famous while the Captain steers the boat."

"Pilots the boat," corrected Mary. "Oh this will all be so much better than a life of typing!"

"Or tutoring," added Luci, with a sigh. "Well, I shall be happy for you, with a side of envy."

"But you said—"

"Envy for the balmy weather and the drinks."

"What have you been doing besides the tutoring," asked Mary, feigning ignorance, though she had heard the whispered rumors of Luci going somewhat astray.

"I've found a group of women I get on with," replied Luci, surprising her. "You have heard of the suffragettes and their causes, no doubt. They have been working on the issue of a woman's right to vote for decades, and are all out for gaining power for women in many areas, something we sorely need. They are outspoken and brave, and look men right in the eye, as equals, and sometimes they look down on them. I am thinking of becoming active in the cause."

"But I thought you *liked* men," blurted Mary, "I've heard you are often seen about with them."

Luci was quiet for a moment, considering the dark side of Mary's history, but decided her friend was mature enough to hear the truth. Perhaps it was the gin that emboldened her. "I like men well enough for sex, but that is where their usefulness stops for me. Free love. No obligation."

"Oh!" was all Mary could manage at first, then growing braver, she asked, "Are you not frightened, Luci?"

"I presume to dare. Look around you. At the time I was born a respectable woman could not enter a place like this alone, though it is nothing but a place to have lunch with a bar. Nothing sinister is going on, just people eating and drinking and talking and laughing. Sometimes I look around at the older women in here, the bold ones of their generation who dare to come in alone, and I wonder, is that my mother? Or that one? My mother was ashamed to have me, doubtless because she was not married to my father. Those were rules, set up by pious men, rules that separated the good women they could exploit in marriage from the bad women they could exploit outside it, rules that separated woman from woman, and mother from child. Yet who is really responsible for my existence? A man. A man who could then refuse that responsibility. Now I break the rules set up by men, knowingly, proudly, and for my own pleasure. I will never marry, or give a man the power over me that men once had over my mother."

"You are brave, Luci. Braver than me. I want the security of a husband, a home of my own, though I never imagined it would be on a boat!"

"Any woman who lives honestly is brave, including you, Mary. You up and left the brute behind that harmed you. You left the community that would judge you as damaged. You've worked hard for your independence, been honest with the man you now love, and have made a whole new life for yourself."

"But will you never let yourself love someone, Luci? Be married? Have a home and children? Will you sacrifice all that for your independence?"

"'I am Lazarus, come from the dead,'" quoted Luci with a smile, "'I shall tell you all.'" And now we should go and register you for wedding presents at Jordan Marsh. You must need many things. They have beautiful linens and crystal. Or perhaps some coffee spoons?"

100.

"THE PRINCE of swords. Let me consider. That card could bode an auspicious or a bad fortune for you, I believe," said Ian. He had wandered down to the kitchen in search of Josiah, restless, having declined yet another evening Mass with Maybelle, and found Himself, most surprisingly hovering over a deck of tarot cards.

"What do you know of these?" asked Josiah, seemingly quite entranced with the pictures. Ian had explained they were for telling fortunes. He had once owned a pack sent to him by Willie, but had tossed them out following his brother's death after randomly flipping over a card revealing the drowned Phoenician sailor.

"How could they tell fortunes?"

To demonstrate Ian said he would try to read Mr. Elder's cards, shuffled the deck and asked Himself to draw five cards and place the first one face up and the other four face down.

The first card up was the Prince of Swords.

"So what would this mean?" asked Mr. Elder.

"I believe the prince of swords was originally called the knight of swords, a crusader by nature, but too hot-headed for his own good. It suggests a man who starts out on a mission quite ruthlessly, but then his own emotions, or his own faults, cause him to fail."

"Whatever is going on in my kitchen?" asked Beatrice as she opened the street door and bustled down the kitchen steps, her arms full of groceries.

Both men rose to assist her, but she waved them away.

"Oh, you found those tarot cards that the dreadful Winston Ward gave to Reggie as a wedding present. Can you imagine? He came through Boston a while back on his way to Cuba…no Haiti, and waylaid Reggie in a cafe. He wanted Reggie to forsake me and go off with him! What an absurd man! It might have come to fisticuffs but my dear husband is too much the gentleman." She laughed at the idea, and set down the groceries next to the men. "I don't want those cards, and I brought them down here to give to the kitchen maid next door. She is young and foolish and I thought she would have some fun out of them. I see Mr. Elder has drawn the prince."

"Yes," Josiah concurred. "It seems I am some kind of a crusader in the short run who cannot accomplish anything in the long run."

"And you, a Harvard professor! How much more accomplished could you be? You see what nonsense they are."

But Mr. Elder was inclined to see the truth in the draw. "We had best get out of your way, Beatrice," he offered. "We will finish up in the parlor, and return the cards for the kitchen maid after we see all that is to be seen in our futures."

"As you wish. I am always pleased to have others in my kitchen. Usually I have only the cats for company."

Ian gathered up the cards and the two men made their way upstairs to continue with their amusement.

Beatrice sat down heavily in the nearest chair. She had watched Himself with interest after what Augustus had suggested. Could he be the model for Prufrock? She had observed hesitancy, but it seemed to be from forgetfulness and there was more and more of that lately. Only yesterday he had asked when dessert might be served having already eaten his peach pie and had the plate removed.

She spied a card that had fallen to the kitchen floor, and bent to pick it up. Mr. Elder had inadvertently dropped a card at her feet. The Death card. Whose death, she wondered? Mr. Elder had drawn it, but she had picked it up. All nonsense, she knew, superstition, not for the educated mind. Still, a chill went through her, and she rested her hand lightly on her rounded abdomen.

101.

No DOUBT about it. The yellow cat was eager for a night in the streets. During the time of the cold white stuff he had been content to stay in the kitchen and watch as the NaughtyKittens were carried away one after the other by cooing humans, leaving only himself and Shoo Shoo. He preferred their life without the little cats. The cold white stuff was gone now and the night air was warm. Shoo Shoo did not share his need for adventure, for the thrill of running away from excited humans, for a challenging back alley fight with another cat now and then. She was sleeping peacefully so he crept up the stairs and through the flap in the door into half deserted streets.

102.

An EASY TOOL. That is what he had been to that bunch of thieves in Haiti. He had been picked up, used, and discarded, thought Winston. They had taken his money and his energies and then driven him off the island. He raged inside whenever he thought of it, and he thought of little else.

So here he was, returned to Boston, almost penniless, but knowing he would soon find work again. He was a clever salesman, and could sell himself to a prospective employer.

Winston found himself by habit back again in the neighborhood of No. 13. He certainly could not return there, but he liked the area. It was near the harbor, decent enough, cheap enough, too. He noticed a vacancy sign at No. 21. A woman who was probably the landlady, an

TO MURDER AND CREATE   155

overweight woman, not too neat in appearance, came out onto the front
stoop taking a cigarette from a packet, tapping it lightly, showing the
movements of an experienced smoker.

Winston was standing next to her in an instant, offering a light.

103.

DEFERENTIAL, that is what we are raised to be the speaker had declared
and Luci agreed. The speech had been a rousing one and chimed well
with Luci's own sentiments. She applauded energetically at the meeting's
end and felt satisfaction knowing that she had found a sisterhood of
strong women. Having saved herself from servitude she had now made
the bold decision to unite with the suffragettes in order to save others,
the women who would waste their youth trying to be good, hoping to
find a man in order to walk straight into the wretched bonds of marriage, the risks of childbearing, the burdens of childrearing, and worst
of all, catering to the endless needs and demands of a husband. Some
husbands were responsible she supposed, but many were rakes, drunks,
gamblers, philanderers, or worse. Luci knew. Knew them all.

What she couldn't make out was how men had come to rule the
world in the first place. They were so bloody stupid most of them. If
they weren't shooting innocent animals they were shooting each other.
Now there was a war boiling over in Europe. It was just men, doing what
other men told them to do, lining up in mud-holes and killing each
other. Women would never do that. Women were smarter than the lot of
them. There was a fierceness in Luci's step as she walked home to No. 21
having joined the ranks of the women agitating for equality, for the vote,
for full participation in the fabric of society.

She had her own private agenda, of course, that she shared with no
one. She knew there was a clinical name for her inclinations, though
she did not consider them an affliction...nymphomania. The long hours
in the library had informed her of this diagnosis. There was nothing
nymph-like about it for she was fully mature. And she was not a maniac,
though she had been temporarily out of her mind in the hospital. It was
not mad to break free of the thoughts that had incarcerated her, first in
her straight-laced life, then in the hospital. Now she was just a single

woman who enjoyed sex. She did not require a diagnosis because sexuality felt healthy, and she was not mentally ill just because she enjoyed the pleasures of her own body. Surely it was a man that had coined the term nymphomania. Doubtless a man who knew all about it from his experiences with women, though his wife surely did not, just like the oh-so-respectable and very married doctor she had been with the night before. She smiled a wry smile. Hippocratic? No. Hypocrites! The lot of them.

In spite of the warning from Mrs. Crofts, Luci had continued to bring home the men she fancied into her room at the top of the stairs. Secrecy added excitement to her adventures but she was more careful nowadays. She would delay entering No. 21, captivating her current choice with promises of pleasures to come, until she knew Mrs. Crofts was deep into her cups. When she was finished with them, the men were turned out as before, into the early morning hours, before the other boarders were awake. Luci Dee collected her sexual experiences as Lucille Davenport had once memorized poems.

In the afternoons, in the evenings, she slept peacefully.

104.

"GLAD TO BE OF USE," said Ian, as he helped Maybelle with the decorations of white paper stars and satin ribbons. Today was the wedding, a first for No. 13, and a big event for Mrs. Gill. The parlor looked like a flower shop, and the furniture had been polished to gleaming, then moved around to provide a short aisle. Father Sweeney would officiate, as both bride and groom had been baptized Catholic in their infancies and he had reluctantly agreed to one confession and communion each before the ceremony. A pianist had been hired. Everything was in order. Ian realized, unhappily, that he was restless. He understood Maybelle's excitement for her world seldom encompassed gaiety. And he understood that a wedding was exciting for the pair involved. He had performed the service himself for dozens, perhaps hundreds, of smiling couples over the years, and it left him little room to wonder why the upcoming event held no enchantment for him.

He had thought that living here, with matters settled as they were between himself and Maybelle would be comfortable. Instead, he was feeling pinned down, constricted, and often just plain bored, but he seemed without the imagination to conceive of a definite change in his life. Willie was impatient with him. He was impatient with himself.

The psychological predicament he was experiencing seemed familiar to him, reminding him of something he had recently heard or seen. Was it something he had read? A play he had attended perhaps? He searched his mind. *Hamlet?* Well, then surely I am not the first man to find himself constrained by uncertainty, he consoled himself. I must take some action on my behalf, but how shall I begin?

105.

POLITIC, CAUTIOUS, AND METICULOUS; Mr. Elder read the words with satisfaction. He had copied the words of the poem on carefully cut out pieces of paper, one phrase upon each piece, and stuck them up along carefully measured lines drawn on all four of his walls. He had moved his cot from the bedroom into the living room so he was now living, night and day, inside the poem. It was deeply comforting to be surrounded with so much love and admiration, however carefully it had needed to be disguised.

Josiah knew that the poem had somehow been a part of Lucille's madness. There was something in it that had spoken to her of repression, of the fear of living the life she actually wanted. Ian Davies had heard her and understood her and helped her to become aware of what she needed to do, and some would say she had begun her recovery in that moment. Others would say she had begun to ruin her life. Either way, it spoke to the power of the poem.

He had observed that Ian was now stuck in the same sort of malaise. Ian had not drawn from the tarot deck, so he had no direction as to how to proceed in life, as he did...Josiah, the Prince of Swords.

He realized that once the poem had driven him into a temporary madness. He had actually plotted to kill Tom Eliot, believing that he had been disgraced by him; and he might have done so had not Ian helped him to see that although he been rejected by Tom, it was because Tom had been terrified of his own nature and the forbidden love he felt for his Professor.

He had recovered from the insanity that the poem had induced, and with great relief recovered his love for the golden boy. What genius, what mastery over the power of words T. S. Eliot possessed! His student. How he adored him.

So now, with the dementia worsening, as he felt his mental powers fading, his memories disappearing, his intellect slipping away by slow degrees, he had wrapped himself up in these precious lines, this hymn to Himself.

106.

FULL OF HIGH SENTENCE, BUT A BIT OBTUSE. The words he had written in Prufrock came back to haunt him and he smiled. For he knew that would be the going opinion of T. S. Eliot, long after this war had ended, and perhaps the next as well. And yes, he was full of high sentence, *and* he was a bit obtuse for otherwise it would be impossible to say just what he meant, for how else was he to write of the unspeakable? Of love without hope, of evil without redemption, and of death without resurrection?

He knew what was happening in his world, in *the* world, and he was prescient. Like the Oracles of old he could see clearly what would become of the future. The poem within him, conceived in grief and nurtured by despair, was ready to begin its journey into being. It would take years to develop, but all that was within his experience must now become his inspiration and flow outward, like a polluted river carrying the wreckage of civilization.

He picked up his pen, held it firmly, committed it to the paper, and, without hesitation, entered the waste land.

107.

AT TIMES, thought Reginald, he was the luckiest man alive, at others he was terrified of what lay ahead, jolted as he was by the prospect of fatherhood, and the necessity of providing safety and sustenance for his wife and child. True, he would have the companionship of Augustus and Lionel, of that he was certain, but the responsibility for Beatrice and the child would be his.

He had never felt quite grown up before. Perhaps the limp had impeded him. It was as if the eleven year old boy he had once been was still held in the clamped jaws of that vicious dog. The injury had literally dogged him. His inability to play sports as a boy was part of it, and as he had matured the girls chose other, more able, boys to fancy.

His love for Beatrice had been sudden, and the awareness that she returned his love was a profound shock. They had fallen into each other's arms without hesitation, given way to the intoxicating experience of romance, married almost without thought, for who needed thought at such a moment? Now reality had come knocking. Was he man enough to prevail? Winston had laughed at him, warned of imminent regret, but he did not feel regret, only fear for their future, which, as the man of the house, rested upon his shoulders alone.

And what house was it to be? He did not wish to raise a child in rented rooms here at No. 13, even as more rooms would soon be available when Mary and the Captain left for their new life at sea. Though Mrs. Gill would surely enjoy playing the grandmother, he did not want his son or daughter to grow up in a world of faded carpets and fading people. They could not displace Lionel and live in Beatrice's family home. Augustus and Lionel were content there and he knew he would never again wish to disrupt the happiness of another.

Electricity scared him because he didn't understand it, but electricity was the way of the future. He would have to find *his* way to being a part of that future. He turned back to his textbook, *Alternating Currents and Interior Lighting*.

When he had brought the book home and begun to study it, Beatrice had read the title over his shoulder and instead of yawning as he expected she might, she read it again, laughed and said: "It sounds like a description of how one must live a life."

108.

INDEED, thought Maybelle, this had been one of the most memorable of days at No. 13. A wedding. All had gone as planned and the happy couple, and they *were* a happy couple, had left for an brief honeymoon on the Cape. Upon their return they would pack up their belongings and leave for the Bahamas where the boat purchased by the Captain was in dry dock for refitting. Maybelle could not imagine living on something that moved up and down and splashed water everywhere, but she was happy that Mary was young enough to give it a try, and that the thought of being with Mary was enough to lure the Captain back to the sea.

Now she sat solidly and dryly with Ian and Josiah in her living room discussing the day's event. Father Sweeney had departed when the bottle of champagne she had allowed to accompany the light refreshments had been emptied after only one round of toasts. Beatrice, Reginald, Lionel and Augustus had made short work of cleaning up and restoring the parlor before going out for a celebratory dinner.

The surprise of the day, for her, had been the arrival of Lucille, looking especially beautiful in blossoming spirits. Lucille and Mary had struck up quite a friendship she knew, so of course she should have expected her to be in attendance. She had been friendly and gracious to Maybelle in a way that echoed their relationship of old.

Lucille had been wearing a dress cut to the latest fashion and with her hair short and dyed a bright shade of red, she had at first glance, been unrecognizable to Father Sweeney who had not seen her since the hospital. Neighborhood gossip had informed Maybelle of her tutoring and involvement with the women's right to vote movement, and there were the rumors, too of other more liberated behaviors that Maybelle simply would not, could not, accept.

After Lucille's hurtful departure from her rooms at No. 13 Maybelle had wept and prayed, and in time she had found forgiveness in her heart. Ian had encouraged this, explaining that some people had to act shockingly in order to act at all. Mr. Elder had counseled her wisely in the kitchen the morning she had felt so at a loss, and she had taken his perspective to heart as well. Lucille was *young*. It was a simple truth, so disguised in good manners and proper behavior that it had come almost as a revelation to Maybelle.

More importantly, Lucille had left a loving note full of appreciation for her time at No. 13 and expressing her true affection. She kept this note next to the photograph of her departed husband.

Well, the new Luci Dee had forgotten her gloves. They rested on the hall table proving to Mrs. Gill that she was still in some ways the old Lucille, and she smiled each time she saw them. She would take them over to No. 21 tomorrow if Lucille had not, by then, returned to retrieve them.

As Maybelle, Ian and Josiah worked their way through a pot of Earl Gray tea and a plate of cookies left over from the reception, they spoke of the summer weather that was surprising them, arriving early with unseasonably warm May days. April had been cold and somewhat grim for all of them, but the longer, sunnier days were cheerful and the wedding preparations along with Beatrice's announcement that there was a baby on the way were welcome distractions. At least these were the musings of Maybelle as she sat contentedly between her two men.

Ian had other thoughts. He had, through many sleepless nights, arrived at a decision. He knew he would be leaving No. 13 and had no way to go about it with any more kindness than Lucille had done. He would follow the Captain and Mary in due time to warmer climes and new adventures aboard ship which pleased Willie greatly. His time here seemed to have come to a natural ending.

Though he was not given to smugness he was glad to have been of service during his stay. Besides helping Lucille back to reality he had kept the Captain alive and able to endure his past misfortune, thus fulfilling his brother Willie's request. The unexpected result was a fortunate life for Mary. He had helped Josiah Elder to know there were many ways to express love. He had helped Maybelle to find her way back to God and to the knowledge that she could be loved at any age. He had supported Reginald and listened to Mary when they talked to him of their various worries and woes. Only Beatrice had not required his attentions, for she was the most capable at living life of the lot. She and Reginald and the baby spoke of the future and he liked the sound of it, but knew he would not be part of it.

He knew that Maybelle was used to people coming and going from her home. She had chosen it as a way of life, and in it she had flourished; offering temporary sanctuary, mothering, spiritual guidance, and nourishment to so many over the years; letting them come, letting them go, with grace or admonishment as the situation required. And she had grown. At his urging she had found kindness for some who were not easy for her to accept, most particularly for Lionel Quill's difference. She had sought and found forgiveness for Lucille, and was beginning to understand that those who did evil, like Winston Ward, had had evil done unto them in ways she could not imagine. And she had allowed Ian to love her. She had uncovered long buried feelings and, although she had turned down his proposal, he knew she cared deeply for him. Ian had realized, when first she had told him of the tree that fell, killing her husband, that it had also broken her heart. He hoped perhaps that he had mended it. Would his departure break it again? He prayed not.

Mr. Elder was not thinking of the wedding. He nodded as the others made observations about it, nodded again and again as they spoke of the weather, Lucille's appearance, the baby that was coming to Beatrice and her husband whose name he could not recall. Was it Roger? Rupert? No great matter. His mind was elsewhere, wandering through half deserted streets and sawdust restaurants. It digressed, thinking of skirts that trail along the floor, it lost itself among some talk of *Hamlet*, it scuttled along at the floors of a silent sea. He would soon reach the safety of his room, the embrace of his poem.

Maybelle had noticed and worried about the decline in Mr. Elder. He was quieter than usual tonight. He had come to dinner at the wrong hour last Thursday. His frayed cuff showed a gravy stain which she had never seen on his impeccable attire before. And there was the potted geranium he had carried home from one of his evening walks, one that did not belong to him and that she had had to return to the disgruntled neighbor who had found it on the front steps. He had said he did not recall taking it, and suggested that the cat might have dragged it there. Maybelle had observed elderly people become senile in the past; her grandmother, an uncle, and she had heard tell of others; but it had never occurred to her that it might be a problem she would need to face under her own roof. She felt a chill. Mr. Elder was dear to her.

"Have you seen that magazine of Lucille's?" he asked suddenly. "The one with the poet's likeness on the cover?"

"Dear me, no," she replied. "I threw the hateful thing out long ago."

"I have lost my own copy," he said sadly, "perhaps among the porcelain."

"That seems very unlikely," replied a startled Maybelle. "It is most probably in your chambers. You must look for it there."

"Ah yes, of course. And there will be time," he said, apropos of nothing that she could discern. She caught the eye of Ian. He looked as concerned as she felt. She wondered what would happen should Josiah's mind deteriorate further, and in short, she was afraid.

109.

ALMOST RIDICULOUS, thought Captain Arlington. Yes, indeed! It was almost ridiculous to be so happy. And scary, too. Surely such excellent luck must end. He knew it was superstition, nonsense actually, to think that bad must always follow good, but wasn't it so? As he looked back over his long life he could make out the pattern if he tried. His mother had died after a jolly day at the beach. That fatal storm had followed a tranquil voyage.

He looked at beautiful Mary sleeping peacefully beside him. He pictured her on the deck of his little ship, which he had named *The Love Song*. He could imagine her black hair blowing in the wind behind her, as she smiled into the sun.

She had already had a life of trouble and hard work, and yes, there would be work aboard ship to keep the passengers content, the vessel clean and well maintained, but so much better than crouching over a typing machine day in day out under the scrutiny of surly bosses.

Mary would outlive him, of course, and he had already been to solicitors to be sure her future would be secure. If I died right now, he thought, I would die a happy man.

He remembered walking through the parlor the day before the wedding. He had spied a pack of tarot cards left upon a table. There had been sailors who played at fortunes with such cards aboard his ship, not that the cards had saved them. Curious, he had flipped over the top card. The World card. He knew its meaning…having your dreams come true, but he did not smile for he had drawn it upside down which warned against achieving that for which you wished.

Just then, Mrs. Gill had entered the parlor, seen the cards, and shrieked. "Evil! Wicked things in my house!"

"They are not mine," he had replied defensively, "They were just here when I came through."

"Those cards are the work of the devil. Filthy things. First that wretched poem and now this. I must not let my house become cursed again. Oh, they must be burnt!" She had swooped up the cards and carried them away.

They were, no doubt only ashes now, but the memory of the card remained with him. Be careful of getting what you wish for, and though he was neither a superstitious man nor a religious man, he offered up a prayer for Mary's safety in the years to come. With a bit of luck and a following wind she might sail contentedly through her life. He vowed that he would do all that was humanely possible to make this a certainty.

110.

ALMOST, AT TIMES, THE FOOL. Yes. That was the line from the poem that best suited the current situation, decided Luci Dee. Here I am, naked as the day I was born, with Winston Ward snoring beside me, the same man whose attentions caused my nervous breakdown, the same hand on the same thigh that ignited my sexual fires. I am indeed the fool.

It had been much easier to invite Winston over from his room across the hall, than it was to maneuver the men she met casually in restaurants and saloons, up and down the darkened stairs. Safer, too, with just one lover, she thought, for she was well informed about unwanted pregnancy and illness and although she took precautions carefully there was always risk.

Fate had ushered Winston into No. 13, then into No. 21, but she herself had ushered him into her bed. They had both been stunned to see each other again, and he had been amazed at the change in her. "I am flabbergasted," he had said, his eyes opening wide as he recognized her.

She had at first hesitated to take him up, for she saw no change in his character or behaviors. He was a rake of the first order, but whenever she had remembered his hand beneath Mrs. Gill's dining room table gently moving up her inner thigh, she was aroused. And there he was. The very man. And he turned out to be one of the best of her sexual partners, always willing, always inventive.

She felt no affection for Winston, nor did she sense any from him towards her. They both knew what they were about. Nevertheless, there would probably be trouble when one or the other became tired of the arrangement. She could always move elsewhere.

Luci and Winston had agreed the night before to sleep in late on this morning. A lovely soft light spilled into the room and over his sleeping features. He was a looker now. She peeled back the coverlet and admired his muscular body, leaner than before. He had told her hard work and bad food in Haiti had taken the weight off him, toughened him up. She rolled her body on top of him, sitting up and astride as he began to waken and respond. They began to move together, giving encouragement each to each, when a light tap was heard upon the door, and then without pause the door swung open. Maybelle Gill stepped boldly into the room waving a pair of Luci's abandoned gloves.

No one spoke.

Luci was too shocked to move. Winston swiftly pushed her to one side and covered her nakedness. Maybelle, uttered a soft moan, closed her eyes, dropped the gloves, clutched at her chest and collapsed.

III.

"I GROW OLD...I GROW OLD..." cried out Maybelle Gill from her semi-comatose state, for that is how she felt as she slowly emerged into consciousness. Old and sad and frightened. She had heard the murmurs of the voices around her as she was moved from Lucille's bedroom at No. 21 to the hospital and then to her own rooms; heart attack brought on by shock, it was thought. She would stand the best chance of recovery in her own home it was said...bed rest, no exertion, hydration...so she lay quietly in her bed at No. 13 with Josiah, Beatrice, Ian, and even Reginald, coming and going, bringing her water and broth and softly spoken words of assurance.

Everyone assumed it was the sight of Lucille and Winston in an act of unmarried sexuality that had caused her heart to fail, her deeply felt morality having all but killed her; but she knew differently. In the moment when she had so cheerily entered the room holding Lucille's gloves aloft, she had been appalled by what she saw, of course; but unutterably horrified by what she had felt...jealousy of Winston Ward.

In that astonishing moment a desire for Lucille's beautiful body to be pressed against her own had surged into her awareness. She wanted to touch the soft, rounded breasts, pull the delicate curves of her waist towards her own, feel the smooth, youthful skin glowing in morning sunlight against her suddenly enlivened body. And now that the moment of their forbidden embrace had been imagined, it could not be repressed. How could she live with such self-knowledge? Or with the wave of regret that had consumed her…oh, such deep regret…for her barren, sexless, loveless, thwarted, Roman Catholic life.

112.

"I SHALL WEAR THE BOTTOMS OF MY TROUSERS ROLLED," Josiah Elder declared, and was determined to do so. Standing in his sitting room, surrounded by the words of the poem, he reached down to roll up his trouser bottoms, but found he was wearing only his wrinkled nightshirt. He thought this exceedingly odd for only a moment ago he had been at a tea party. There had been coffee spoons clinking in porcelain cups and there had been cakes and ices. Or perhaps that had been in a dream. It was difficult to tell these days just what was real and what was imagined.

He had gone upstairs to speak with the doctor following the man's last visit to Mrs. Gill. He had not been comforted. The doctor had told him with icy authority that his confusion would get worse, his memories would disappear, his ability to function would continue to decline, and he must face his fate like a man.

He reached for the pills that he kept safely in his trouser pockets. Pills he had purchased with the idea he might use them to kill Tom Eliot, but again encountered the seam of his nightgown, not the pocket of his pants. Why had he wanted to kill Tom? Well, no great matter. The pills he had purchased for murder would now serve to make an end of himself, relieving him of his humiliations when he could no longer appear normal.

The doctor had said that because he had no immediate family, when he became a threat to himself or others, he would be put away, sent to a poorhouse. No, he had thought. I would rather die. He liked to hold the glass vial in his hand, rattle the pills about. The poison made him feel he was still in charge of his own life.

He crawled back into his bed, thinking of Maybelle recuperating on the floor above him. He should again go and make a visit. No, he was too tired. He would lie still and let the brown fog of sleep roll over him. The papers attached to the surrounding walls, each with a phrase from his poem flapped gently, buffeted by a current of air that came in from under the door as someone entered or left the house. Perhaps it was the yellow cat. The poem seemed to be waving to him, and he knew it needed revision. He would work on it tomorrow.

113.

"SHALL I PART MY HAIR BEHIND?" asked Reginald. He wanted to look his best for the job interview.

"You are fine as you are," answered Beatrice. "Mature. Experienced. Trustworthy." And she kissed him gently, leaning in over the table, bumping her rounded belly as she did so. They were having a private breakfast in the kitchen, the last for a while as Mary and the Captain would be rejoining the house guests tomorrow to gather up their belongings and make their move. At present Mr. Elder declined breakfasts and Ian took his upstairs in the room with Mrs. Gill.

All of this will soon be at an end, thought Reginald, for with the help of Augustus they had located an affordable apartment in a nearby neighborhood. Augustus had been hired to convert an old boarding house into a group of small, modern flats. They could acquire one through his connections if Reginald landed a steady electrician's job, so the pressure was on.

Beatrice, distracted of late, he assumed by her pregnancy and the added care of Mrs. Gill, had been supportive, but was not as eager for the move as he was himself. He supposed she might think it easier to give birth in familiar surroundings.

"Do you remember the pack of Tarot cards that Winston Ward gave us for a wedding present?" she asked, surprising him, as this was the farthest thing from his mind at the moment.

"Yes. What about them?" he inquired, putting down his buttered toast, realizing his nervousness had left him with no appetite.

"I picked a stray one up off the floor. Mrs. Gill burned the pack, saying they were the work of the devil, but I came across the one I had retrieved in my apron pocket this morning." She drew out the card and placed it in front of him on the kitchen table, next to the neglected toast. It was the Death card. "It frightened me."

Reginald had heard that pregnant women were subject to irrational fears and superstitions, and he knew his duty.

"There is nothing whatever to fear, Beatrice," he said, taking up the card and ripping it into small pieces. He rose and put the shreds in the bin, then stood behind her, enclosing her in reassuring arms. "No one is going to die. Not you, not me, and not our child." He said these words as if they were a certainty, not a hope, and felt her shoulders relax, accepting his confidence. This was what husbands were meant to do, he thought, put aside their own fears and be a strength to their families.

"You are quite right," she concurred. "It just gave me the shivers when I came across it so unexpectedly. I had forgotten it was in that pocket. It is a hideous image."

"Well, think no more about it. I must go now and have my interview. A kiss for luck, please." And she gladly obliged.

After he was gone, Beatrice smiled, thinking of his sweet attempt to shore up her nerves, which had achieved the salubrious effect of calming his own. But what did men know of childbirth?

In the pantry corner the two cats batted around a small piece of the Death card that had missed the bin.

114.

Do I dare to eat a peach? Mary asked herself. Her roiling stomach, which she knew to be morning sickness, probably wouldn't abide it. She smiled greenly at Earnest, who she had yet to tell of the happy news. Lost in his own thoughts he peeled and sliced the fruit for her.

"In the Caribbean, my dear," he said, "we shall dine on guavas and pineapples and mangoes. Oh, to be on the water again, with the waves beneath us, rising and falling with every step, but you will soon get your sea legs, I'm sure. You will learn to love its eternal motion."

At the moment she could think of nothing worse.

115.

I SHALL WEAR WHITE FLANNEL TROUSERS, AND WALK UPON THE BEACH, thought the Captain, unaware of Mary's delicate condition, and continuing his happy imaginings of their future. Just the two of us alone on the gently rocking boat at night, and once the pleasure cruises became known, wealthy people would be aboard in the daytimes offering stimulating conversations and an excuse for wine at luncheon. They would arrive with large sums of money.

He could not think of a better future, and he banished superstitious thoughts of life's unfortunate possibilities from his mind.

Mary had left the breakfast table abruptly at the first bite of the peach. Women's ways, he thought and ate the rest of the peach himself.

116.

I HAVE HEARD THE MERMAIDS SINGING. They lure me away. And I have heard my brother's voice, urging me to be off.

It was with some sadness that Ian packed his valise. He knew he must go now or he would be imprisoned in No. 13, caring for an invalid Maybelle Gill for the rest of her life. His departure while she was so ill could be judged as heartless, almost cruel. He judged it so himself. It went against his nature which had always been to comfort those he loved, and many of those he did not.

Willie insisted. *The years are closing in on ya, mate,* he said. *She missed her chance when she turned you down. She just doesn't fancy you. She prefers her invisible God. Now what does that tell you?*

If he was to breathe fresh air, have new adventures, taste life in all its richness before he died, he must go, as Lucille had gone before him. He believed that every human being lived a common story throughout their lives, whether they were exemplary or depraved: there was love, followed by loss, and if one were not broken by it, love again, and then loss, endlessly repeating. An angel would stay at No. 13, he knew. Ian Davies was a righteous man, but he was not an angel.

However, there was one thing he must do before taking his leave. He must kill Josiah Elder.

117.

Eᴀᴄʜ ᴛᴏ ᴇᴀᴄʜ, thought Father Sweeney. God handed a fate to each soul, but it was seldom a fair one in the opinion of most people. He, after years of listening and forgiving from his little wooden chamber held a different view. What people made of their fate was what mattered. Did they grow, mature, become wise and charitable, or shrivel and become bitter? No one, not a single person he had ever known, had walked through life without tragedy, without loss, grief, illness, decline, no matter how good they were, how devout, how deserving of a better fate. There were those that flourished in spite of adversity, and those that rotted in seeming luxury.

His own life had been as difficult as that of anyone he had absolved. He was often lonely, often in doubt. He drank too much, he thought about women too much, and once or twice he had strayed into a lustful bed, feeling afterwards "the expense of spirit in a waste of shame" as Shakespeare had written it.

Now he quietly and prayerfully tried to make the best of what God chose to give him in this life. As a young lad, when his parents had died in a fire, his life had changed. Everything became dark, and he had become withdrawn and surly. The rejection in late adolescence by the only woman he had allowed himself to love sent him spinning into a depression from which he thought he would not emerge. He thought of suicide. A kindly uncle had paid for him to travel to Europe in the hope of a cure, explaining he should try to improve himself through the experience, to bring a better self back to whomever he would love on return, an idea that had repelled him.

It was in France visiting Chartres Cathedral where he had been called upon by God, and the love he was graced to feel there, pouring into him upon a river of light from a hundred jeweled windows, taught him to be grateful for all of life, including his sufferings. It was there that he became a priest at heart.

The loneliness of his vocation had helped him to understand other solitary souls who came to him on bended knee, and to deal with them all with compassion. If we don't help one another bear our fates, then we are truly lost. This he believed.

He worried now for Maybelle Gill who was in ill health, her boarders departing one by one. Even Ian Davies, her imagined angel, would fly. Her oldest friend, Mr. Elder, was becoming senile, worse by the day, and her faith in herself had been shaken in some way he did not know. It was all so unfair. Perhaps God would grace her with his love, now when she needed it most. Perhaps not.

118.

"I DO NOT THINK THAT we should call the baby John," said Beatrice. "John Sterling is too plain. Augustus is right that we should not give him a fancy literary name, but John, no. I don't care for it. How about Samuel? The two S's are nice together."

"Samuel Sterling." Reginald tried it out and liked it. "And if it's a girl?"

"Susanna?"

"That's one too many S's. How about Abigail?"

"No. Something short and sweet, I think."

"Jane?"

"That's pretty. Jane Sterling. It's very nice. Samuel or Jane it will be. That's settled then."

Beatrice turned on the radio to pleasant music and knitted as they chatted here in the rooms she kept tidy and cozy. Reginald, feeling content, perused his paper and smoked his pipe. He had secured the electrician's job. His wife was continuing her studies. His baby was on the way. An apartment for them was being finished. All was well with the Sterlings.

Would it last? Did he dare to presume that his happiness would continue? The afternoon, the evening, sleeps so peacefully, mused Reginald. And, yes, he would presume.

119.

THEY WILL SING TO ME. Although they did not as have words yet to think with, the twins Samuel and Jane Sterling, knew this to be true. They knew it in their souls as they drifted in warm amniotic fluid and listened to the hum of their parents' gentle voices beneath the music from a farther room.

120.

I HAVE SEEN THEM all for the last time, thought Luci Dee. She was leaving Mrs. Crofts of No. 21, leaving Winston, leaving Boston and moving to New York City where surely she would find strong single women like herself, full of spirit and determination with whom to march into this newly minted century.

She would not see Maybelle Gill or Ian Davies or Mary Prior and the Captain, or Reginald and Beatrice Sterling, or Himself ever again. It was better so. They might like her, maybe even love her, but they could never begin to understand her. Winston thought he did, but really he was as ignorant as the rest, knowing her only physically. He thought her indecent, but she knew her enjoyment of sexuality was not indecent. He was. Like so many men. She had enjoyed him, even sleeping with him once more after the disastrous moment when Mrs. Gill appeared; but then he had spoken with more detail about his time in Haiti and his inhumanity and racism had sickened her, after which she had spurned him. Until that moment she had experienced him as simply a rogue, lacking in character, but what he spoke of so lightly was sordid.

Bewildered by her rejection he had nevertheless persisted, asking if he might pay her visits whenever his new sales job brought him through New York City, but she had said absolutely not.

The piece of her that was still Lucille was sorry for the part she had played in Mrs. Gill's sudden heart failure, but Maybelle had had no right to come bursting into the room of Luci Dee unannounced. She was sure Mrs. Crofts had told her where the room was located and had maliciously encouraged Maybelle to go right in. Well, lineup all the landladies right alongside all the nuns, along with all the white men who thought themselves superior to everyone else who lived, and march them to hell, she thought.

The last thing she put into her suitcase was her folder of newly written poems. Poems about women. Women coming alive, women learning to love themselves, love their bodies, love one another. Even women loving men for in spite of her angers she knew she was heterosexual to the core. It was, in a way, a curse.

In spite of all she knew and had experienced she believed that good men existed, that one day she might even meet a man who could love her just as she was, single and free, and unashamedly sexual. She had to believe such a man was possible the way Mrs. Gill needed to believe in God. When we believe in something, she mused, almost *anything*, no matter how unlikely, the world seems to make a little more sense to us.

Believing in herself had once seemed impossible but here she was. Her talent was deep within her, she knew, though it was reluctant to emerge. The verses she wrote now were acceptable for a beginner, but they held promise. She was certain that if she kept writing then one day she would produce a poem of real worth, one to challenge woeful old Prufrock in his rolled up trousers.

Luci looked around the room and feeling no hesitation, she went down the stairs with a light step. Her life, she knew, was hers to squeeze into a ball and roll wherever she damn well pleased.

She had forgotten her gloves. She would not need them anyway.

121.

Riding seaward on the waves Mary Prior surprised herself. She had never felt better in her life. She hadn't known there was air like this, warm and rich and fresh all at once, carrying the mingled perfumes of the tropics. The gentle roll of the Caribbean had soothed the baby in her womb, and miraculously cured her morning sickness. The child would be born a sailor. The sky was a dome of blue perfection, and the sun licked deliciously on her salty skin. The seemingly endless expanse of water stretching outwards towards the ever unreachable horizon seemed to connect her to the universe, the infinite, the divine. She felt the warm sea inside her and outside her as one body of water, and she floated there, gently swaying, full of wonder. She understood now why her husband had longed for this life.

The Captain, for in some ways she still thought of Earnest as The Captain, had at first been taken aback by the news that they were to become parents. It had not been part of the life he had imagined for them. A baby was not it at all.

"Why I am old enough to be the child's grandfather," he had protested.

"Yet young enough to be its father," she had replied with a smile. He had gotten through the initial shock, carried along inevitably towards acceptance on the current of his love for her. Now they looked forward together to the child's arrival.

"If it's a boy we will call him Willie," he declared one evening as they enjoyed a delicious fish stew and a bottle of wine.

"Why 'Willie?'" she had asked.

"It is a story that I shall tell you at another time," he replied, "or perhaps I shall let Ian Davies tell it to you when he arrives."

They were both pleased to think about the impending visit from their friend, whom they intended to ask to be the child's godfather.

In his letter Ian had enthusiastically accepted the Captain's offer to take him aboard as First Mate. Mary, in her condition, could no longer work as crew, and she would be too busy after the child arrived. He had apologized for being detained by events in Boston, and said he would be along shortly. He had not specified what these events were and she hoped that Mrs. Gill was gaining strength and all would be well at No. 13, albeit with a new cast of characters.

It had been a lucky place for Mary. It was the place where she had first spoken of The Terrible Thing and where, with the Captain's understanding, she had left that nightmare behind her forever.

122.

COMBING THE WHITE HAIR OF Mrs. Gill was like combing a cloud, Ian mused. Her head rested upon a pillow, a shawl wrapped around her shoulders, a knitted blanket left behind by Lucille tucked around her feet. Ian was reminded of his parents' last moments, and those of his brother Willie's. Father Sweeney was on his way, and he was thankful he had not mentioned his intended departure from No. 13 to Maybelle before she had taken this final, serious turn for the worse. At least the abandonment of Maybelle Gill would not be on his conscience.

In a period of lucidity she had called her solicitor and willed No. 13 to him. He, in turn, had discreetly given it to Beatrice and Reginald so the fate of the house was settled. It would become a family home for a loving couple, its rooms filling up with children and friends and cats, where the delicious dinners that Beatrice provided would be enjoyed, and the paintings of Lionel Quill, who was becoming quite successful, would adorn the walls. A series he had painted depicting The Seven Terraces in Dante's *Purgatorio* had been well received by the Boston art critics and pushed him into prominence. Doubtless, more homely subjects would be chosen for No. 13.

Ian heard the arrival of Father Sweeney in the hallway and called out for him to enter.

Entering the bedroom Father Sweeney saw a loving couple before him. Maybelle wore an immaculate white robe, her hair combed, her features at rest, holding the hand of the retired clergyman she had come to love, who now gently adjusted her shawl. He had no idea, and never would, of the turbulent currents of thought and emotion that had, nevertheless, produced this moment.

Maybelle, to the extent that she was lucid, found herself surprisingly ready to depart Boston and ascend to heaven. Her affairs were in order and No. 13 was in responsible hands. Babies, conceived in the room at the top of the stairs would soon be born, to make the world a happier place, or so she hoped.

She had seen her life flash before her eyes in Lucille's bedroom, both what it was and what it never could have been. She had seen all the love she had been denied. She had seen the face of the devil in Winston's knowing leer; and though the scene had been heart-wrenching, it was God's familiar voice she had heard as she fell...understanding, forgiving, consoling. She lingered in life long enough to make her peace with the world, with the mild pleasures and deep disappointments that had come of her choices, born of her beliefs and her devotion to God.

Maybelle Gill had tried, always, even during her brief lapse of faith, to be a good woman and she knew her efforts counted for something in God's judgment, however misshapen she had discovered herself to be in that dreadful, revelatory moment. Death would lighten her heart. Death would heal her soul. She imagined that Leon Gill, uncrushed, might await her in heaven. Would he still be young and handsome as he had been on their honeymoon, or would he have grown old and wise drifting around on the clouds?

Lucille floated into her mind and she wished her well, not daring to linger at any length upon her image. She whispered a goodbye to dear Mr. Elder, Himself, in his room below; and opened her eyes to the sadly smiling face of Ian the Protestant, who was the last of God's earthly gifts. Then she closed her eyes on life with all its endless confusions.

The Reverend Ian Davies stood aside, and Father Sweeney approached to give the last rites to an unprotesting Maybelle Gill.

123.

THE WAVES BLOWN BACK across the sands of Margate strand were soothing to T. S. Eliot. He stood alone among the rocks, close to the water's ever-changing edge. He had come alone to think and to write, far from the distractions of the city.

Everything was all right now. Nothing in his misery of a life had changed; not his mistaken wife, nor his misshapen body; not the hollowness of his relationships or the shallowness of his previous poems; and none of it was of any importance. No one could harm him now for the new poem was alive within him, its steady heartbeat thrumming. It devoured every unkind voice he had ever heard, every misfortune he had suffered, every unacceptable feeling he had harbored, and transformed them into raw, ragged beauty.

In the years ahead, as he searched deeper and deeper, asking the overwhelming questions as Professor Elder had commanded, the poem would grow into the magnificent beast it was destined to become. Time was no great matter. The poem would be timeless. And the name of its author, T. S. Eliot, would live forever. He knew this and was at peace.

He watched the water and the rocks, now glowing in the violet light of sunset.

He watched the waves, back and forth, back and forth....

Shantih shantih shantih.

124.

WHEN THE WIND BLOWS THE WATER in this direction, the Captain observed, it could mean a bad storm approaching. He knew this was the kind of storm that had once brought him to tragedy and humiliation, his shipmates to untimely death. A picture of cheerful, adventurous bosun Willie arose briefly in his mind. It was his responsibility to live, to remember Willie as he had promised. And he must also protect his wife and their coming child who would carry the name Earnest Willie Arlington.

Now, once again wearing the immaculate whites of a Captain, he raised anchor and with a hand firmly on the wheel, an arm tightly around Mary, he made for safe harbor.

125.

WHITE AND BLACK kittens appeared this time, not yellow like himself, noticed Tom. He never knew why or when Shoo Shoo would create these creatures. They came and went at intervals. Shoo Shoo kept her secrets to herself.

126.

"WE HAVE LINGERED long enough," said Mr. Elder. "It is time for us to begin."

Josiah's periods of awareness were less frequent now, and his wish to die here in his room, surrounded by his poem had been repeated to Ian with more urgency each time his mind was clear. His horror at being removed to a poorhouse had haunted him for months, and he had sought the help of the minister, to deliver him from such a horrible fate.

Now Ian had joined him in his chamber, marveling at the shards of paper encircling the room. Reading a few of the words he soon recognized that they were from the poem which had so disturbed Lucille, written out and pinned against the walls. The poem by T. S. Eliot, which now seemed to have fully inhabited the remaining mind of Mr. Elder.

Josiah handed the vial of pills to Ian. His instructions had been clear enough.

"Ask me to swallow one every few minutes until they are gone. It doesn't matter if I remember why you do so. I will be working on my poem. There is still time for decisions and revisions. You read it aloud to me as we go along so I can amend it as necessary. It is the best poem I have ever written and I want it to be perfect when I die."

If I was a Catholic, thought Ian, I could not do this thing for it would be deemed a mortal sin. I know it is against all Christian thought to help a man to his death, but how could I, Rev. Ian Davies, not help a suffering man depart this life with the grace and dignity he desires, for it was not prayer and holy oils that was needed, but poison. Of course, he had qualms when he had at first been asked. He imagined any moral person would be hesitant, but Mr. Elder had been persuasive, pleading simply for mercy, and he could not deny mercy to a man who had done much of value in his life, and no appreciable harm. Ian must act as the angel of death.

And so they began, Ian reading softly. "Let us go then, you and I, when the evening is stretched out upon the sky—"

Josiah interrupted abruptly. "Why look at me! I'm like a patient etherized upon a table. I'll use that. It is astonishingly original. Put it in right there and go on."

"—the evening stretched out upon the sky like a patient etherized upon a table—"

"Yes, yes. That is good."

"Let us go through certain half-deserted streets..."

Josiah spoke less and less as the pills began to work and their strange ritual proceeded slowly into the hours of the night.

"I am J. Alfred Prufrock! Come from the dead," he shouted after the seventh dose. "Come back to tell you all. I shall tell you all." Then when it became difficult for him to speak he lay still on his narrow bed, listening while Ian moved quietly around the room reciting the poem off the paper tatters.

127.

"IN THE CHAMBERS OF THE SEA, BY SEAGIRLS WREATHED WITH SEA-WEED RED AND BROWN," read Ian aloud as Mr. Josiah Elder allowed himself to sink deeper towards oblivion.

128.

"TILL HUMAN VOICES WAKE US," murmured Mr. Elder, and as the poem moved towards its ending, he closed his eyes. An image floated briefly into his mind, a young man, entering his classroom, full of life, golden with promise. Who, he wondered, could that be? Josiah's last breath gently rustled the bits of poetry pinned to the wall closest to his bed.

129.

"AND WE DROWN." whispered the Reverend Ian Davies, concluding the last stanza as a benediction, for he knew he was now alone in the room.

The silence was filled with one overwhelming question.

Oh, do not ask, "what is it?"

THE LOVE SONG OF J. ALFRED PRUFROCK
BY T. S. ELIOT

S'io credessi che mia risposta fosse
A persona che mai tornasse al mondo,
Questa fiamma staria senza piú scosse.
Ma perciocché giammai di questo fondo
Non tornò vivo alcun, s'i'odo il vero,
Senza tema d'infamia ti rispondo.

Let us go then, you and I,
When the evening is spread out against the sky
Like a patient etherized upon a table;
Let us go, through certain half-deserted streets,
The muttering retreats
Of restless nights in one-night cheap hotels
And sawdust restaurants with oyster-shells:
Streets that follow like a tedious argument
Of insidious intent
To lead you to an overwhelming question…

Oh, do not ask, "What is it?"
Let us go and make our visit.

In the room the women come and go
Talking of Michelangelo.

The yellow fog that rubs its back upon the window panes,
The yellow smoke that rubs its muzzle on the window panes,
Licked its tongue into the corners of the evening,
Lingered upon the pools that stand in drains,
Let fall upon its back the soot that falls from chimneys,
Slipped by the terrace, made a sudden leap,
And seeing that it was a soft October night,
Curled once about the house, and fell asleep.

And indeed there will be time
For the yellow smoke that slides along the street,
Rubbing its back upon the window panes;
There will be time, there will be time
To prepare a face to meet the faces that you meet;
There will be time to murder and create,
And time for all the works and days of hands
That lift and drop a question on your plate:
Time for you and time for me,
And time yet for a hundred indecisions,
And for a hundred visions and revisions,
Before the taking of a toast and tea.

In the room the women come and go
Talking of Michelangelo.

And indeed there will be time
To wonder, "Do I dare?" and, "Do I dare?"
Time to turn back and descend the stair,
With a bald spot in the middle of my hair—
(They will say: "How his hair is growing thin!")
My morning coat, my collar mounting firmly to the chin,
My necktie rich and modest, but asserted by a simple pin—
(They will say: "But how his arms and legs are thin!")
Do I dare
Disturb the universe?
In a minute there is time
For decisions and revisions which a minute will reverse.

For I have known them all already, known them all:
Have known the evenings, mornings, afternoons,
I have measured out my life with coffee spoons;
I know the voices dying with a dying fall
Beneath the music from a farther room.
       So how should I presume?

    And I have known the eyes already, known them all—
The eyes that fix you in a formulated phrase.
And when I am formulated, sprawling on a pin,
When I am pinned and wriggling on the wall,
Then how should I begin
To spit out all the butt-ends of my days and ways?
       And how should I presume?

    And I have known the arms already, known them all—
Arms that are braceleted and white and bare
(But in the lamplight, downed with light brown hair!)
    Is it perfume from a dress
    That makes me so digress?
Arms that lie along a table, or wrap about a shawl.
       And should I then presume?
       And how should I begin?

                • • • • • •

    Shall I say, I have gone at dusk through narrow streets,
And watched the smoke that rises from the pipes
Of lonely men in shirt-sleeves, leaning out of windows?...

I should have been a pair of ragged claws
Scuttling across the floors of silent seas.

                • • • • • •

And the afternoon, the evening, sleeps so peacefully!
Smoothed by long fingers,
Asleep...tired...or it malingers,
Stretched on the floor, here beside you and me.
Should I, after tea and cakes and ices,
Have the strength to force the moment to its crisis?
But though I have wept and fasted, wept and prayed,
Though I have seen my head (grown slightly bald) brought in upon a
  platter,
I am no prophet—and here's no great matter;
I have seen the moment of my greatness flicker,
And I have seen the eternal Footman hold my coat, and snicker,
  And in short, I was afraid.

And would it have been worth it, after all,
After the cups, the marmalade, the tea,
Among the porcelain, among some talk of you and me,
Would it have been worth while,
To have bitten off the matter with a smile,
To have squeezed the universe into a ball
To roll it towards some overwhelming question,
To say: "I am Lazarus, come from the dead,
Come back to tell you all, I shall tell you all"—
If one, settling a pillow by her head,
  Should say: "That is not what I meant at all;
   That is not it, at all."

And would it have been worth it, after all,
Would it have been worth while,
After the sunsets and the dooryards and the sprinkled streets,
After the novels, after the teacups, after the skirts that trail along the
  floor—
And this, and so much more?—
It is impossible to say just what I mean!
But as if a magic lantern threw the nerves in patterns on a screen:
Would it have been worth while
If one, settling a pillow or throwing off a shawl,

And turning toward the window, should say: "That is not it at all,
    That is not what I meant, at all."

        · · · · · ·

No! I am not Prince Hamlet, nor was meant to be;
Am an attendant lord, one that will do
To swell a progress, start a scene or two,
Advise the prince: no doubt, an easy tool,
Deferential, glad to be of use,
Politic, cautious, and meticulous;
Full of high sentence, but a bit obtuse;
At times, indeed, almost ridiculous—
Almost, at times, the Fool.

        · · · · · ·

I grow old...I grow old...
I shall wear the bottoms of my trousers rolled.

    Shall I part my hair behind?   Do I dare to eat a peach?
I shall wear white flannel trousers, and walk upon the beach.
I have heard the mermaids singing, each to each.
I do not think that they will sing to me.

I have seen them riding seaward on the waves,
Combing the white hair of the waves blown back
When the wind blows the water white and black.

We have lingered in the chambers of the sea
By seagirls wreathed with seaweed red and brown
Till human voices wake us, and we drown.

ACKNOWLEDGMENTS

I wish to acknowledge my invaluable sources of support in the writing of *To Murder and Create,* first among them, Ann Davies and Hatti Figge who read along as the novel developed offering excellent comments; Michael, Meredith, and Daniel Bergmann who give me every imaginable kind of support in my literary efforts and in my life; my cousin Milton Deemer, and my friends Carol Waldman and Bruna Nardelli who send me daily encouragement. I am most fortunate in my superlative publishers, Mary Bahr and Ulrich Baer, who dare to disturb the universe at Warbler Press. There are not enough ways to say thank you in the thesaurus.

Printed in Great Britain
by Amazon